Christopher Marlowe's Tamburlaine: Parts 1 and 2: Retellings

David Bruce

Published by David Bruce, 2022.

This is a work of fiction. Similarities to real people, places, or events are entirely coincidental.

CHRISTOPHER MARLOWE'S TAMBURLAINE: PARTS 1 AND 2: RETELLINGS

First edition. July 18, 2022.

Copyright © 2022 David Bruce.

ISBN: 979-8201413446

Written by David Bruce.

Table of Contents

Cover Photo for Christopher Marlowe's *Tamburlaine: Parts 1 and 2: Retellings*:

https://pixabay.com/en/adult-tattoos-body-dark-face-1867489/

Dedicated to Carl Eugene Bruce and Josephine Saturday Bruce

***

Educate Yourself
   Read Like A Wolf Eats
   Be Excellent to Each Other
   Books Then, Books Now, Books Forever

***

In this retelling, as in all my retellings, I have tried to make the work of literature accessible to modern readers who may lack some of the knowledge about mythology, religion, and history that the literary work's contemporary audience had.

Do you know a language other than English? If you do, I give you permission to translate this book, copyright your translation, publish or self-publish it, and keep all the royalties for yourself. (Do give me credit, of course, for the original retelling.)

I would like to see my retellings of classic literature used in schools, so I give permission to the country of Finland (and all other countries) to buy (or get free) one copy of this eBook and give copies to all students forever. I also give permission to the state of Texas (and all other states) to buy (or get free) one copy of this eBook and give copies to all students forever. I also give permission to all teachers to buy (or get free) one copy of this eBook and give copies to all students forever.

Teachers need not actually teach my retellings. Teachers are welcome to give students copies of my eBooks as background material. For example, if they are teaching Homer's *Iliad* and *Odyssey*, teachers are welcome to give students copies of my *Virgil's* Aeneid: *A Retelling in Prose* and tell students, "Here's another ancient epic you may want to read in your spare time."

TAMBURLAINE, PART 1

CAST OF CHARACTERS (Part 1)

The Prologue.

Male Characters

Mycetes, King of Persia.

Cosroe, his brother.

Persian Lords:

- Ceneus.

- Meander.

- Menaphon.

- Ortygius.

- Theridamas.

Tamburlaine, a Scythian shepherd.

His followers:

- Techelles.

- Usumcasane (nickname: Casane).

Bajazeth, Emperor of the Turks.

Bajazeth's Tributary Kings:

- King of Algiers.

- King of Fez.

- King of Morocco.

Alcidamus, King of Arabia.

Sultan of Egypt.

Governor of Damascus.

Median Lords (Lords of the country named Media):

- Agydas.

- Magnetes.

Capolin, an Egyptian military commander.

Philemus, a messenger.

A spy.

Female Characters

Zenocrate, daughter of the Sultan of Egypt.

Anippe, her maid.

Zabina, wife to Bajazeth.

Ebea, her maid.

Minor Characters

Virgins of Damascus, Messengers, Pashas, Lords, Citizens, Moors, Soldiers, Attendants.

TERMS

Marlowe used the word "Soldan"; this book uses the word "Sultan."

Marlowe used the word "Argier"; this book uses the word "Algiers."

Marlowe used the word "Bassoes," which means Bashaws or Pashas; this book uses the word "Pashas." A Pasha is a high-ranking Turkish official.

Marlowe uses Roman names for the gods:

- Jupiter's (Jove's) Greek name is Zeus.
- Juno's Greek name is Hera.
- Minerva's Greek name is Athena.
- Diana's Greek name is Artemis.
- Neptune's Greek name is Poseidon.
- Dis' Greek name is Hades.

NOTA BENE

The real Tamburlaine was named Timur, and he was known as Timur the Lame. (Marlowe's Tamburlaine has no physical disabilities.) He was born in Uzbekistan, although Marlowe makes him a Scythian shepherd. His dates are 9 April 1336 – 18 February 1405. In real life, Timur was a Turko-Mongol conqueror.

In Marlowe's play, the Ottoman Turks rule Asia Minor.

In Marlowe's play, the Egyptians rule Syria.

In Marlowe's play, to the East of Syria is Persia.

In Marlowe's play, the country named Media is part of the Persian Empire.

In Marlowe's play, the Persians rule Babylon.

In Marlowe's play, Scythia is to the north.

In the Prologue, Marlowe says that his play will not have rhyming doggerel but will instead use a higher language. In fact, his play uses heroic blank verse.

THE PROLOGUE (Part 1)

From jigging veins of rhyming mother-wits,
    And such conceits as clownage keeps in pay,
    We'll lead you to the stately tent of war,
    Where you shall hear the Scythian Tamburlaine
    Threat'ning the world with high astounding terms
    And scourging Kingdoms with his conquering sword.
    View but his picture in this tragic glass,
    And then applaud his fortunes as you please.

•••

In more modern language:
    Away from jigging doggerel verses of rhyming uneducated mother-wits,
    And away from such tricks with which buffoons and clowns earn their pay,
    We'll lead you to the stately tent of war,
    Where you shall hear the Scythian Tamburlaine
    Threatening the world with high astounding language
    And scourging Kingdoms with his conquering sword.
    View but his picture in this tragic looking glass,
    And then applaud his fortunes as you please.

CHAPTER 1 (Part 1)

— 1.1 —

King Mycetes of Persia and Cosroe, his brother, were meeting at the Persian court, along with the Persian lords Ceneus, Meander, Menaphon, Ortygius, Theridamas, and others.

"Brother Cosroe," King Mycetes said, "I find myself aggrieved, yet insufficient to express the same, for it requires a great and thundering speech."

One meaning of the word "insufficient" is "incompetent." This is a good description of King Mycetes of Persia. He is insufficient in many areas of expertise, including the making of speeches.

King Mycetes continued, "Good brother, tell the reason for my grief to my lords. I know you have a better intelligence than I."

Instead of talking about the grief that afflicted King Mycetes, his brother talked about the grief that afflicted Persia: Persia had a weak King.

Cosroe, his brother, said, "Unhappy Persia, that in former ages has been the seat of mighty conquerors such as Cyrus the Great, who in their prowess and their diplomacy have triumphed over Egypt in Africa and the territory of Europe, where the Sun dares scarcely appear because of freezing sleet and congealed, frozen, cold snow, is now to be ruled and governed by a man at whose day of birth Cynthia with Saturn joined — and Jupiter, the Sun, and Mercury refused to shed their influence in his fickle brain!"

Cosroe was complaining that the planets were in unfavorable astrological positions when King Mycetes was born. The planets that had the most influence on him were the Moon (Cynthia) and Saturn. The Moon changes constantly, and the astrological result is that King Mycetes has a changing, fickle temperament. Saturn's astrological influence resulted in King Mycetes having a melancholic temperament. (A saturnine person is dull and gloomy.) Cosroe wished that other planets had influenced King Mycetes. Jupiter, the planet associated with greatness and justice, would have made him majestic and magnanimous. The Sun, the "planet" associated with wisdom, would have made him wise. (This society called the Sun and the stars planets.) Mercury, the planet associated with a mercurial temperament, would have made him witty and eloquent.

Cosroe continued, "Now Turks and Tartars shake their swords at you, King Mycetes, and at Persia, meaning to mangle all your provinces."

By "Turks and Tartars," Cosroe meant the Ottoman Turks and the Scythian warriors led by Tamburlaine. Both groups were threatening Persia.

The Scythians were a branch of the Tartars.

"Brother, I see your meaning well enough," King Mycetes said, "and through your citing of astrological planets I perceive you think I am not wise enough to be a King. But I refer myself to my noblemen who know my wit, and can be witnesses.

"I might command you, Cosroe, to be slain for this.

"Meander, might I not do that?"

The Persian lord Meander replied, "Not for so small a fault, my sovereign lord."

"I don't mean to command his death, but yet I know I might do it," King Mycetes said. "Yet live, Cosroe; yes, live; Mycetes wills it so.

"Meander, you, my faithful counselor, declare the cause of my mentally produced grief, which is, God knows, about that Tamburlaine, who, like a fox in midst of harvest time, preys upon my flocks of travelers within Persia, and, as I hear, intends to pull my plumes and tear down my pride.

"Therefore, it is good and fitting to be wise and mentally prepared."

"Often have I heard your majesty complain about Tamburlaine, that fierce, rebellious Scythian thief who robs your merchants from the capital city of Persepolis as they tread by land to the Western Isles," Meander said. "And within your territory Tamburlaine with his lawless band of soldiers daily commits barbarous, uncivilized outrages, hoping (misled by dreaming prophecies) to reign in Asia, and with barbarous arms to make himself the monarch of the East.

"But before Tamburlaine can march in Asia or display his nomadic banners and army in the Persian fields, your grace ordered Theridamas, placed in command of a thousand horse-mounted soldiers, to apprehend and bring him captive to your highness' throne."

King Mycetes said, "Completely true to your nature you speak, and like yourself, my lord, whom I may term a Damon because of your love."

By calling Meander a Damon, King Mycetes was calling him a friend. Damon and Pythias were close friends. Pythias was sentenced to death by Dionysius, tyrant of Syracuse, but he asked to return to his home for a while in order to settle his affairs. Dionysius agreed on the condition that someone else stay as hostage to be executed in his place if Damon did not return. Pythias volunteered to be the hostage, impressing Dionysius, and Damon in fact returned after settling his affairs, further impressing Dionysius, who pardoned him.

King Mycetes continued, "Therefore it is best, if so it pleases you all, to send my thousand horse-mounted soldiers immediately to apprehend that paltry Scythian.

"How do you like this, my honorable lords? Is it not a kingly resolution?"

Cosroe said, "It cannot be otherwise than kingly because it comes from you."

"Then hear your orders, valiant Theridamas," King Mycetes said. "You are the chiefest captain of King Mycetes' army, the hope of Persia, and the very legs whereon our state leans, as on a staff that holds us up and foils our neighbor foes.

"You shall be the leader of these thousand cavalry, whose foaming spite, with rage and high disdain, have sworn the death of wicked Tamburlaine.

"Go frowning forth, but come smiling home, as did Sir Paris with the Grecian dame."

Paris, a Trojan Prince, visited King Menelaus of Sparta and ran away with his wife, Helen, and took her to Troy. She became known as Helen of Troy; the Trojan War was fought over her.

King Mycetes continued, "Return with speed; time passes swiftly away. Our life is frail, and we may die today."

Theridamas replied, "Don't doubt, my lord and gracious sovereign, that before the Moon renews her borrowed light and one month passes, Tamburlaine and his Tartarian gang shall either perish at our warlike hands or plead for mercy at your highness' feet."

"Go, valiant Theridamas," King Mycetes said. "Your words are swords, and with your looks you conquer all your foes. I long to see you return from there, so that I may view these milk-white steeds of mine all laden with the heads of killed men, and from their knees even to their hooves below smeared with blood — that makes a dainty show."

"Then now, my lord, I humbly take my leave," Theridamas said.

"Theridamas, farewell ten thousand times," King Mycetes said.

Theridamas exited.

"Ah, Menaphon," King Mycetes said, "why do you stay thus behind when other men press forward for fame and renown? Go, Menaphon, go into Scythia, and foot by foot follow Theridamas."

"No, please let him stay," Cosroe said. "A greater task is suitable for Menaphon than warring with a thief. Make him Viceroy of Assyria, so that he may win the Babylonians' hearts, which will revolt from Persian government unless they have a wiser King than you."

King Mycetes said, "'Unless they have a wiser King than you'? These are his words, Meander; set them down."

He wanted the insulting words to be written down so that they would not be forgotten. At some time in the future, King Mycetes might want to severely punish Cosroe for his misdeeds and insulting words.

"And add these words to them," Cosroe said. "All in the Persian Empire lament to see the folly of their King."

King Mycetes said, "Well, here I swear by this my royal seat, my throne —"

"You may do well to kiss it then," Cosroe interrupted.

Cosroe insultingly wanted King Mycetes to kiss the part of the throne that he sat on.

King Mycetes continued, "— richly decorated with silk as best beseems my rank, to be revenged for these contemptuous words. Oh, where are duty and allegiance now? Fled to the Caspian Sea or the ocean? Shall I call thee brother? No, I shall call you a foe, a monstrous birth of nature, shame to thy ancestors, who dares to presume to mock thy sovereign."

In this culture, a man of higher rank would use words such as "thee" and "thy" to refer to a servant.

King Mycetes continued, "Meander, come with me. I am abused, Meander."

Everyone exited except Cosroe and Menaphon.

"How are you now, my lord?" Menaphon asked. "Daunted and amazed to hear the King thus threaten like himself? The King is acting like a King."

"Ah, Menaphon, I don't care about his threats," Cosroe said. "Persian noblemen and captains of the garrisons of Media have laid a plot to crown me Emperor of Asia.

"But it is this that torments the very essence of my vexed and troubled soul: To see our neighbors who were accustomed to quake and tremble at the name of the Persian monarch now sit and laugh our rule to scorn.

"And this is that which might make me burst into tears: Men from the farthest equinoctial line — the equator — have swarmed in troops into eastern India, lading their ships with gold and precious stones, and they have gotten their spoils from all our provinces. They have looted us with impunity."

"This should persuade your highness to rejoice," Menaphon said, "since fortune gives you opportunity to gain the title of a conqueror by curing this maimed empire. Because Africa and Europe border on your land and touch your dominions, how easily may you with a mighty army pass into Greek-inhabited western Asia Minor, as did Cyrus once, and cause the Byzantines to withdraw their forces home to defend Constantinople, lest you subdue that city, which is the pride of Christendom."

A trumpet sounded.

"But, Menaphon, what is the meaning of this trumpet's sound?" Cosroe asked.

"Behold, my lord, Ortygius and the rest bringing the crown to make you Emperor!" Menaphon said.

Ortygius and Ceneus entered, bearing a crown. Others were also present.

"Magnificent and mighty Prince Cosroe," Ortygius said, we, in the name of other Persian noblemen and commoners of this mighty monarchy, present you with the imperial diadem."

Ceneus said, "The warlike soldiers and the gentlemen who heretofore have filled Persia's capital, Persepolis, with African commanders captured on the battlefield, whose ransom made Persia's soldiers so rich that they marched in coats of gold, with costly jewels hanging at their ears and shining precious stones upon their lofty crests, now are living idle in the walled towns, lacking both pay and martial discipline. They are beginning, in troops, to threaten civil war and openly exclaim against King Mycetes.

"Therefore, to prevent all sudden mutinies, we will crown your highness Emperor, at which the soldiers will experience more joy than the Macedonians did at the spoil of great King Darius III and his wealthy host."

In 333 B.C.E., Alexander the Great and his Macedonian soldiers captured Darius III's baggage train and his family at the Battle of Issus.

"Well, since I see the imperial rule of Persia droop and languish in my brother's government," Cosroe said, "I willingly receive the imperial crown and vow to wear it for my country's good, in defiance of all who shall bear malice toward my position."

Ortygius said, "And in assurance of desired success, we here crown you Monarch of the East, Emperor of Asia and Persia, Great Lord of Media and Armenia, Duke of Africa and Albania, Mesopotamia and Parthia, East India and the recently discovered isles, Chief Lord of all the wide, vast Black Sea, and of the ever-raging Caspian lake. Long live Cosroe, mighty Emperor!"

The Persian Empire was large, but these titles exaggerated the extent of that empire.

"And may Jove never let me longer live than I may seek to repay your love, and cause the soldiers who thus honor me to triumph over many provinces," Cosroe said. "By the use of the soldiers' desires of discipline in arms, I doubt not shortly but to reign as sole King, and with the army of Theridamas, to where we, my lords, immediately will hasten, to stand secure against my brother's force."

Cosroe had been crowned Emperor, but his brother was still alive, and so there was another claimant to the throne of Persia.

Ortygius replied, "We knew, my lord, before we brought the crown, intending your investiture so near the residence of your despised brother, that the lords would not be so exasperated as to injure or suppress your worthy title. But in case they would actually rebel, ten thousand cavalry are in readiness to carry you away from here in spite of all suspected enemies."

"I know it well, my lord," Cosroe said, "and I thank you all."

"Sound up the trumpets, then," Ortygius said. "God save the King!"

In Scythia, north of the Black Sea, Tamburlaine talked with Zenocrate (the daughter of the Sultan of Egypt), Techelles and Usumcasane (Tamburlaine's followers), Agydas and Magnetes (lords of Media and attendants to Zenocrate), and other lords. Soldiers and treasure chests were present.

Tamburlaine, a bandit with 500 armed followers, had taken Zenocrate, Agydas, and Magnetes prisoner.

Dressed as a shepherd, Tamburlaine said to Zenocrate, "Come, lady, don't let this dismay your thoughts. The jewels and the treasure we have taken shall be safeguarded and preserved, and you will be better treated and enjoy greater splendor than if you had arrived in Syria and were even in the circle of the arms of your father, the mighty Sultan of Egypt."

In her reply, Zenocrate referred to Tamburlaine as "thou" because he seemed to be a man of lower social status than her own.

"Ah, shepherd," Zenocrate said, "pity my distressed plight — if, as thou seem to be, thou are so lowly a man as a shepherd — and seek not to enrich thy followers by lawless theft from a defenseless maiden, who, travelling with these Median lords to Memphis, capital of Egypt, from my uncle's country of Media, where all my youth I have been brought up, have passed the army of the mighty Turk, carrying a safe-passage document sealed with the official seal and bearing the signature of the mighty Turk himself — the head of the Turkish Empire. This document gives us safe and unimpeded passage as we travel through the Turkish Empire as we travel to Memphis in Africa."

The Median lord Magnetes said, "And since we have arrived in Scythia, besides rich presents from the mighty Cham, the Emperor of Tartary, we have his highness' letters to command aid and assistance if we stand in need."

"Cham" is a now obsolete form of "Khan," as in Genghis Khan (c. 1162 – August 18, 1227), the first Khan of the Mongol Empire, which after his death became the largest contiguous empire in history. (The British Empire was larger, but non-contiguous.) In the late 1200s, the Mongol Empire broke up into smaller territories that engaged in power struggles, but in 1304, all of the leaders of the various territories approved a peace treaty and accepted the supremacy — at least nominally — of Yuan Emperor Temür. Tamberlaine's dates are 9 April 1336 – 18 February 1405.

This group of travellers was well prepared. It had safe-passage documents from both the mighty Turk who headed the Turkish Empire (the Ottoman Empire) and from a mighty Cham, aka Khan — the Emperor of Tartary.

"But now you see these letters and commands are countermanded by a greater man," Tamburlaine said, "and through my provinces you must expect to have letters of conduct from me and my mightiness, if you intend to keep your treasure safe.

"But since I love to live at liberty, as easily may you get the Sultan's crown as any prizes out of the territory in my sphere of control. For the prizes are friends that help to nurture my power, until men and Kingdoms help to strengthen it, and the prizes must maintain my life exempt from servitude."

Tamburlaine needed loot to pay his soldiers and repel anyone who sought to capture or kill him.

He then asked Zenocrate, "But tell me, madam, is your grace betrothed?"

"I am, my lord," Zenocrate replied. "I use 'my lord' because you imply that you are a lord."

"I am a lord, for so my deeds shall prove, and yet I am a shepherd by my parentage," Tamburlaine said. "But, lady, this fair face and heavenly hue of yours must grace the bed of him who conquers Asia and means to be a terror to the world, measuring the limits of his empire by east and west, as Phoebus Apollo does his course as he drives the Sun-chariot across the sky."

Tamburlaine, who intended to conquer the world, removed his shepherd's cloak and revealed the armor he was wearing underneath. He dropped the shepherd's cloak on the ground, and said, "Lie here, you clothes that I disdain to wear! This complete set of armor and this curved sword are equipment more suitable to Tamburlaine. And madam, whatsoever you think of this outcome — your capture — and this very expensive loss you have incurred, both may make you Empress of the East.

"And these men of mine — Techelles and Usumcasane — who seem to be only simple countrymen, may have the leading of so great an army as with their weight shall make the mountains quake, even as when windy exhalations, fighting for passage, joust within the earth."

People in this society believed that the pressure of gasses within the earth causes earthquakes.

Techelles said, "As princely lions when they rouse themselves, stretching their paws and threatening herds of beasts, so Tamburlaine looks in his armor. I think I see Kings kneeling at his feet, and he with frowning brows and fiery looks kicking their crowns from off their captive heads —"

Usumcasane said, "— and making you and me, Techelles, Kings — we who even to death will follow Tamburlaine."

"That is nobly resolved and decided, sweet friends and followers!" Tamburlaine said. "These lords — Zenocrate's attendants, the lords from Media — perhaps scorn our value and worthiness, and think we prattle with deranged states of mind, but since they believe us — we who in our imaginations bear empires on our spears, with dreams that are as lofty as the clouds — to be of so little worth, they shall be kept our forced followers, until with their eyes they see us as Emperors."

"The gods, defenders of the innocent, will never cause to prosper your intended plans, that thus oppress poor friendless travelers," Zenocrate said. "Therefore at least allow us liberty, even as you hope to be made forever famous by becoming and living in the future as Asia's mighty Emperor."

The Median lord Agydas said, "I hope our lady's treasure and our own may serve for ransom for our freedom. Return to us our mules and camels, without their loads of valuables, so that we may travel to Syria, where her betrothed lord, Alcidamus, the King of Arabia, awaits the arrival of her highness' person."

This was possibly an arranged marriage because Zenocrate had spent her earlier life in Media. Chances are, Zenocrate and Alcidamus have never met.

The Median lord Magnetes added, "And wherever we repose, we will report only good things about Tamburlaine."

"Disdains Zenocrate to live with me?" Tamburlaine said. "And disdain you, my lords, to be my followers? Do you think I value this treasure more than you do and more than I value you? Not all the gold in India's wealthy arms shall buy the meanest soldier in my train.

"Zenocrate, who is lovelier than Juno (the love of Jove), who is brighter than the Rhodope Mountains famed for their silver mines, and who is fairer than whitest snow on Scythian hills, your person is worth more to Tamburlaine than the possession of the Persian crown, which gracious stars have promised at my birth."

At Tamburlaine's birth, omens forecast a notable future for him.

Tamburlaine continued, "A hundred Tartars shall attend on you, who will be mounted on steeds swifter than Pegasus, the winged horse. Your garments shall be made of Median silk, adorned with precious jewels of my own, more rich and valuable than Zenocrate's.

"With milk-white deer you shall be drawn upon an ivory sleigh amid the frozen pools, and scale the icy mountains' lofty tops, which with your beauty will be soon melted.

"My martial prizes, with five hundred men won on the fifty-headed Volga's waves, all of these we shall offer to Zenocrate, and then I will offer myself to fair Zenocrate."

The Volga River has many heads, or major tributaries; it is continental Europe's longest river.

Techelles asked, "What now? Are you in love?"

"Techelles, women must be flattered," Tamburlaine said, "but this is she with whom I am in love."

One of Tamburlaine's soldiers arrived, shouting, "News! News!"

"What is it now?" Tamburlaine asked. "What's the matter?"

"A thousand Persian horsemen are at hand, sent from the King of Persia to overcome us all," the soldier answered.

"What now, my lords of Egypt and Zenocrate?" Tamburlaine asked. "Must your jewels now be restored again, and I who triumphed so be overcome? What do you say, lordlings? Is not this your hope?"

"We hope that you yourself will willingly restore them," Agydas said diplomatically.

"Such hope, such fortune, have the thousand horsemen," Tamburlaine said.

In other words, the thousand cavalry of the King of Persia have the same hope, and the same chance of a successful outcome, as you have — none at all. Tamburlaine was confident of victory against the cavalry although his men were outnumbered and on foot.

Tamburlaine continued, "Be quiet, my lords, and sweet Zenocrate. The only way you will leave me is for me to be forced to let you go.

"They are one thousand horsemen! We are five hundred foot soldiers!"

He added sarcastically, "Odds too great for us to stand against."

He then asked the soldier-messenger, "But are they rich? And is their armor good?"

Tamburlaine was thinking about booty.

The soldier replied, "Their plumed helmets are made out of beaten gold, their swords are enameled, and about their necks hang massive chains of gold down to the waist. In every part they are exceedingly splendidly and richly dressed."

Tamburlaine asked, "Then shall we fight courageously with them, or would you rather I should play the orator?"

He was mockingly asking if he should attempt to make a peace treaty with them. Or perhaps he was asking if he should defeat them with words.

Techelles took "play the orator" differently, as if Tamburlaine were asking whether he should make a big dramatic speech to persuade his troops to fight valiantly. In Tamburlaine's case, his men did not need such motivation.

"No," Techelles said. "Cowards and fainthearted runaways look for orations when the foe is near. Our swords shall play the orators for us. They will do the talking for us."

"Come, let us meet them at the foot of the mountain," Usumcasane said, "and with a sudden and hot alarm drive all their horses headlong down the hill."

The foot of the mountain is its lower part. The Scythians could drive all their enemies' horses down the rest of the mountain.

"Come, let us march," Techelles said.

"Wait, Techelles," Tamburlaine said. "Ask for a parley first."

Tamburlaine's soldiers entered.

Tamburlaine ordered, "Open the travellers' trunks, yet be sure to guard the treasure securely. Lay out our golden wedges — our golden ingots — to view so that their reflections may amaze and dazzle the Persians."

His men opened the trunks and spread out the wealth so that the Persians could see and be impressed by it.

Tamburlaine continued, "We will look friendly on the Persians when they come, but if they offer quarrelsome words or violence, we'll fight, even at odds of five hundred men-at-arms to one, before we part with our possession of this treasure.

"And against the Persians' general we will lift our swords, and either slit his greedy thirsting throat, or take him prisoner, and his golden chain shall serve as his manacles until he be ransomed home."

"I hear them come," Techelles said. "Shall we encounter them in battle?"

"Keep all your positions, and don't stir a foot," Tamburlaine ordered. "I myself will bide the danger of the brunt of any attack."

He would stand in front of his soldiers.

Theridamas and other Persians arrived.

"Where is this Scythian called Tamburlaine?" Theridamas asked.

"Whom do you seek, Persian? I am Tamburlaine."

Why ask "Whom do you seek?" when Theridamas had already said he sought Tamburlaine? Tamburlaine knew that Theridamas thought that he was seeking somebody who was only a Scythian shepherd and not at all impressive.

Surprised and impressed by Tamburlaine's looks, Theridamas thought, *Tamburlaine! A Scythian shepherd so embellished with nature's pride and richest equipment of body and mind! His looks menace Heaven and dare the gods. His fiery eyes are fixed upon the earth as if he now devised some stratagem, or meant to pierce Avernus' darksome vaults in order to pull the triple-headed dog from Hell.*

In one of his famous labors, Hercules had taken Cerberus, the three-headed guard dog, out of Hades and into the Land of the Living. Avernus was a lake located at one of the entrances into Hades. The "darksome vaults" are dark, gloomy cave passages through which souls pass on the way to the Land of the Dead.

"Noble and mild this Persian seems to be, if outward appearance allows us to judge the inward man," Tamburlaine said softly to Techelles. "He is gently noble."

Techelles replied softly, "His deeply felt emotions make him compassionate. His nature is inclined to pity."

Tamburlaine said loudly so that Theridamas could hear him, "With what a majesty he rears his looks!"

He then said directly to Theridamas, "In you, you valiant man of Persia, I see the folly of your Emperor. Are you only the captain of a thousand horsemen? I see by the character engraved in your brows, and by your martial face and splendid appearance, that you deserve to have the leading of an army."

Tamburlaine was playing the orator here and flattering Theridamas in an attempt to win a victory without killing anyone.

He added, "Forsake your King and join with me, and we will triumph over all the world. I hold the Fates bound fast in iron chains, and with my hand I turn Fortune's wheel about, and sooner shall the Sun fall from his sphere than Tamburlaine be slain or overcome."

The mythological three Fates determined the length of human life. Clotho spun the thread of life, Lachesis measured the thread of life, and Atropos cut the thread of life.

Lady Fortune had a wheel that she spun and that determined one's success or lack of success in life.

The Ptolemaic theory of the universe put Earth at the center. The Sun, stars, and planets were encased in concentric spheres that revolved around the Earth.

Tamburlaine continued, "Draw forth your sword, you mighty man-at-arms, intending only to scratch my charmed skin, and Jove himself will stretch his hand from Heaven to ward off the blow and shield me safe from harm."

He pointed to the golden ingots and said, "See how he rains down heaps of gold in showers, as if he meant to give my soldiers pay; and as sure and grounded evidence that I shall be the Monarch of the East, he sends this Sultan's daughter, rich and splendid, to be my Queen and majestic Empress.

"If you will stay with me, renowned man, and lead your thousand horsemen under my military management, then besides your share of this Egyptian prize, those thousand horsemen shall sweat with the martial spoil from the Kingdoms we conquer and from the cities we sack.

"We both will walk upon the lofty cliffs, and Christian merchant ships that along with Russian ships plow up huge furrows in the Caspian Sea shall lower their topsails to show respect to us as lords of all the lake.

"We both will reign as consuls of the earth, and mighty Kings shall be our senators."

Tamburlaine was referring to ancient Roman times, when Rome was led by two consuls and had a senate. In those days, Rome had a great empire.

He continued, "Jove sometimes disguised himself in a shepherd's cloak, and by those steps by which he has scaled the heavens, we may become immortal like the gods."

For Jove to become King of the gods, he had to kill his father, Saturn.

Tamburlaine continued, "Join with me now in this my lowly condition — I call it lowly because, since I am still obscure, the nations that are far away don't admire and marvel at me — and when my name and honor shall be spread as far as Boreas, god of the North Wind, claps his as-strong-as-brass wings and blows, or as far as the fair northern constellation known as Boötes sends his cheerful light, then you shall be my partner and sit with Tamburlaine in all his majesty."

The constellation Boötes is also known as the Herdsman or the Plowman or the Wagoner. The brightest star in Boötes is Arcturus, which is known as the guardian of the constellation Ursa Major, the Big Bear, because it is so close to it in the night sky. The Big Dipper is part of Ursa Major.

"Not Hermes, god of eloquence and spokesman of the gods, could use persuasive speech more movingly," Theridamas said.

"Nor are Apollo's oracles more true than you shall find my boasts reliable and firmly based," Tamburlaine said.

Apollo's oracle at Delphi in Greece was famous for oracular sayings. People from all over the ancient world consulted it. Interpreting the oracle, however, could be tricky. In 546 BCE or 547 BCE, Croesus, the King of Lydia, was thinking about attacking Persia, then ruled by Cyrus the Great. He sent an emissary to the Delphic Oracle to ask whether he should do that. The Delphic Oracle responded that if he attacked Persia, "A mighty empire will fall." Croesus regarded the oracle as propitious, and he attacked Persia. A mighty empire did fall; unfortunately, the mighty empire that fell was his own empire.

Techelles said, "We are his friends, and if the Persian King should offer us immediate dukedoms to exalt our social standing, we would think it a loss to accept a dukedom in exchange for that which we are assured of by our friend Tamburlaine's success."

Usumcasane said, "And we all expect Kingdoms at the least, besides the honor in assured conquests, where Kings shall crouch and bow to our conquering swords and armies of soldiers stand amazed at us, when with their frightened tongues they shall confess that these are the men whom all the world admires."

"What strong enchantments entice my yielding soul!" Theridamas said. "Ah, these resolute noble Scythians! But shall I prove a traitor to my King?"

Tamburlaine said, "No, but you will prove to be the trusty friend of Tamburlaine."

Theridamas said, "Won with your words, and conquered with your looks, I yield myself, my men, and my horses to you, to be partaker of your good or ill fortune, as long as life is in Theridamas."

And so Theridamas became a traitor to King Mycetes of Persia. Soon, Tamburlaine and Theridamas would fight against King Mycetes.

"Theridamas, my friend, take here my hand, which is as good as if I swore by Heaven and called the gods to witness my vow," Tamburlaine said.

They shook hands.

Tamburlaine continued, "Thus shall my heart be always combined with your heart, until our bodies decompose and return to the elements, and both our souls climb up to celestial thrones.

"Techelles and Casane, welcome him."

"Casane" is a nickname for "Usumcasane."

Techelles said, "Welcome, renowned Persian, to us all."

Usumcasane said, "May Theridamas long remain with us."

"These are my friends in whom I rejoice more than does the King of Persia in his crown," Tamburlaine said. "And by the love of Pylades and Orestes, whose statues we adore in Scythia, I swear that you — Theridamas — and they shall never part from me before I crown you Kings in Asia."

Pylades and Orestes were close friends who were willing to die for each other. Pylades helped Orestes murder his mother, Clytemnestra, and then shared his exile. (Some versions of the myth state that Orestes alone murdered his mother and then visited Pylades; the two men then traveled together.) They were captured while in Scythia. Their captors wanted to offer the gods a human sacrifice, and Pylades and Orestes each offered to die to save the other.

"Make much of them, gentle Theridamas," Tamburlaine said, "and they will never leave you until the death."

Theridamas said, "Neither you, nor them, thrice noble Tamburlaine, shall lack my heart to be with gladness pierced to do you honor and offer you security and protection. I am gladly willing to die for you."

Tamburlaine said, "A thousand thanks, worthy Theridamas.

"And now, fair madam, and my noble lords, if you will willingly remain with me, you shall have honors as your merits deserve, or else you shall be forced to remain with me as slaves."

"We yield to you, fortunate Tamburlaine," Agydas said.

"As for you then, madam, I have no doubt that you will choose to remain with me," Tamburlaine said.

"I, wretched Zenocrate, must be pleased of necessity and have no choice!" she said.

CHAPTER 2 (Part 1)

— 2.1 —

Cosroe and the Persian lords Menaphon, Ortygius, and Ceneus talked together. Other soldiers were present. Cosroe knew that Theridamas had defected to Tamburlaine's side. Three armies were in play now: Cosroe's, Tamburlaine's, and King Mycetes'. Cosroe was planning on joining forces with Tamburlaine. Cosroe planned to be the main commander, and he planned to make Tamburlaine his regent — a deputy King under him.

Cosroe said, "Thus far are we towards Theridamas and valiant Tamburlaine, the man of fame, the man who in the forehead of his fortune bears figures of renown and miracle."

Tamburlaine was an impressive-looking man, as Theridamas had earlier acknowledged. Some men look extraordinary.

Cosroe continued, "But tell me, Menaphon, since you have seen him, what is his stature, and what is his body like?"

Menaphon answered, "He is tall of stature, and straightly fashioned, which like his desire is aspiring upwards and divine. He is so large of limbs, his joints are so strongly knit, and he has such a breadth of shoulders as might by main force bear old Atlas' burden."

The mythological Atlas was a Titan who held the sky up on his shoulders.

Menaphon continued, "Between his manly shoulders is placed a pearl — his head — that is worth more than all the world. In his head ingenious sovereignty of art — divine creation — fixed his piercing instruments of sight, whose fiery circles bear encompassed a Heaven of heavenly bodies in their spheres that guides his steps and actions to the throne where honor sits invested royally."

According to Menaphon, Tamburlaine's eyes are spheres within which is a Heaven of fortuitous astrological planets that guide his ambitious career.

Menaphon continued, "He is pale of complexion, and when he was created, he was filled with passion so that he thirsts after sovereignty and loves weapons.

"When his lofty brows frown, they presage death, and when they are smooth, they presage amity and life.

"Above his brows hangs a knot of amber hair, wrapped in curls, as the fierce Greek warrior Achilles' hair was. On Tamburlaine's hair the breath of Heaven delights to play, making it dance with playful majesty."

Achilles was the greatest warrior of the Trojan War.

Menaphon continued, "Tamburlaine's arms and fingers, long and sinewy, betoken valor and excess of strength.

"In every part Tamburlaine is proportioned like *the* man who would make the world subdued to himself."

"Well have you portrayed in your lively description the face and body of a wondrous man," Cosroe said. "Nature's gifts strive with good fortune and his positive astrological stars to make him famous in accomplished worth, and his merits well show him to be the master of his fortune and the King of men. He is the man who could persuade, at such a sudden critical moment, using his valor and his life, a thousand foes sworn to be his enemy to desert their King and join his side although the thousand foes outnumbered his army.

"So then, when our armies in points of swords are joined in battle against my brother, King Mycetes, and closed within range of the killing projectile, although the path and the gate are narrow that lead to the palace of my brother's life, proud is my brother's fortune if we don't pierce it."

Cosroe was metaphorically referring to King Mycetes' body as a besieged city and his heart as a palace. No matter how well defended the palace was, Cosroe intended to pierce it.

Cosroe continued, "And when the princely Persian diadem shall overweigh my brother's weary, witless head and fall, like ripened fruit, with shakes of death, then in fair Persia noble Tamburlaine shall be my regent, and remain as my deputy King."

Ortygius said, "In a happy hour we will set the crown upon your kingly head. You are the man who seeks our honor by joining with Tamburlaine, the man ordained by Heaven to further every action to the best."

Ceneus said, "He who with shepherds and a little booty dares, in disdain of wrong and tyranny, to defend his freedom against a monarchy, what will he be able to accomplish when he is supported by a King, is leading a troop of gentlemen and lords, and is enriched with treasure to encourage and gratify his highest thoughts?"

"And worthy Tamburlaine shall get all of that," Cosroe said. "Our army will be forty thousand strong when Tamburlaine and brave Theridamas have met us by the river Araris. All of us will be joined together to meet the witless King Mycetes, who now is marching near to Parthia and is weakly armed with unwilling soldiers, to seek revenge on Tamburlaine and me. To Tamburlaine, sweet Menaphon, direct me immediately."

"I will, my lord," Menaphon said.

King Mycetes and Meander talked together. Other lords and soldiers were present.

"Come, my Meander, let us get to this business," King Mycetes said. "I tell you truly, my heart is swollen with wrath because of this same thievish villain, Tamburlaine, and because of that false Cosroe, my traitorous brother.

"Wouldn't it grieve a King to be so abused and have a thousand horsemen taken away? And, which is worse, to have his diadem sought for by such contemptible knaves as do not love and respect him?

"I think it would. Well, then, by the heavens I swear, Aurora shall not peep out of her doors until after I have captured Cosroe and have killed proud Tamburlaine with the point of a sword."

He was using poetic language — "Aurora shall not peep out of her doors" — to say that he would accomplish these things before the next dawn.

King Mycetes then said, "You tell the rest, Meander; I have finished speaking."

Meander said, "Then, having passed Armenian deserts now, and pitched our tents under the Georgian hills, whose tops are covered with Tartarian thieves who lie in ambush, waiting for a prey, what should we do but bid them to battle immediately and rid the world of those detested troops?

"We should do battle now, for if we let them linger here a while, they may gather strength by power of fresh supplies of men. This country swarms with vile, fierce, violent, outrageous men who live by rapine and by lawless spoil. They would be fit soldiers for the wicked Tamburlaine.

"In addition, this man, who could with gifts and promises inveigle a man who led a thousand horsemen — Theridamas — and make him a traitor to his King, will quickly win such men as are like himself.

"Therefore cheer up your minds; prepare to fight. He who can capture or slaughter Tamburlaine shall rule the province of Albania along the west coast of the Caspian Sea.

"He who brings King Mycetes the head of that traitor, Theridamas, shall have a government in Media, south of the Caspian Sea, in addition to the spoils that will come from Theridamas and all his train of soldiers.

"But if Cosroe (as our spies say, and as we know) remains with Tamburlaine, his highness' pleasure is that he should live and be reclaimed with princely lenity and mercy. Take him alive."

A spy entered and said, "A hundred horsemen of my company, scouting abroad upon these level and open plains, have viewed the army of the Scythians. These hundred horsemen report that the Scythians' army far exceeds King Mycetes' army."

Meander said, "Suppose the Scythians' army has an infinite number of soldiers. They lack martial discipline, and they all will be running headlong after greedy spoil. They value booty more than victory, and so they will be like the cruel brothers of the earth, sprung from the sowed teeth of venomous dragons. Their careless swords shall lance their fellows' throats as they fight over the booty and make us triumph in their overthrow."

Meander was referring to an ancient myth:

The ancient Greek hero Cadmus slew a dragon, and he followed the goddess Minerva's orders to sow the teeth of the dragon. He did so, and armed warriors grew from the teeth and were about to attack him. He threw a stone among them, and they attacked and killed each other over the stone.

Meander believed that winning booty would be more important than winning the battle to Tamburlaine's soldiers, and the soldiers would even kill each other in their pursuit of booty.

King Mycetes asked about the armed warriors who grew from sowed dragon's teeth, "Tell me, sweet Meander, were there really such brethren who sprang from the teeth of venomous dragons?"

"So poets say, my lord," Meander replied.

"And it is a pretty toy to be a poet," King Mycetes said. "Well, well, Meander, you are deeply read, and having you, I surely have a jewel.

"Go on, my lord, and give your orders, I say. Your intelligence will make us conquerors today."

Meander ordered the troops, "So then, noble soldiers, we will entrap these thieves who live confounded and confused in disordered troops if wealth or riches may prevail with them.

"We have our camels laden with gold, which you who are only common soldiers shall fling in every corner of the field. While the base-born Tartars pick up the gold, you, who are fighting more for honor than for gold, shall massacre those greedy-minded slaves.

"After their scattered army is subdued and you march on their slaughtered carcasses, then you shall share equally the gold that bought their lives, and live like gentlemen in Persia.

"Strike up the drum and march courageously. Fortune herself sits upon our helmets."

"He tells you truly, my masters," King Mycetes said. "So he does."

Cosroe, Tamburlaine, Theridamas, Techelles, Usumcasane, Ortygius, and others talked together. Cosroe and Tamburlaine had agreed to fight together against King Mycetes.

"Now, worthy Tamburlaine," Cosroe said, "I have placed in your proven good fortune all my hope. What do you think shall come of our undertakings, man? Just as if your words came from a sacred oracle skilled at foretelling the future, I will be satisfied with what you judge will happen."

Tamburlaine replied, "And in doing so, you are not even a little mistaken, my lord, for fates and oracles of Heaven have sworn to royalize and make famous the deeds of Tamburlaine, and make blest those who share in his undertakings.

"And don't doubt that if you favor me and let my fortunes and my valor exert some authority over your martial deeds, the world will strive with hosts of men-at-arms to swarm to the banner and side I support. The soldiers of Xerxes, who by fame and legend are said to have drunk dry the mighty Parthian river Araris, was only a handful to the number of soldiers we will have."

King Xerxes of Persia invaded Greece in 480 B.C.E. with such a large army of soldiers that they were said to have drunk rivers dry. Three hundred Spartans (the total number of Greeks was approximately 7,000) slowed down his army enough at Thermopylae that the Greeks were able to unite and gather forces and then defeat the Persians at sea at Salamis.

Tamburlaine continued, "Our quivering lances shaking in the air and projectiles like Jove's dreadful thunderbolts, enfolded in flames and fiery smoldering mists, shall threaten the gods more than Cyclopean wars."

The Olympian gods defeated the Titans in the Battle of the Titans. Cyclopes were huge, as were the Titans. Apparently, Tamburlaine was confusing Cyclopes and Titans.

He continued, "And with our Sun-bright armor, as we march we'll chase the stars from Heaven and dim their eyes that stand and muse at our admired arms. Our Sun-bright armor will shine so much that the night will be so bright that the stars can't shine."

Theridamas said to Cosroe, "You see, my lord, what working — effective — words he has, but when you see his actions top and surpass his speech, your speech either will be stopped with astonishment or will so extol his worth that I shall be commended and excused for putting myself and my poor army under his command."

He pointed to Techelles and Usumcasane and said, "And these, his two renowned friends, my lord, would make one thrust against obstacles and strive to be retained in such a great degree of amity and friendship."

Techelles said, "With duty and with amity we yield our utmost commitment and service to the fair Cosroe."

Cosroe replied, "I esteem your service as much as I do a portion of my crown — a part of my empire.

"Usumcasane and Techelles both, when she — Nemesis, goddess of vengeance and punishment — who rules within the golden gates of her temple in Rhamnus, Attica, and makes a passage for and assists all prosperous arms shall make me the sole Emperor of Asia, then your merits and deservings and valors shall be advanced to positions of honor and nobility."

Tamburlaine said, "Then hasten, Cosroe, to be King alone, so that I with these my friends and all my men may triumph in our long expected fate. The King, your brother, is now hard at hand. Meet with the fool, and rid your royal shoulders of such a burden as outweighs the sands and all the craggy rocks of the Caspian Sea."

A messenger entered and said, "My lord, we have discovered the enemy ready to charge you with a mighty army."

Cosroe said, "Come, Tamburlaine, now sharpen your winged sword, and lift your lofty arm into the clouds, so that it may reach the King of Persia's crown and set it safe on my victorious head."

Tamburlaine lifted his sword and said, "See where it is, the keenest sword that ever made passage through Persian arms. These are the wings — my arms — that shall make it fly as swiftly as does the lightning or the breath of Heaven, and kill as surely as it swiftly flies."

"Your words assure me of fitting success," Cosroe said. "Go, valiant soldier, go before and charge the fainting army of that foolish King of Persia."

"Usumcasane and Techelles, come," Tamburlaine said. "We are enough to scare the enemy, and more than needs to make an Emperor."

The battle had started, and King Mycetes, standing alone, held his crown in his hand and tried to find a place to hide it.

King Mycetes said, "Accursed be whoever first invented war! They knew not, ah, they knew not, simple men, how those who were hit by pelting cannon shot stand staggering like a quivering aspen leaf fearing the force of the north wind Boreas' boisterous blasts. In what a lamentable case would I be, if nature had not given me wisdom's lore, for Kings are clouts that every man shoots at and our crown is the pin that thousands seek to cleave and split."

A clout is the center of a target in archery. The pin in the center holds the target in place. Being able to hit and split the pin is a mark of an excellent archer.

He continued, "Therefore in policy I think it good to hide the crown secretly — this is a good stratagem, and uncharacteristic of any man who is a fool. This way I shall not be recognized, or if I am recognized, they cannot take away my crown from me. I will hide it here in this ordinary hole."

Tamburlaine entered, saw him, and said, "Fearful coward! Straggling from the camp, when Kings themselves are present in the battlefield?"

King Mycetes said, "You lie."

"Base villain, do you dare to call me a liar!" Tamburlaine said.

"Leave me!" King Mycetes said. "I am the King. Go! Don't touch me! You break the law of arms, unless you kneel and cry to me, 'Mercy, noble King!'"

"Are you the witty, intelligent, capable King of Persia?" Tamburlaine asked sarcastically.

"Yes, indeed, I am," King Mycetes replied. "Have you any request to make to me?"

"I would entreat you to speak just three wise words," Tamburlaine said.

This was an insult: Tamburlaine did not think that King Mycetes was capable of speaking even three wise words.

"So I can, when I see my time," said King Mycetes, who had not had time to put his crown in the hole.

Tamburlaine took the crown from him and asked, "Is this your crown?"

"Yes. Have you ever seen a fairer crown?"

"You will not sell it, will you?"

"Say another such word, and I will have you executed," King Mycetes said. "Come, give it back to me."

"No," Tamburlaine said. "I took it prisoner."

"You lie; I gave it to you."

"Then it is mine."

"No," King Mycetes said. "I mean I let you keep it."

By "keep," he meant "hold."

"Well, I mean you shall have it again," Tamburlaine said.

He gave King Mycetes the crown and said, "Here, take it for a while; I lend it to thee until I may see thee hemmed with armed men. Then thou shall see me pull it from thy head. Thou are no match for mighty Tamburlaine."

Tamburlaine used "thee," "thy," and "thou" when talking to King Mycetes. In this society, these were words that a nobleman would use when talking to a servant.

He exited.

Alone, King Mycetes said, "Oh, gods, is this Tamburlaine the thief? I marvel much that he did not steal the crown and carry it away."

Trumpets sounded for the battle to resume.

Cosroe, Tamburlaine, Theridamas, Menaphon, Meander, Ortygius, Techelles, and Usumcasane met together. Others were present.

"Wait, Cosroe. Take this," Tamburlaine said, handing him the late King Mycetes' crown. "Wear two imperial crowns."

Some Persian noblemen had crowned Cosroe Emperor of Asia — they also gave him many other titles — when he had first revolted against his brother, the King of Persia. Now he was about to wear the crown of the King of Persia.

Tamburlaine added, "Think yourself invested now as royally, even by the mighty hand of Tamburlaine, as if as many Kings as could surround you with greatest pomp had crowned you Emperor. Being crowned by me is like being crowned by as many Kings as could surround you."

"So do I think of it like that, thrice-renowned man-at-arms," Cosroe said, "and none shall protect the crown but Tamburlaine. I make you my regent of Persia and general lieutenant of my armies.

"Meander, you who were our brother's guide, and the chiefest counselor in all his acts, since he is yielded to the stroke of war and has died in battle, on account of your submission to us we with thanks pardon your former opposition to me and give you equal place in our affairs."

"Most fortunate Emperor, in humblest terms I vow my service to your majesty, with the utmost commitment and vigor of my faith and duty," Meander said.

Cosroe said, "Thanks, good Meander.

"So then, Cosroe, reign and govern Persia in her former pomp.

"Now send ambassadors to your neighbor Kings, and let them know that the Persian King has changed from one who didn't know what a King should do to one who can command what belongs to a King.

"And now we will go to fair Persepolis with twenty thousand proven soldiers. The lords and captains of my brother's camp with little slaughter take Meander's course of action, and gladly yield to my gracious rule.

"Ortygius and Menaphon, my trusty friends, now I will reward your good service and your allegiance and promote you to positions with greater power."

"And as we have always aimed at your benefit," Ortygius said, "and sought for your royal state all the honor that it deserved, so will we with our powers and our lives endeavor to preserve and prosper it."

"I will not thank you, sweet Ortygius," Cosroe said. "Better replies than mere words shall prove my purposes. Actions shall do that.

"And now, lord Tamburlaine, my brother's troops I leave to you and to Theridamas. You will follow me to fair Persepolis. Then we will march to all those Indian gold and jewel mines that my witless brother lost to the Christians, and we will ransom them and gain fame and profit.

"And until you catch up to me, Tamburlaine, since you are staying behind to bring to order all the scattered troops, farewell, lord regent and his happy friends.

"I long to sit upon my brother's throne."

"Your majesty shall shortly have your wish," Meander said, "and ride in triumph through Persepolis."

Everyone except Tamburlaine, Theridamas, Techelles, and Usumcasane exited.

"And ride in triumph through Persepolis!" Tamburlaine said. "Isn't it splendid to be a King, Techelles? Usumcasane and Theridamas, isn't it surpassingly splendid to be a King, and ride in triumph through Persepolis?"

"Oh, my lord, it is sweet and full of pomp," Techelles said.

"To be a King is half to be a god," Usumcasane said.

"A god is not as glorious as a King," Theridamas said. "I think the pleasure the gods enjoy in Heaven cannot compare with kingly joys on earth:

"To wear a gold crown set with pearls,

"To wear a crown whose special powers carry with it life and death,

"To ask and have, command and be obeyed, and

"When looks breed love, with looks to gain the prize — such attractive power shines in Princes' eyes."

"Why, what do you say, Theridamas, will you be a King?" Tamburlaine asked.

"No," Theridamas said. "Although I praise it, I can live without it."

"What do my other friends say?" Tamburlaine asked. "Will you be Kings?"

"Yes, if I could, with all my heart, my lord," Techelles said.

"Why, that's well said, Techelles," Tamburlaine said. "So would I. And so would you, my good sirs, would you not?"

"What then, my lord?" Usumcasane asked.

"Why then, Casane," Tamburlaine replied, "shall we wish for anything the world affords in the greatest rarity and shall we then rest, faint and destitute, without trying to get it?

"I think we should not.

"I am strongly convinced that if I should desire the Persian crown, I could attain it with a wondrous ease. And wouldn't all our soldiers soon consent, if we should aim at such a high office?"

"I know they would with our persuasions," Theridamas said.

"Why, then, Theridamas," Tamburlaine said, "I'll first try to get the Persian Kingdom for myself. Then I'll try to get you made King of Parthia, Techelles made King of Scythia, and Usumcasane made King of Media.

"And if I prosper, all shall be as sure as if the Turk, the Pope, Africa, and Greece came immediately creeping on their knees to us with their crowns."

The Turk was the Turkish Emperor (Bajazeth), the Pope was the head of Christianity, the Sultan of Egypt represented the most powerful country in Africa, and most Emperors of the Byzantine Empire were from Greece. In the later centuries of the Byzantine Empire, Western Christians often called the Byzantine Emperor the Emperor of the Greeks. If these four potentates submitted to Tamburlaine, he could claim that he was Emperor of the (Known-to-Him) World.

"Then shall we send a messenger to this triumphing King, Cosroe, and ask him to battle for his new crown?" Techelles asked.

Usumcasane advised, "Let's do it quickly then, before his room be hot."

His advice was to battle Cosroe quickly before he had time to sit in his throne and make it hot with the heat from his butt. In this society, the word "room" could mean a seat set aside for someone.

"It will prove to be a pretty jest, indeed, my friends," Tamburlaine said.

"A jest to charge on twenty thousand men!" Theridamas said. "I judge the enterprise to be far more momentous."

"Judge by yourself, Theridamas, not me," Tamburlaine said, "for immediately Techelles here shall hasten to tell Cosroe to fight before he travels too far and before we expend more labor than the gain will requite.

"Then you shall see the Scythian Tamburlaine make but a jest to win the Persian crown. Winning the crown will be like winning an easy game.

"Techelles, take a thousand horsemen with you, and tell Cosroe to turn back to war with us, who made him King only because it entertained us. We will not cowardly steal upon him, but instead give him warning and time to gather more warriors.

"Make haste, Techelles; we will follow you.

"Theridamas, what do you say about this?"

"Let's do it, I say," Theridamas said. "Count me in."

This was the second time Theridamas was a traitor to a King of Persia.

Cosroe, Meander, Ortygius, and Menaphon talked together. Other soldiers were present.

Cosroe said, "What does this devilish shepherd mean to aspire with such a Giantly presumption, to cast up hills — pile one mountain on top of another — against the face of Heaven, and dare the force of angry Jupiter?

"But just as Jupiter thrust them underneath the hills, and pressed out fire from their burning jaws, so will I send this monstrous slave to Hell, where flames shall forever feed upon his soul."

The Giants had fought to oust the Olympian gods and take their place as rulers. Cosroe was comparing himself to Jupiter, King of the gods, and Tamburlaine to one of the Giants.

The Giants piled Mount Pelian on top of Mount Ossa in order to reach the abode of the gods. Ovid's *Metamorphoses* I.151-176 tells the story of The Battle of the Giants, in which Jupiter threw thunderbolts at the Giants and hurled Mount Pelian down from the top of Mount Ossa and buried the Giants. The Battle of the Giants ended with Jupiter and the other Olympian gods triumphant. Mount Pelian and Mount Ossa are in Greece.

According to mythology, the Giant Enceladus is buried under Mount Etna. According to Pseudo-Apollodorus' *Bibliotheca* 1.38, Enceladus fled and the goddess Minerva threw the island of Sicily, where Mount Etna is located, at him.

According to another myth, Typhon, who had a hundred heads that emitted fire, is buried under Mount Etna.

Many versions of myths exist, and they often conflate figures or contradict other myths. Also, of course, people sometimes misremember myths.

Meander said to Tamburlaine, "Some powers divine and heavenly, or else infernal and hellish, mixed their angry seeds at his conception, for he was never sprung from the human race, since with the spirit of his fearsome pride, he dares so without fears and doubts to rule, and openly professes his ambition."

Ortygius said, "No matter what god, or fiend, or spirit of the earth, or monster turned to a manly shape, or of what substance or temperament he is made, whatsoever star or state govern him, let us put on our fitting steeled-to-battle minds, and in detesting such a devilish thief, let us in love of honor and defense of right be armed against the hate of such a foe, whether he grows from Earth, or Hell, or Heaven."

"Nobly resolved, my good Ortygius," Cosroe said. "And since we all have sucked and inhaled one wholesome air, and since we will decompose with the same proportion of elements that make up our bodies, I hope we are similar in vowing our loves to equal death and life."

In other words: While alive we breathe the same air, and after death we decompose into the same elements, and therefore I hope that all of us will vow our friendships to each other to equal life and death. Let us be willing to live and to die together as we fight in battle.

Cosroe continued, "Let's encourage our soldiers to encounter him, that grievous image of ingratitude, that fiery thirster after sovereignty, and burn him in the fury of that flame that nothing can quench but bloodshed and absolute power.

"Resolve, my lords and loving soldiers, now to save your King and country from decay and destruction.

"Then strike the drum, drummer.

"All the stars that determine the extent of my mortal life, I ask you to direct my weapon to Tamburlaine's barbarous heart, his heart that thus opposes him against the gods and scorns the powers that govern Persia."

In the battle, King Cosroe of Persia was wounded, captured, and defeated. After the battle, the wounded Cosroe was in the custody and presence of Tamburlaine, Theridamas, Techelles, and Usumcasane. Others were present.

Cosroe said, "Barbarous and bloody Tamburlaine, thus to deprive me of my crown and life! Treacherous and false Theridamas, even at the morning of my happy state — the beginning of my reign as King — when I was scarcely seated in my royal throne, you worked my downfall and untimely end!

"A strange pain torments my grieved soul, and death arrests the organ of my voice. Death, entering at the breach your sword has made, sacks and pillages every vein and artery of my heart.

"Bloody and insatiate Tamburlaine!"

Tamburlaine replied, "The thirst of reign and sweetness of a crown, a thirst that caused the eldest son of heavenly Ops to thrust his doting father from his throne, and place himself in the imperial Heaven, moved me to command soldiers and wage war against your royal state. What better precedent is there than mighty Jove? Why shouldn't I follow his example?"

Jupiter, aka Jove, led the rebellion of the gods against Saturn and supplanted him as the chief god. Ops was Jupiter's mother. Tamburlaine was mistaken when he said that Jupiter was the oldest son of heavenly Ops; actually, Jupiter was the youngest son.

Tamburlaine continued, "Nature, that framed us from four elements (earth, air, water, and fire) warring within our breasts for supremacy, teaches us all to have aspiring minds. Our souls, whose faculties can comprehend the wondrous architecture of the world and measure every wandering planet's course, always climbing after infinite knowledge, and always moving just like the restless spheres, direct us to wear out ourselves and never rest, until we reach the ripest fruit of all, that perfect bliss and sole happiness — the sweet fruition of an earthly crown."

"And that is what made me join with Tamburlaine," Theridamas said. "For gross and like the weighty Earth is a man who does not move upwards, and who does not intend to soar above the highest rank by princely deeds. Unless a man is ambitious, he is a clod of dirt."

Techelles added, "And that is what made us, the friends of Tamburlaine, lift our swords against the Persian King."

Usumcasane said, "For as when Jove thrust old Saturn down, Neptune and Dis each gained a crown, so do we hope to reign in Asia, if Tamburlaine is placed as King in Persia."

After the god Saturn was overthrown, three gods cast lots to divide much of the world. Jupiter got the sky, Neptune got the sea, and Dis got the Land of the Dead. Now that Tamburlaine had become King of Persia, Theridamas, Techelles, and Usumcasane hoped to become Kings.

Cosroe said, "The strangest men whom nature ever made! I don't know how to take their tyrannies and outrageous actions.

"My bloodless body grows chill and cold, and with my blood my life slides through my wound. My soul begins to take her flight to Hell and summons all my senses to depart. The heat and moisture that did feed each other, for want of nourishment to feed them both, are dry and cold; and now does ghastly death with greedy talons clutch my bleeding heart and like a Harpy tears at my life."

His blood was hot and moist, but it was leaving his body, leaving it cold and dry.

The mythological Harpies were rapacious birds with the heads of women.

Cosroe continued, "Theridamas and Tamburlaine, I die — and may fearsome vengeance light upon you both!"

He died.

Tamburlaine took the crown of the King of Persia from Cosroe's head and put it on and said, "Not all the curses that the Furies breathe shall make me leave so rich a prize as this."

The mythological Furies were avenging monsters that punished major crimes such as a son's murder of a father or a mother.

Tamburlaine then asked, "Theridamas, Techelles, and the rest, who do you think now is King of Persia?"

All shouted, "Tamburlaine! Tamburlaine!"

Tamburlaine, now the King of Persia, said, "Even if Mars himself, the angry god of war, and all the earthly potentates conspire to dispossess me of this diadem, yet I will wear it as great commander of this eastern world in despite of them, if you only say that Tamburlaine shall reign."

All shouted, "Long live Tamburlaine, and long may he reign in Asia!"

Tamburlaine said, "So; now it is more surer on my head than if the gods had held a parliament, and all the gods had pronounced me to be King of Persia."

39

CHAPTER 3 (Part 1)

— 3.1 —

Bajazeth met with the King of Fez, the King of Morocco, and the King of Algiers in great pomp. Bajazeth was the Emperor of the Turks. The Kings of Fez, Morocco, and Algiers were tributary Kings who were subservient to him. Others, including Pashas, who were high-ranking Turkish officials, were present.

Fez, Morocco, and Algiers are all located on the north coast of Africa; this region is known as the Barbary Coast.

Currently, the Turks were besieging Constantinople.

Bajazeth said, "Great Kings of Barbary and my stately Pashas, we hear that the Tartars and the eastern thieves, under the conduct of one Tamburlaine, presume to skirmish with me, your Emperor, and think to tear us from our fear-inspiring siege of the famous Grecian city Constantinople.

"You know that our army is invincible. As many circumcised Turks we have, and warlike bands of apostate Christians who have converted to Islam as has the Ocean or the Mediterranean Sea small drops of water in high tides when the Moon begins to join into one her semicircle horns and become a full Moon.

"Yet we would not be challenged by a foreign power, nor raise our siege before the Grecians yield or breathless lie dead before the city walls."

The King of Fez advised, "Renowned Emperor and mighty general, what if you sent the Pashas of your guard to command Tamburlaine to remain in Asia, and if he does not, to threaten death and deadly arms as from the mouth of mighty Bajazeth?"

Bajazeth ordered a Pasha, "Hurry, my Pasha, and go quickly to King Tamburlaine of Persia. Tell him that your lord, the Turkish Emperor, the dread lord of Africa, Europe, and Asia, the great King and conqueror of Graecia, Ocean, Mediterranean, and coal-black Black Sea, the high and highest monarch of the world, wills and commands — do not say that I entreat, ask, or beg — him not once to set his foot in Africa or advance his banners in Graecia lest he incur the fury of my wrath."

Some of Bajazeth's titles were titular.

He continued, "Tell Tamburlaine I am content to make a truce because I hear he bears a valiant mind. But if, presuming on his feeble army, he would be so mad as to wage war with me, then stay with him — say that I ordered you to do so — and if, before the Sun has measured Heaven with triple circuit and three days have passed, you have not returned to greet us again, we intend to take the morning of the fourth day as a message that he, Tamburlaine, will not be reclaimed and obey me, and we intend to come and fetch you in despite of him."

The Pasha replied, "Most great and powerful monarch of the Earth, your Pasha will accomplish your behest and show your pleasure to the Persian, as befits the legate of the stately Turk."

The Pasha exited.

The King of Algiers said, "They say he is the King of Persia, but if he dares to attempt to disrupt your siege of Constantinople, it would be requisite that he should be ten times more powerful than he is, for all flesh quakes at your magnificence."

"True, King of Algiers, and all flesh trembles at my looks," Bajazeth said.

The King of Morocco said, "The spring is hindered by your smothering host of soldiers, for they are so numerous that neither can rain fall upon the earth, nor can the Sun cast his virtuous, life-giving beams thereon. The ground is covered as with a mantle with such multitudes of your soldiers."

"All this is as true as holy Mahomet," Bajazeth said, "and all the trees are blasted and laid waste with our breaths."

The King of Fez asked, "What does your greatness think best to be done in pursuit of the city's overthrow? What needs to be done for us to conquer Constantinople?"

Bajazeth said, "I will command that the drafted trench diggers and fortification builders of Algiers cut off the water that by leaden pipes runs to the city from the mountain Carnon. Two thousand horsemen shall forage up and down, so that no relief or succor can come by land, and my galleys will keep all the sea under control and countermand any approaches of the enemy by sea. Then shall our footmen lie within the trench, and with their cannons as large mouthed as the entrance of Orcus — Hell — batter the walls, and we will enter in, and thus the Grecians shall be conquered."

Agydas and Zenocrate talked together. Zenocrate's maid, Anippe, was present, as were others. Agydas, Zenocrate, and Anippe were all prisoners of Tamburlaine. Agydas was a Median lord who was doing his best to look after Zenocrate and keep her safe.

Agydas said, "Madam Zenocrate, may I presume to know the cause of these unquiet fits that work such trouble to your accustomed rest and keep you from sleeping? It is more than a pity that such a heavenly face should by heart's sorrow grow so wan and pale, when your offensive abduction by Tamburlaine — which of your whole displeasures and troubles should be the greatest — has seemed to be digested and gotten over long ago."

Zenocrate replied, "Tamburlaine's abduction of me has been digested and gotten over long ago, just as his exceeding favors to me have deserved. They may even have made the Queen of Heaven — Juno, Jupiter's wife — content just as they have changed my first-conceived disdain for Tamburlaine.

"But a deeper passion feeds my thoughts with ceaseless and disheartening thoughts that dye my looks so lifeless and pale as they are, and that might, if my extremes had full events — if my most violent fears fully became reality — make me the ghastly image of death."

Agydas said, "May eternal Heaven sooner be dissolved, and all that pierces the Moon goddess Phoebe's silver eye — all that the Moon looks down on — be dissolved before such an event happens to Zenocrate!"

Zenocrate addressed her own life and soul, "Ah, life and soul, always hover in Tamburlaine's breast, and leave my body as without senses as the earth, or else unite yourselves to his life and soul so that I may live and die with Tamburlaine!"

Tamburlaine, along with Techelles and others, quietly entered the room. Unseen, they eavesdropped.

"With Tamburlaine?" Agydas said. "Ah, fair Zenocrate, don't let a man so vile and barbarous, who withholds you from your father in contemptuous defiance and keeps you from the honors of a Queen, allowing you instead to be supposed his worthless concubine, be honored with your love except out of necessity — pretend to love him if you have to.

"Provided that now your father, the mighty Sultan of Egypt, hears of you, your highness needs not doubt but in short time he will, with Tamburlaine's destruction, redeem you from this deadly servitude."

Zenocrate said, "Agydas, stop wounding me with these words, and speak of Tamburlaine as he deserves. The treatment we have had from him is far from being indignity or servitude, and might in noble minds be accounted princely."

"How can you fancy one who looks so fierce and is only disposed to martial stratagems?" Agydas said. "Tamburlaine is a man who, when he shall embrace you in his arms, will tell you how many thousands of men he slew, and when you look for amorous discourse and words of love, he will rattle forth his deeds of war and bloodshed, which are too harsh a subject for your dainty ears."

Zenocrate said, "As looks the Sun through the river Nile's flowing stream, or when the morning holds the Sun in her arms, so looks my lordly love, fair Tamburlaine. His talk is much sweeter than the Muses' song that they sung for honor against the Pierides."

Pierus, a Thracian, had nine daughters — the Pierides — whom he named after the nine Muses, goddesses of music, dance, and other arts. Out of excessive pride, they challenged the Muses to compete with them in song. Of course, the Muses won, and they punished the Pierides by turning them into magpies. Book 5 of Ovid's *Metamorphoses* tells this myth.

Zenocrate continued, "His talk is much sweeter than when Minerva did with Neptune strive."

Minerva and Neptune competed to see who would be the patron deity over the Greek region named Attica, which included Athens. The contest was to see who could confer the most benefit on Attica; that deity would become Attica's patron deity. Poseidon struck a rock and water poured out of it, but the water was salt water and not of much benefit. (Another version of the myth says that he gave the gift of Attica's first horse, but much of Attica is hilly.) Minerva then caused Attica's first olive tree to grow from the ground, and since olives are very beneficial, she won the contest. Minerva's Greek name is Athena (Athens is named after her), and she is the goddess of wisdom.

Zenocrate continued, "And higher would I raise my estimate of my worth than the worth of Juno, sister and wife to Jupiter, the highest god, if I were wedded to mighty Tamburlaine."

Agydas said, "Yet don't be so inconstant in your love, but let the young Arabian — the King of Arabia, Alcidamas, to whom you are betrothed — live in hope, after your rescue to enjoy his choice.

"You see, at first the King of Persia, when he was a shepherd, seemed to love you much. But now, in his majesty as King of Persia, he leaves behind those loving looks, those words of favor, and those comfortings, and he gives you no more than common courtesies."

Zenocrate said, "That is the reason for the tears that so stain my cheeks: I doubt his love through my unworthiness. I am afraid that I am unworthy of his love, and I am afraid that he does not love me."

Her fear of not deserving Tamburlaine's love was apparent in the mythological tales she told. The daughters of Pierus did not deserve to win the contest with the Muses, and Neptune did not deserve to win the contest with Minerva. Zenocrate was afraid that she did not deserve to win the contest with other women for Tamburlaine's love.

Tamburlaine went to her, and took her away lovingly by the hand. As he exited, he looked wrathfully at Agydas, but said nothing.

Everyone except Agydas exited.

Agydas knew that Tamburlaine was a formidable enemy. He could condemn Agydas to death, and that death need not be a quick death.

Alone, Agydas said to himself, "Betrayed by Fortune and suspicious love, threatened with frowning wrath and jealousy, surprised with fear of hideous revenge, I stand aghast; but I am most astonished to see his anger shut in secret thoughts and wrapped in the silence of his angry soul.

"Upon his brows was portrayed ugly death, and in his eyes that shine like comets — evil omens threatening revenge — was portrayed the fury of his heart. His shining eyes cast a pale complexion on his cheeks.

"Imagine a seaman seeing the Hyades gather an army of Cimmerian clouds."

The Hyades were seven stars representing nymphs who were said to bring rain, and the Cimmerians were a people who were believed to always live in darkness. Agydas was saying that the sailor knew that bad weather was coming because of the current location of the stars that made up the Hyades and because dark clouds were gathering.

Agydas continued, "Auster and Aquilon — the south wind and the north wind — with winged steeds, all sweating, joust in the watery heavens. With shivering spears they create thunderclaps, and from their shields they strike flames of lightning."

In this society, people believed that collisions of winds and clouds caused thunder and lightning.

Agydas continued, "The afraid sailor lowers his sails and sounds the main, measuring the height of the sea's waves, lifting his prayers to the heavens for aid against the terror of the winds and waves.

"Just like that sailor, so fares Agydas because of Tamburlaine's lately felt frowns that sent a tempest to my daunted thoughts and make my soul foretell her overthrow."

Carrying an unsheathed dagger, Techelles entered the room. Usumcasane accompanied him.

Techelles gave Agydas the dagger and said, "See, Agydas, see how King Tamburlaine greets you. He tells you to prophesy what this dagger imports."

Agydas replied, "I have already prophesied that, and now I suffer Tamburlaine's killing frowns of suspicion and love. He didn't need to confirm my fear with words, for words are vain where working tools — such as this dagger — present the naked action of my threatened end.

"Tamburlaine's greeting, which is this dagger, says, 'Agydas, you shall surely die, and of extremities elect the least — choose the least horrible death.'"

Talking about himself in the third person, he continued, "More honor and less pain you may procure if you die by this determined hand of yours rather than wait for the torments Tamburlaine and Heaven have sworn. So then hasten, Agydas, and prevent the plagues that your prolonged fates may draw on you.

"Go wander free from fear of the tyrant's rage, removed from the torments and the Hell wherewith he may torture your soul, and let Agydas by Agydas die, and with this stab slumber eternally."

He stabbed himself and died.

Techelles said, "Usumcasane, see how rightly the man has hit the meaning of my lord and King's greeting."

Usumcasane replied, "Indeed, and Techelles, his suicide was manly done. And, since he was so wise and honorable that he killed himself without fuss, let us give him now the bearing hence, and call for him to have a triple-worthy burial."

"Agreed, Casane," Techelles said. "We will honor him."

They carried away Agydas' body.

Tamburlaine, Techelles, Usumcasane, Theridamas, a Pasha, and Zenocrate met together. Anippe and others were present. The Pasha was the one who Bajazeth had sent to Tamburlaine.

Tamburlaine said, "Pasha, by this time your lord and master knows that I intend to meet him in Bithynia on the coast of the Black Sea. See how he comes!"

He was sarcastic: Bajazeth had not yet come.

Tamburlaine continued, "Tush, Turks are full of brags and they menace more than they can well perform."

He said sarcastically, "He meet me in the field and take you away from here!"

Then he added, "Alas, poor Turk, his fortune is too weak to encounter with the strength of Tamburlaine. View well my camp, and speak without bias. Don't my captains and my soldiers look as if they mean to conquer Africa?"

"Your men are valiant, but their number is few, and they cannot terrify Bajazeth's mighty army," the Pasha said. "My lord is the great commander of the world. Besides fifteen Kings who pay tribute to him, he has now in arms ten thousand Turkish soldiers, mounted on strong, vigorous Mauritanian steeds, brought to the war by men of Tripoli. He also has two hundred thousand footmen who have served in two pitched battles fought in Graecia. And to end this war quickly, he can, if he thinks it good to do so, withdraw as many more from his garrisons to follow him."

Techelles said, "The more horsemen he brings, the greater is the spoil, for when they perish by our warlike hands, we mean to set our footmen on their steeds and plunder all those stately Turkish soldiers."

"But will those Kings accompany your lord?" Tamburlaine asked.

"Such as his highness wants to accompany him will do so, but some must stay to rule the provinces he has recently subdued," the Pasha answered.

Tamburlaine said to Techelles, Usumcasane, and Theridamas, "Then fight courageously; their crowns are yours. This hand shall set them on your conquering heads, the heads of you who made me Emperor of Asia."

Usumcasane said, "Let him bring infinite millions of men, unpeopling western Africa and Greece, yet we feel sure of the victory."

Theridamas said, "We feel sure that Tamburlaine, who in a moment vanquished two Kings — Mycetes and Cosroe — who were mightier than the Turkish Emperor, shall drive Bajazeth out of Europe and pursue his scattered army until they yield or die."

"Well said, Theridamas!" Tamburlaine said. "Speak in that mood, for 'will' and 'shall' — rather than 'may' and 'might' — best fit Tamburlaine, whose smiling stars give him assured hope of martial triumph, even before he meets his foes.

"I who am termed the scourge and wrath of God, the only fear and terror of the world, will first subdue the Turkish Emperor, and then set free those Christian captives that the Turks keep as slaves, burdening their bodies with your heavy chains, and feeding them with thin and slender fare. These are the naked captives who row galleys about the Mediterranean Sea, and, when they chance to breathe and rest a space, are punished with bastinadoes — cudgels — so grievously that they lie panting on the galley's side, and strive for life at every stroke the Christian rowers make with the oar or the Turkish master gives with the bastinado.

"These are the cruel pirates of Algiers, that damned troop, the scum of Africa, inhabited with straggling runagates — vagabonds, apostates, and deserters — who make quick havoc of the Christian blood.

"But, as I live, that town of Algiers shall curse the time that Tamburlaine set foot in Africa."

Bajazeth arrived with his wife, Zabina, and her maid, Ebea, along with his Pashas and three tributary Kings: those of Fez, Morocco, and Algiers.

Bajazeth ordered, "Pashas and Turkish soldiers of my guard, attend upon the person of your lord, the greatest potentate of Africa."

Tamburlaine ordered, "Techelles and the rest, prepare your swords. I mean to fight a battle with that Bajazeth."

Insulted at being called by his name, not by his titles, Bajazeth said, "Kings of Fez, Morocco, and Algiers, he calls me Bajazeth, whom you call lord! Note the presumption of this Scythian slave!"

He then said to Tamburlaine, "I tell thee, villain, those who lead my horse have in addition to their names titles of dignity, and thou dare to bluntly call me Bajazeth?"

Tamburlaine replied, "Know, thou Turk, that those who lead my horse shall lead thee captive through Africa, and thou dare to bluntly call me Tamburlaine?"

Bajazeth said to his tributary Kings, "By my kinsman Mahomet's sepulcher, and by the holy Koran I swear, he shall be made a chaste and lust-lacking eunuch, and in my harem — my women's apartments — he will tend my concubines. And all his captains, who thus proudly and arrogantly stand, shall draw the chariot of my Empress, whom I have brought to see their overthrow."

"By this my sword that conquered Persia, thou fall shall make me famous through the world," Tamburlaine said. "I will not tell thee how I'll handle thee, but every common soldier of my camp shall smile to see thy miserable state."

The King of Fez said, "What means the mighty Turkish Emperor to talk with one as base as Tamburlaine?"

The King of Morocco said, "You Moors and valiant men of Barbary, how can you suffer these indignities?"

The King of Algiers said, "Leave aside words, stop talking, and let them feel your lances' points, which glided through and pierced the bowels of the Greeks."

"Well said, my brave tributary Kings," Bajazeth said. "Your threefold army and my huge army shall swallow up these base-born Persians."

Techelles said, "Puissant, renowned, and mighty Tamburlaine, why are we inactive, thus prolonging all their lives?"

"I long to see those crowns won by our swords," Theridamas said, "so that we may reign as Kings of Africa."

Usumcasane said, "What coward would not fight for such a prize?"

"All of you fight courageously, and you will be Kings," Tamburlaine said. "I speak it, and my words are oracles."

Bajazeth said to his wife, "Zabina, you are the mother of three boys braver than Hercules, who in his infancy crushed the jaws of venomous serpents."

Juno hated Hercules because he was her husband's bastard son. She sent two serpents to strangle him when he was an infant, but the already strong Hercules strangled the snakes.

Bajazeth continued, "These three sons' hands are made to grip a warlike lance. Their broad shoulders are fit for complete armor. Their limbs are larger and of a bigger size than all the brats that sprung from Typhon's loins.

Typhon was the father of the Nemean lion, the three-headed dog named Cerberus, the two-headed dog named Orthrus, the Chimera, the Lernaean Hydra, and the Theban Sphinx.

Bajazeth continued, "These three sons, when they come to their father's age, will batter turrets with their manly fists.

"Zabina, sit here upon this royal chair of state, and on your head wear my imperial crown, until I bring this sturdy Tamburlaine and all his captains bound in captive chains."

"May such good fortune happen to Bajazeth!" Zabina said as she sat on the chair of state and Bajazeth set his crown on her head.

Tamburlaine and Bajazeth had been using "thee," "thy," and "thou" when talking to each other. In this society, these were words that a high-ranking person would use when talking to a servant. Bajazeth's wife and Tamburlaine's consort, Zenocrate, would speak to each other in the same way.

Tamburlaine said, "Zenocrate, the loveliest maid alive, fairer than rocks of pearl and precious stone, Tamburlaine's only paragon and consort, whose eyes are brighter than the lamps of Heaven and whose speech is more pleasant than sweet harmony, who with your looks can clear the darkened sky and calm the rage of thundering Jupiter — sit down by Zabina, and be adorned with my crown, as if you were the Empress of the world.

"Don't move, Zenocrate, until you see me march victoriously with all my men, triumphing over Bajazeth and these his tributary Kings, whom I will bring as vassals to your feet.

"Until then, take my crown, extol my worth, and wage a war of words with Zabina, as her husband and I will wage a war of weapons."

As Tamburlaine set his crown on Zenocrate's head, she said, "And may my love, the King of Persia, return with victory and free from wounds!"

Bajazeth said to Tamburlaine, "Now shall thou feel the force of Turkish weapons, which lately made all Europe quake for fear. I have of Turks, Arabians, Moors, and Jews, enough to cover all Bithynia. Let thousands die! Their slaughtered carcasses shall serve as walls and bulwarks and fortifications for the rest. And just like the heads of the Hydra, so my army, subdued, shall stand as mighty as before."

The Hydra was a monster with nine heads. Each time one head was cut off, another appeared in its place. Bajazeth was saying that each time one of his soldiers fell in battle, another soldier would take his place.

Bajazeth continued, "If my soldiers should yield their necks to the sword, thy soldiers' arms could not endure to strike as many blows as I have heads for thee. Thou know not, foolish hardy Tamburlaine, what it is to meet me in the open field. My soldiers are so numerous that they will leave no ground for thee to march upon."

Tamburlaine replied, "Our conquering swords shall lead the way we use to march upon the slaughtered foe, trampling their guts with the hooves of our horses, brave horses bred on the white Tartarian hills. My army is like Julius Caesar's army, which never fought without having the victory."

Tamburlaine now referred to the Battle of Pharsalus, fought on 9 August 48 BCE, in which Julius Caesar's army decisively defeated his rival Pompey's army: "Nor in Pharsalus was there such hot war as these, my followers, willingly would have.

"Legions of spirits, gliding in the air, direct our projectiles and our weapons' points and make your strokes wound the senseless air, and when Victory sees our bloody banners spread, then Victory begins to spread her wings and take her flight, alighting upon my milk-white tent in triumph.

"But come, my lords, to weapons let us fall. The field is ours, the Turkish Emperor, his wife, and all."

Tamburlaine exited with his followers.

Bajazeth said, "Come, Kings and Pashas, let us glut our swords that thirst to drink the feeble Persians' blood."

Bajazeth exited with his followers.

Now Zabina and Zenocrate began to insult each other, using "thou," "thy," "thine," and "thee."

Zabina said, "Base concubine, must thou be placed by me who am the Empress of the mighty Turk?"

Zenocrate replied, "Disdainful Turkess, and irreverent fat woman, do thou call me concubine, who am betrothed to the great and mighty Tamburlaine?"

"To Tamburlaine, the great Tartarian thief!" Zabina said.

"Thou will repent these intemperate words of thine when thy great Pasha-master and thyself must plead for mercy at Tamburlaine's kingly feet, and plead to me to be your advocates," Zenocrate said.

"And plead to thee?" Zabina said. "I tell thee, shameless girl, thou shall be the laundress to my waiting maid."

She asked her maid, "How do you like her, Ebea? Will she serve?"

Ebea, Zabina's maid, answered, "Madam, she thinks perhaps she is too refined, but I shall make her wear other clothing and make her dainty fingers fall to work."

Zenocrate said to her own maid, "Do you hear, Anippe, how your drudge talks, and how my slave, her mistress, menaces?"

Zenocrate was saying that after Tamburlaine won the battle, Zabina would be her slave, and Ebea — the drudge — would be Anippe's slave.

She continued, "Both for their sauciness shall be employed to prepare the common soldiers' food and drink, for we will scorn that Zabina and Ebea should come near ourselves."

Anippe said, "Yet sometimes let your highness send for them to do the work my chambermaid disdains."

They listened to the sounds of trumpets and the battle, and waited a while.

Zenocrate then prayed, "You gods and powers who govern Persia, and made my lordly love — Tamburlaine — become Persia's worthy King, now strengthen him against the Turkish Bajazeth, and let his foes, like flocks of fearful roes — small deer — pursued by hunters, flee his angry looks, so that I may see him come out of this battle as conqueror."

Zabina prayed, "Now Mahomet, solicit God himself, and make him rain down murdering shots from Heaven to dash the Scythians' brains, and strike dead those who dare to battle with Bajazeth, who offered jewels to your sacred shrine when first he warred against the Christians."

They listened again to the trumpets and the battle.

Zenocrate said, "By this time the Turks lie weltering in their blood, and Tamburlaine is lord of Africa."

If Tamburlaine were to defeat Bajazeth, he would control much of North Africa.

Zabina said, "Thou are deceived. I heard the trumpets sound as when my Emperor overthrew the Greeks and led them captive into Africa. Immediately will I treat thee as thy pride deserves: Prepare thyself to live and die as my slave."

Zenocrate replied, "Even if Mahomet should come from Heaven and swear that my royal lord is slain or conquered, Mahomet still could not persuade me of anything except that Tamburlaine lives and will be conqueror."

Bajazeth arrived, fleeing from Tamburlaine, who pursued him and caught up to him. They fought, and Tamburlaine was victorious.

Tamburlaine said, "Now, King of Pashas, who is the conqueror?"

"Thou," Bajazeth said, "by the fortune of this damned defeat."

"Where are your three brave tributary Kings?" Tamburlaine asked Bajazeth as Theridamas, Techelles, and Usumcasane arrived.

Techelles answered the question: "We have their crowns; their bodies strew the battlefield."

"Each man has a crown?" Tamburlaine said. "Why, kingly fought, indeed. Deliver them to my treasury."

Zenocrate said, "Now let me offer to my gracious lord again his royal crown, so highly won."

"No, Zenocrate, you keep it," Tamburlaine said, "but take the Turkish crown from Zabina, and crown me Emperor of Africa."

"No, Tamburlaine," Zabina said. "Although now thou has got the best of us, thou yet shall not be lord of Africa."

Theridamas said, "Give her the crown, Turkess; it is best for you that you do so."

He took it from her, and gave it to Zenocrate.

Zabina said, "Injurious villains, thieves, runagates, how dare you thus abuse my majesty?"

Theridamas gave the crown to Zenocrate and said, "Here, madam, you are Empress; Zabina is not."

"True, Zabina is not Empress now, Theridamas," Tamburlaine said. "Zabina's time is past. The pillars that have bolstered up those terms have fallen in clusters at my conquering feet."

The word "terms" meant both "titles" and "statues of the kind known as busts."

Zabina said, "Although Bajazeth is a prisoner, he may be ransomed."

"Not all the world shall ransom Bajazeth," Tamburlaine said.

"Ah, fair Zabina," Bajazeth said, "we have lost the battle, and never have I, the Turkish Emperor, had so great a defeat by any foreign foe.

"Now will the Christian miscreants be glad, ringing with joy their superstitious bells, and making bonfires for my overthrow. But before I die, those foul idolaters shall make me bonfires with their filthy bones, for although the glory of this day is lost, Africa and Greece have garrisons enough to make me sovereign of the earth again."

"Those walled garrisons I will subdue," Tamburlaine said, "and write myself great lord of Africa.

"So from the east unto the furthest west shall Tamburlaine extend his puissant, powerful arm. The galleys and those pillaging small pirate ships called brigandines, that yearly sail to the Venetian gulf and hover in the Straits of Otronto, which separate Italy and Greece, in order to wreck Christians' ships, shall lie at anchor in the Isle Asant off the west coast of Greece until the Persian fleet and men-of-war, sailing along the oriental sea, have sailed around the Indian continent, even from Persepolis to Mexico, and from there to the Straits of Gibraltar."

In other words, they will sail from Persia across the Indian Ocean and the Pacific to Mexico and then to the Straits of Magellan at the bottom of Argentina (or to Mexico, where they would then build a canal to the Atlantic Ocean), and then sail across the Atlantic Ocean to Gibraltar.

Tamburlaine continued, "The two fleets of ships will meet at Gibraltar and join their force in one, keeping in awe and intimidating the Bay of Biscay near Portugal and all the ocean by the British shore, and by this means I'll win the world at last."

Bajazeth said, "Yet set a ransom on me, Tamburlaine."

Tamburlaine replied, "What, do thou think that Tamburlaine esteems thy gold? Before I die, I'll make the Kings of India offer their mines to sue for peace to me. And they will dig for treasure to appease my wrath."

He then ordered, "Come, bind them — Bajazeth and Zabina — both, and one of you lead in the Turk. Let my love's maid lead away the Turkess. Let Anippe lead away Zabina."

Some soldiers bound Bajazeth and Zabina.

Bajazeth said, "Ah, villains, do you dare to touch my sacred arms? Oh, Mahomet! Oh, sleepy, lethargic Mahomet!"

Zabina said, "Oh, cursed Mahomet, who makes us thus the slaves to rude and barbarous Scythians!

"Come, bring them in," Tamburlaine ordered, "and for this happy conquest let us triumph, exult, and celebrate a martial feast."

CHAPTER 4 (Part 1)

— 4.1 —

The Sultan of Egypt, Zenocrate's father, met with three or four Lords, an Egyptian military commander named Capolin, and a messenger in Memphis, Egypt.

The Sultan of Egypt said, "Awaken, you men of Memphis! Hear the clang of Scythian trumpets! Hear the immense cannons named basilisks, which roaring shake Damascus' turrets down!"

Damascus, Syria, is far from Memphis, Egypt, but the Sultan of Egypt was imagining that the sounds of Tamburlaine's siege of Damascus could be heard in Memphis.

He continued, "The rogue of Volga — Tamburlaine — holds Zenocrate, the daughter of the Sultan of Egypt — me — for his concubine, and with a troop of thieves and vagabonds, he has spread his banners to our high disgrace, while you, fainthearted base Egyptians, lie slumbering on the flowery banks of the Nile, just like unafraid crocodiles that rest while thundering cannons rattle on their skins."

The messenger said, "Mighty Sultan, if your greatness could see the frowning looks of fiery Tamburlaine, who with his terror and his imperious eyes commands the hearts of his associates, it might amaze your royal majesty."

The Sultan of Egypt said, "Villain, I tell you that even if Tamburlaine were as monstrous and unnatural as Demogorgon, a demon Prince of Hell, the Sultan would not flinch and jump a foot from him.

"But tell me, what kind of army does he have?"

The messenger replied, "Mighty lord, he has three hundred thousand men clad in armor, upon their prancing steeds, disdainfully with insolent paces trampling on the ground.

"He also has five hundred thousand footmen threatening to shoot arrows and throw spears, shaking their swords, their spears, and their iron bills. They stand, surrounding their standard banner, as bristle-pointed as a thorny wood."

A bill is a long-handled weapon that consists of a pole and a hook for unseating horsemen; it has a spike at the end of the pole.

The messenger continued, "Their large warlike instruments of assault and their artillery exceed the forces of their martial men."

The Sultan of Egypt said, "Even if their numbers equaled the number of the stars, or the number of ever-drizzling drops of April showers, or the number of withered leaves that autumn shakes down, yet the Sultan would by his conquering power so scatter and consume them in his rage, that not a man should live to rue their fall."

Capolin said, "So might your highness, had you time to organize your fighting men, and raise your royal army, but Tamburlaine by speedy travel takes advantage of your unreadiness."

"Let him take all the advantages he can," the Sultan of Egypt said. "Even if all the world conspired to fight for him — indeed, even if he were a devil, as he is no man — yet in revenge of fair Zenocrate, whom he detains to spite us, this arm should send him down to Erebus — Hell — to shroud his shame in the darkness of the night."

The messenger said, "May it please your mightiness to understand that his resolution and determination far exceeds that of all other men.

"The first day when he pitches down his tents before a city he intends to conquer, white is their hue, and he bears on his silver crest a snowy feather speckled white, to signify the mildness of his mind that, if quickly satiated with spoil, refuses blood. If the city surrenders on the first day, he will kill no one.

"But when Aurora, goddess of the dawn, mounts the second time, and the second day begins, as red as scarlet are his banners, tents, and armor. Then his kindled wrath must be quenched with blood and he will not spare any who can manage arms. If the city surrenders on the second day, he will kill only those who are capable of fighting in battle.

"But if these threats don't move the surrender and cause the city to submit to him, black are his banners, black is his pavilion — his ceremonial tent — and black are his spear, his shield, his horse, his armor, his plumes, and his jet-black feathers that menace death and Hell. If the city surrenders on the third day, he will kill everyone without respect of sex, degree, or age: He will raze all his foes with fire and sword."

The Sultan of Egypt said, "Merciless villain, peasant ignorant of military codes of honor or martial discipline! Pillage and murder are his usual trades: The slave usurps the glorious name of war.

"See to it, Capolin, that the fair Arabian King Alcidamas, who is betrothed to my daughter, Zenocrate, and who has been disappointed by this slave who has my fair daughter — the recipient of Alcidamas' princely love — may have quick notice to go to war in allegiance with us, and be revenged for Zenocrate's disparagement and disgrace."

Tamburlaine, Theridamas, Techelles, Usumcasane, Zenocrate, and Anippe stood together. Two Moors — Muslims from North Africa — pulled in Bajazeth, who was in a cage. Bajazeth's wife, Zabina, followed him. Tamburlaine was besieging Damascus, the capital of Syria. This was the first day of the siege, and Tamburlaine was wearing white.

Tamburlaine ordered, "Bring out my footstool."

The Moors took Bajazeth out of the cage.

Bajazeth said, "You holy priests of heavenly Mahomet — you priests who, sacrificing, slice and cut your flesh, staining his altars with your purple blood — make Heaven frown and every fixed star suck up poison from the Moorish marshlands, and pour it in this boastful tyrant's throat!"

Vapors that rose from marshlands were thought to be unhealthy. People in this culture believed that stars sucked up the vapors.

Tamburlaine said, "The chiefest god, First Mover of that sphere encased with thousands of ever-shining lamps — stars — will sooner burn the glorious frame of Heaven than it would so conspire my overthrow."

Aristotle thought of God as the First Mover: God set the universe in motion. The Primum Mobile was the sphere that moved and caused motion in all the other spheres within it. Outside the Primum Mobile was the Empyrean, the dwelling place of God: Paradise.

Tamburlaine continued, "But, villain, thou who wishes this to me, fall prostrate on the low disdainful earth, and be the footstool of great Tamburlaine, so that I may rise into my royal throne."

Bajazeth replied, "First shall thou rip my bowels with thy sword and sacrifice my heart to death and Hell, before I yield to such a slavery."

Tamburlaine said, "Base villain, vassal, slave to Tamburlaine, you are unworthy to embrace or touch the ground that bears the honor of my royal weight. Stoop, villain, stoop! Stoop, for so bids me, the man who may command thee to be torn into pieces, or scattered like the lofty cedar trees struck with the voice of thundering Jupiter."

Such trees are blasted with lightning.

Bajazeth said, "Then, as I look down to the damned fiends, fiends, look on me; and may you, Pluto, dread god of Hell, with a scepter made of ebony strike this hateful earth, and make it swallow both of us — Tamburlaine and me — at once!"

Bajazeth knelt.

As Tamburlaine stood on him to reach his chair, Tamburlaine said, "Now clear the triple region of the air, let the air be clear and transparent, and let the majesty of Heaven behold their scourge and terror tread on Emperors."

People in this culture divided the atmosphere into three regions: 1) low and warm because the Sun warms the ground, 2) middle and cold like the tops of mountains, and 3) high and hot because close to the sphere of fire that some people in this culture believed to exist between the Earth and the Moon.

Sitting in his chair, Tamburlaine began to talk about astrological stars; in astrology, stars are the heavenly bodies and include planets.

He said, "Smile, stars that reigned at my nativity, and dim the brightness of your neighboring lamps. Disdain to borrow light from Cynthia — the Moon — for I, the chiefest lamp of all the earth, first rising in the east with mild aspect, but fixed perpetually now in the meridian line that is noon, will send up fire to your turning spheres and cause the Sun to borrow light from you."

Tamburlaine meant that his brightness would give light to the stars and would outshine the Sun, forcing the Sun to borrow light from the stars. He was also saying that he had reached the high point — the high noon — of his fortunes and that he intended to stay there. And he was saying that he had started his career with a mild aspect: The stars that reigned at his nativity had given him a mild disposition. Apparently, Tamburlaine believed that he was mild as long as he got exactly what he wanted; unfortunately for Bajazeth, what he wanted was to humiliate him and keep him as a caged slave.

Tamburlaine continued, "My sword struck fire from Bajazeth's coat of steel, even in Bithynia, when I took this Turk, as when a fiery meteor, wrapped in the bowels of a freezing cloud, fighting for a passage out, makes the sky crack and casts a flash of lightning to the earth."

People in this society believed that thunder and lightning were caused when compressed fire trapped in a cloud found a way out.

He continued, "But before I march to wealthy Persia, or leave Damascus and the Egyptian fields, as was the fame of Phaëthon, Clymene's brainsick son, who almost burned the axle-tree of Heaven, so shall our swords, our lances, and our arrows and other missiles fill all the air with fiery meteors."

The axle-tree of Heaven is an axis on which the Earth rotates and the spheres that make up the universe revolve. This society believed that the Earth was at the center of the universe and the planets and stars were embedded in crystalline spheres that revolved around the Earth.

Phaëthon, the mortal son of the Sun-god, asked for a gift, which his father swore an inviolable oath to give to him. The gift was to be allowed to drive the Sun-chariot across the sky. Because his father had sworn an inviolable oath, he had to grant it. The mortal Phaëthon was unable to control the immortal horses that pulled the Sun-chariot, and it veered wildly across the sky and almost burned the Earth. Jupiter prevented the destruction of the Earth by killing Phaëthon with a thunderbolt.

The polished weapons of Tamburlaine's soldiers flashed and made the air seem as if it were filled with fiery meteors. The lightning bolts that Jupiter threw to kill Phaëthon looked like fiery meteors.

Tamburlaine said, "Then, when the sky shall grow as red as blood, it shall be said I myself made it red in order to make myself think of nothing but blood and war."

Zabina, the wife of Bajazeth, said, "Unworthy King, that by thy cruelty unlawfully has usurped the Persian seat, dare thou, who never saw an Emperor before thou met my husband on the battlefield, being thy captive, thus abuse his royal person, keeping his kingly body in a cage? For Bajazeth, roofs of gold and Sun-bright palaces should have been prepared to receive his grace! And dare thou tread on him beneath thy loathsome feet? The Kings of Africa have kissed the feet of Bajazeth."

Techelles said to Tamburlaine, "You must devise some worse torment, my lord, that will make these captives rein their uncontrolled tongues."

Tamburlaine said, "Zenocrate, pay better attention to your slave and control her."

Zenocrate replied, "Zabina is my handmaid's slave, and my handmaid shall see to it that these abuses stop flowing from her tongue. Berate her, Anippe."

Anippe, Zenocrate's maid, said to Zabina, "Let these be warnings for you then, my slave, about how you abuse the person of the King. Stop, or else I swear to have you whipped stark naked."

Bajazeth said, "Great Tamburlaine, made great in my overthrow, ambitious pride shall make thee fall as low, for treading on the back of Bajazeth, who should be horsed — mounted — on four mighty Kings."

Tamburlaine said, "Thy names and thy titles and thy dignities have fled from Bajazeth and remain with me, who will maintain my ambitious pride against a world of Kings."

The Moors put Bajazeth back in the cage.

Bajazeth said to Tamburlaine, "Is this a place for mighty Bajazeth? May ruin light on him who helps thee thus."

Tamburlaine said, "There, while he lives, shall Bajazeth be kept, and wherever I go Bajazeth will thus be in triumphal procession pulled.

"And thou, Zabina, his wife, shall feed him with the scraps my servants shall bring thee from my table, for he who gives him any other food than this shall sit by him and starve to death himself.

"This is my mind, and I will have it so. Not all the Kings and Emperors of the earth, if they would lay their crowns before my feet, shall ransom him or take him from his cage.

"The ages that shall talk of Tamburlaine, even from this day to Plato's wondrous year, shall talk about how I have treated Bajazeth."

Plato believed that the planets and stars had an original starting position for their movement. In *Timaeus* (especially see section 39), Plato's wondrous year is the time it takes for the planets and stars to return back to their original starting position. Translator W.R.M. Lamb calls the wondrous year "the Great World-Year, which is completed when all the planets return simultaneously to their original starting points. Its length was variously computed: Plato seems to have put it at 36,000 years." Tamburlaine was calling "Plato's wondrous year" the year in which the return to original positions would occur.

Tamburlaine continued, "These Moors who drew him from Bithynia to fair Damascus, where we now remain, shall lead him with us wherever we go.

"Techelles, and my loving followers, now we may see Damascus' lofty towers, which are like copies of the Egyptian Pyramids that with their beauties grace the Memphian fields. The golden statue of their sacred feathered bird, the ibis, that spreads her wings upon the city walls, shall not defend it from our battering shot. The townsmen dress richly in silk and cloth of gold as if attending a masquerade, and every house is like a treasury. The men, the treasure, and the town are ours."

Theridamas said, "Your tents of white are now pitched before the gates, and gentle flags of amity are displayed. I don't doubt that the governor will yield and surrender Damascus to your majesty."

"If he does," Tamburlaine said, "he shall have his life, and all the rest shall have their lives.

"But if he waits until the second day when the bloody flag is raised aloft on my vermilion — red — tent, he dies, and also die those fighting men who kept us out so long.

"And if on the third day they see me march in black array, with mournful, drooping pennons hanging down their heads, then even if that city contained all the world, not one person should escape, but all would perish by our swords."

"Yet you would have some pity for my sake," Zenocrate said, "because it is my and my father's country. Damascus is a city in territory that my father the Sultan controls."

"Not for the world, Zenocrate, if I have sworn otherwise," Tamburlaine said.

He then ordered the Moors, "Come, bring along the Turk."

They exited.

The Sultan of Egypt and King Alcidamus of Arabia met with the Egyptian military leader Capolin. Many soldiers with streaming colors were present. Alcidamus and Zenocrate had been engaged before Tamburlaine captured her.

The Sultan of Egypt said, "I think we march as the ancient Greek hero Meleager did, surrounded with brave knights from Argolis in Greece as we chase the savage Calydonian boar."

Meleager was one of the Argonauts, the heroes who traveled on the first ship, the *Argo*, in search of the Golden Fleece. After successfully completing this quest, he returned home and organized the hunt for the dangerous Calydonian boar that the goddess Diana had sent to punish the citizens for not showing her the honor she wanted. A woman, Atalanta, wounded the boar, and Meleager killed it and awarded the boar's hide to her. A brother and an uncle of Meleager objected to the hide being awarded to a woman, and in a quarrel Meleager killed them, a deed that led to his own death. When Meleager was born, the Fates told his mother that he would live only until a piece of wood in the fire burned up. His mother took out the piece of wood, put out the flame, and put the piece of wood in a secure place. But after she learned that Meleager had killed one of her brothers and one of her sons, she burned the piece of wood and Meleager died.

The Sultan of Egypt continued, "Or we march like Cephalus, with brave Theban youths, against the wolf that angry Themis — the personification of divine order — sent to waste and spoil the sweet fields of Greek Aonia, where Thebes and Mount Helicon are located."

Usually, the beast is called a fox, not a wolf. Cephalus hunted the beast with his hunting dog, which was a gift from his wife, but both the beast and the hunting dog were transformed into stone. Why? Both the beast and the hunting dog had super powers. The beast was unable to be caught, and the hunting dog always caught its prey. Faced with an irreconcilable paradox, Jupiter turned the two animals into stone. The beast is called the Teumessian fox or the Cadmean vixen, and the hunting dog is named Laelaps.

Cephalus and Procris, his wife, were two ancient lovers whose love ended tragically. He was accustomed to spend much time hunting, but his wife became jealous and thought he was going to see a lover, and so one day she secretly followed him to spy on him. Cephalus heard a rustling in the shrubbery, thought it was caused by an animal, threw his javelin, which never missed and which was another gift from his wife, and killed her.

In both stories, the beast is a scourge of a divine being; in both stories, success is followed by disaster.

Now the Sultan of Egypt began to describe Tamburlaine's army of five hundred thousand footmen as if it were a hunted monster:

"A monster of five hundred thousand heads joined in rapine, piracy, and spoil, the scum of men, the hate and scourge — enemy — of God, raves and rages in territory controlled by Egypt, and militarily molests us.

"King of Arabia, my lord, it is the bloody Tamburlaine, a fierce, cruel felon, and a base-bred thief, raised to the Persian crown by murder, who dares challenge us in our territories. To tame the pride of this presumptuous beast, join your Arabians with the Sultan's power; let us unite our royal bands in one and hasten to stop Damascus' siege.

"It is a blemish to the majesty and high estate and status of mighty Emperors that such a base usurping vagabond should defy a King, or wear a princely crown."

King Alcidamus of Arabia replied, "Renowned Sultan, have you lately heard about the overthrow of mighty Bajazeth in the border regions of Bithynia? Have you heard about the slavery with which Tamburlaine persecutes the noble Turk and his great Empress, Zabina?"

"I have, and I sorrow for his disastrous misfortune," the Sultan of Egypt said. "But, noble lord of great Arabia, be so persuaded that the Sultan is no more dismayed with tidings of Bajazeth's downfall than when a ship's pilot stands in a safe harbor, and views a foreigner's ship torn apart in the winds and smashed against a craggy rock.

"Yet in compassion to his wretched state and condition, I make a sacred vow to Heaven and him, confirming it with Isis' holy name, that Tamburlaine shall rue the day, the hour, wherein he wrought such ignominious wrong to the hallowed person of a Prince, or kept the fair Zenocrate so long, as his concubine, I fear, to feed his lust."

King Alcidamus of Arabia replied, "Let grief and fury hasten revenge. Let Tamburlaine for his offences feel such plagues as Heaven and we can pour on him. I long to break my spear upon his crest and test the weight — strength — of his victorious arm. For Fame, I fear, has been too prodigal and generous in sounding through the world his praise — Fame has been partial to Tamburlaine."

The Sultan of Egypt asked, "Capolin, have you surveyed our armies?"

Capolin answered, "Great Emperors of Egypt and Arabia, the number of your hosts united is a hundred and fifty thousand horsemen and two hundred thousand footmen. These are brave men-at-arms, courageous and full of hardiness, as frolicsome and merry as the hunters in the chase of savage beasts amid the desolate woods."

King Alcidamus of Arabia said, "My mind foretells fortunate success, and, Tamburlaine, my spirit foresees the utter ruin of thy men and thee."

"Then rear your standards," the Sultan of Egypt said. "Let your sounding drums direct our soldiers to Damascus' walls.

"Now, Tamburlaine, the mighty Sultan comes and leads with him the great Arabian King to dim thy baseness and obscurity, your low birth that is famous for nothing but theft and spoil, and to raze and scatter thy inglorious crew of Scythians and slavish Persians."

Tamburlaine, wearing scarlet, walked over to a banquet. With him were Theridamas, Techelles, Usumcasane, and Zenocrate. Bajazeth was brought in, in a cage pulled by Moors. Zabina followed him.

Tamburlaine said, "Now our bloody colors hang by Damascus, casting hues of blood-red upon the heads of the citizens of Damascus while they walk quivering on their city walls, half dead for fear before they feel my wrath.

"So then let us freely banquet and carouse and drink heartily full bowls of wine to the god of war, who intends to fill your helmets full of gold, and make Damascus' spoils as rich to you as was to Jason the golden fleece that hung in the Kingdom of Colchis, located on the east coast of the Black Sea.

"And now, Bajazeth, have thou any stomach?"

The word "stomach" means 1) appetite, 2) anger, and 3) courage.

"Yes," Bajazeth replied. "I have such a stomach, cruel Tamburlaine, that I could willingly feed upon thy bloody, raw heart."

"Nay," Tamburlaine said. "Thine own heart is easier to come by. Pluck out that, and it will serve to feed thee and thy wife.

"Well, Zenocrate, Techelles, and the rest, fall to your victuals and eat."

"Fall to," Bajazeth said, "and may your meat never be digested!

"Ye avenging Furies, who can turn invisible, dive to the bottom of Avernus' pool at the entrance of Hell and in your hands bring hellish poison up, and squeeze it in the cup of Tamburlaine!"

The Furies had the power of being invisible to people other than the particular person whom they were punishing. This is seen in Aeschylus' *Oresteia*: At the end of *The Libation Bearers*, the second play in Aeschylus' trilogy, only Orestes can see the Furies.

Bajazeth continued, "Or, winged snakes of the Lernaean Hydra, cast your stings, and leave your venoms in this tyrant's dish!"

The Hydra in the region of Lerna was a poisonous serpentine water monster with nine heads. Hercules killed the Hydra and used its venom to poison his arrows. The heads of the Hydra were figuratively "winged" because they were so quick.

Bajazeth's wife, Zabina, said, "And may this banquet prove as ominous as Procne's to the adulterous Thracian King who fed upon the substance of his child."

King Tereus of Thrace violently raped Philomena, who was the sister of his wife, Procne. To keep Philomena from telling anyone about the rape, Tereus cut out her tongue. Philomena weaved her story into a tapestry, which Procne saw, thus learning what had happened. To get revenge, Procne killed, cooked, and fed her and Tereus' son to Tereus.

Zenocrate asked Tamburlaine, "My lord, how can you tolerate these outrageous curses that are made by these slaves of yours?"

Tamburlaine replied, "I tolerate the curses to let these slaves of mine see, divine Zenocrate, that I glory in the curses of my foes — I have the power from the imperial and empyreal Heaven to turn them all upon their own heads."

Techelles said to Zenocrate, "Please, give them permission to curse, madam; this kind of speech is a good refreshment to them."

Theridamas said, "But if his highness would let them be fed, it would do them more good."

Tamburlaine said to Bajazeth, "Sirrah, why don't you fall to? Are you so daintily brought up that you cannot pull out your heart and eat your own flesh?"

Tamburlaine used both "sirrah" and "you" to refer to Bajazeth. "Sirrah" was used to refer to a male of lower status, such as a servant, than the speaker. "You" was formal and respectful, and Tamburlaine was mocking Bajazeth by using it.

"Before that happens, legions of devils shall tear thee in pieces," Bajazeth said.

Usumcasane said, "Villain, do thou know to whom thou speak?"

Tamburlaine said to Usumcasane, "Oh, let him alone."

He then put some food on the end of his sword and held it out to Bajazeth and said, "Here; eat, sir; take it from my sword's point, or I'll thrust it to thy heart."

Bajazeth took the food, threw it down, and stomped on it.

Theridamas said, "He stamps it under his feet, my lord."

"Take it up, villain, and eat it," Tamburlaine said, "or I will make thee slice the muscles of thy arms into strips of meat and eat them."

"Nay, it would be better if he killed his wife," Usumcasane said, "and then she shall be sure not to be starved, and he shall be provided for a month's food beforehand."

Tamburlaine showed his dagger to Bajazeth and said, "Here is my dagger. Kill her while she is fat, for if she lives just a little while longer, she will fall into a wasting disease because of anguish, and then she will not be worth the eating."

Theridamas asked Bajazeth, "Do thou think that Mahomet will allow this?"

Techelles said, "It is likely that he will allow it, when he cannot stop it."

"Go to it," Tamburlaine said. "Fall to and eat your food.

"What, not a bit? Perhaps he has not been watered today. Give him some water to drink."

Animals are watered; Tamburlaine was treating Bajazeth like an animal.

The Moors gave Bajazeth water to drink, but he flung it on the ground.

Tamburlaine said, "Fast and starve, and welcome, sir, until hunger makes you eat.

"What do you think, Zenocrate? Don't the Turk and his wife make a splendid show at a banquet?"

"Yes, my lord," Zenocrate said.

She was sad and thinking about her husband's invading her father's territory, including Damascus, and the death and destruction that would occur.

"I think it is a great deal better than a company of performing musicians," Theridamas said.

"Yet music would do well to cheer up Zenocrate," Tamburlaine said.

He asked her, "Please tell me, why are you so sad? If you will have a song, the Turk Bajazeth shall strain his voice and sing. But why are you sad?"

Zenocrate replied, "My lord, to see my father's town besieged, the country wasted where I myself was born — how can it but afflict my very soul? If any love remain in you, my lord, or if my love to your majesty may merit favor at your highness' hands, then raise your siege from fair Damascus' walls, and with my father make a friendly truce."

Tamburlaine replied, "Zenocrate, even if Egypt were Jupiter's own land, yet I would with my sword make Jupiter stoop, bow down, and submit to me.

"I will confute and prove wrong those blind geographers who make a triple region of Africa, Europe, and Asia in the world, excluding regions that I mean to travel and chart and with this pen — my sword — reduce them to a map, renaming the provinces, cities, and towns, after my name and your name, Zenocrate.

"Here at Damascus I will make the point that shall begin the perpendicular."

Some medieval maps were of the T-in-O variety. A T was placed in an O, dividing the map into three areas. Usually, at the top was Asia, and below were Europe (left) and Africa (right). Jerusalem, as the spiritual center of the world, was placed at the top middle of the T, where the perpendicular bar met the horizontal bar. Tamburlaine was boasting that he would put Damascus instead of Jerusalem in that spot.

Or possibly he meant by "perpendicular" the initial meridian of some maps. The position of the initial meridian varied, and Tamburlaine may have been saying that he would put Damascus on that meridian.

Tamburlaine continued, "And would you have me buy your father's love with such a loss? Tell me, Zenocrate."

"May honor always wait on and serve happy, fortunate Tamburlaine," she replied, "yet give me permission to plead for my father, my lord."

"Be happy," Tamburlaine said. "His person shall be safe, I shall not take his life, and the same is true for all the friends of fair Zenocrate — if with their lives they will be pleased to yield, or may be forced to make me Emperor; for Egypt and Arabia must be mine."

He then said to Bajazeth, "Eat, you slave; thou should think thyself happy to be fed the scraps from my dinner plate."

Bajazeth said, "My empty stomach, full of idle heat, draws blood from my feeble parts" — he was starving and so his body was feeding on itself — "preserving life by hastening cruel death. My veins are pale, my sinews hard and dry, my joints benumbed; unless I eat, I die."

"Eat, Bajazeth," Zabina said. "Let us live in spite of them, in hope that some merciful power or lucky intervention will pity and liberate us."

Bajazeth began to eat the food he had stomped on.

Tamburlaine held out a clean plate to him and said, "Here, Turk; will thou have a clean trencher?"

A trencher is a wooden plate.

"Yes, tyrant, and more food," Bajazeth said.

"Slow down, sir, you must be dieted," Tamburlaine said. "Too much eating will make you sick."

"So it would, my lord," Theridamas said, "especially since he has so small a space to walk in and so little exercise."

Servants brought in three crowns.

Tamburlaine said, "Theridamas, Techelles, and Casane, here are the delicacies you desire to finger, are they not?"

"Yes, my lord," Theridamas said, "but none save Kings must feed with these."

"It is enough for us to see them," Techelles said, "and for only Tamburlaine to enjoy them."

Tamburlaine proposed a toast, "Well, here is now to the Sultan of Egypt, the King of Arabia, and the Governor of Damascus."

These people wore three crowns that he intended to enjoy.

They drank.

Tamburlaine then said to Theridamas, Techelles, and Usumcasane, "Now, take these three crowns, and pledge your loyalty to me, my tributory Kings."

As he handed out the crowns, he said:

"I crown you here, Theridamas, King of Algiers.

"I crown you here, Techelles, King of Fez.

"And I crown you here, Usumcasane, King of Morocco."

He then said to Bajazeth, "What do you say to this, Turk? These are not your tributory Kings."

"Nor shall they long be thine, I promise them," Bajazeth said.

Tamburlaine said, "Kings of Algiers, of Fez, and of Morocco, you who have marched with happy, fortunate Tamburlaine as far as from the frozen region of Heaven — the tops of snowy mountains in the far north — to the watery, dewy morning's ruddy red abode in the East, and from there by land to the torrid zone between the Tropic of Cancer and the Tropic of Capricorn" — Tamburlaine was vastly exaggerating the distance they had traveled together — "deserve these titles I endow you with because of your valor and your fortitude.

"Your non-noble births shall be no blemish to your reputations and honors, for virtue — power and ability — is the fountain from which honor springs, and they whom the personified Virtue invests as Kings are worthy of being Kings."

Theridamas said, "And, since your highness has so graciously granted us these crowns, if we do not deserve them with greater excellence in our bearings and actions than formerly we have possessed, take them away again, and make us slaves."

"Well said, Theridamas," Tamburlaine said. "When holy Fates shall establish me in strong Egypt, we intend to travel to the Antarctic pole, conquering the people underneath our feet — those in the Southern Hemisphere — and be renowned as never Emperors were.

"Zenocrate, I will not crown you yet — not until with greater honors I am graced."

CHAPTER 5 (Part 1)

— 5.1 —

The Governor of Damascus met with three or four citizens, and with four virgins holding branches of laurel in their hands.

The Governor of Damascus said, "Still does this man, or rather god, of war, batter our walls and beat our turrets down, and to resist with longer stubbornness, or hope of rescue from the Sultan of Egypt's army, would only bring our willful overthrow, and make us despair of saving our threatened lives.

"We see that Tamburlaine's tents have now been altered terrifyingly to the last and cruelest hue. His coal-black colors, everywhere raised high, threaten our city with a general slaughter that no one will escape.

"And if we would in accordance with common rites of war offer our lives to his mercy, I fear that he will follow the custom peculiar to his sword and his mode of warfare, which he observes as an essential part of his reputation, intending by doing so to terrify the world.

"I fear that not until after we are dead will he allow himself to make any change in his established military practice or feel pity.

"I fear that he will follow his own custom and slaughter all of us because we did not surrender to him earlier.

"Therefore, for these our innocent, harmless virgins' sakes, whose honors and whose lives rely on him, let us have hope that their pure prayers and entreaties, their tearful cheeks, and their heartfelt humble moans will melt his fury into some pity, and persuade him to treat us like a loving conqueror would."

The Governor of Damascus was hoping the virgins would make Tamburlaine both feel pity and change his custom of slaughtering all the citizens of a city that surrendered to him on or after the third day of his siege.

The first virgin said, "If humble entreaties or prayers, uttered with tears of wretchedness and blood shed from the heads and hearts of all our female sex, some of whom are your wives, and some of whom are your children, might have entreated your stubborn, obdurate breasts to think to take some care of our safety while only danger and not certain destruction beat upon our walls, these more than dangerous promises of our death — Tamburlaine's black tents and banners — would have never been erected as now they are, nor would you depend on such weak helps as we virgins are. You should have surrendered earlier."

The women of Damascus had pleaded for the city to be surrendered earlier, but their pleas had not been effective.

The Governor of Damascus replied, "Well, lovely virgins, consider our concern for our country, our love of honor, our repugnance at the thought of being enslaved to foreign powers and rough imperious yokes. We would not with too much cowardice or fear — before all hope of rescue was denied — submit yourselves and us to servitude."

The Governor of Damascus was loath to surrender to Tamburlaine because of honor and because of fear of enslavement as long as there was hope that the Sultan of Egypt would rescue them.

He continued, "Therefore, since your safeties and our own, your honors, liberties, and lives were weighed in equal care and balance with our own, endure as we endure the malice of our astrological stars that have been malignant toward us. Endure also the wrath of Tamburlaine and the power of wars, or be the means the overruling powers of Heaven have kept in reserve to alleviate this hot crisis, and bring us pardon in your cheerful looks."

The second virgin prayed, "Then here, before the majesty of Heaven and the holy patrons of Egypt, on our knees and with submissive hearts we entreat grace to our words and pity to our looks so that this plan may prove propitious, and so that through the eyes and ears of Tamburlaine we may make him feel in his heart that a merciful outcome to the siege is possible.

"Grant that these signs of victory we yield may bind the temples of his conquering head to hide the folded furrows of his brows as his anger fades, and envelop his displeased countenance with propitious looks of pity and mercy."

The virgins were holding branches of laurel that they were going to make into a wreath that Tamburlaine would wear if he showed pity to them and to the other citizens of Damascus.

She continued, "Leave us, my lord, and loving countrymen. What simple virgins may persuade, we will. We will do our best to persuade Tamburlaine to save all of our lives."

The Governor of Damascus replied, "Farewell, sweet virgins, on whose safe return depend our city, liberty, and lives."

The virgins of Damascus had left the city and were now in Tamburlaine's camp. Tamburlaine, Theridamas, Techelles, Usumcasane, and others walked over to the virgins. Tamburlaine was wearing black clothing, and he was very melancholy.

He said, referring to the virgins, "What! Are the turtledoves frightened out of their nests? Alas, poor fools, must you be the first who shall feel the destruction of Damascus I have sworn?

"The city rulers know my customs of warfare. Couldn't they as well have sent you out when first appeared my milk-white flags, through which sweet mercy threw her gentle beams, casting them on Damascus' disdainful eyes as now when fury and incensed hate flings slaughtering terror from my coal-black tents, and tells truly that your submission comes too late?"

The first virgin said, "Most happy King and Emperor of the Earth, image of honor and nobility, for whom the divine powers have made the world and on whose throne the holy Graces sit" — the three Graces, aka Charities, were goddesses of charm, beauty, and gracefulness — "in whose sweet person is comprised the sum of nature's skill and heavenly majesty, pity our plights!

"Oh, pity poor Damascus!

"Pity our old people, within whose silver hairs honor and reverence evermore have reigned.

"Pity the marriage bed, where many a lord, in the prime and glory of his loving joy, embraces now with tears of pity and blood the apprehensive body of his fearful wife, whose cheeks and hearts, so tormented with fearful imaginings that they think that your powerful, never-resting arm will part their bodies and deprive their souls of heavens of comfort that they might enjoy as they age.

"Now all the people of Damascus grow pale and withered to the death, for grief because our ruthless Governor of Damascus has thus refused the mercy of your hand, whose scepter angels kiss and Furies dread. All the people of Damascus also grieve for the loss of their liberties, their loves, or their lives. We regret that the Governor of Damascus did not earlier surrender to you.

"Oh, then, for these, and for such as we ourselves, for us, for infants, and for all our lives, which never nourished thought against your rule, pity, oh, pity, sacred Emperor, the prostrate homage of this wretched town" — the virgins prostrated themselves before Tamburlaine — "and take in sign thereof this gilded wreath, whereto each man in a position of ruling authority has given his hand, and has wished, as worthy subjects, to have the happy opportunity to ceremonially adorn your royal brows and crown you with this wreath even as with the true Egyptian diadem."

If Tamburlaine were to accept and wear the wreath, then that would mean that he had accepted the virgins' petition to him and he would not kill the citizens of Damascus. The wreath was also a symbol of the intention of the citizens of Damascus to regard him as their legitimate ruler.

Tamburlaine replied, "Virgins, in vain you labor to prevent that which my honor swears shall be performed. Behold my sword. What do you see at the point?"

The first virgin replied, "Nothing but fear and deadly steel, my lord."

Tamburlaine said, "Your full-of-fear minds are thick and misty then, for there sits Death; there sits imperious Death, traveling his circuit along the slicing edge of my sword."

Tamburlaine was comparing Death to a traveling judge whose circuit — accustomed path as he traveled from one court to another — was the path traveled by Tamburlaine's sword as he fought in battle.

He continued, "But it pleases me that you shall not see him there. He now is seated on my horsemen's spears, and on their points his fleshless skeletal body feeds."

Then he ordered, "Techelles, immediately go charge — order — a few of them to charge these dames and present to the virgins my servant, Death, sitting in scarlet — a red judge's robe, and blood — on their ready spears."

The virgins begged, "Oh, pity us!"

"Away with them, I say, and show them Death," Tamburlaine ordered.

Techelles and some soldiers took the virgins away.

Tamburlaine said, "I will not spare these proud Egyptians, nor change my customary martial practices for all the wealth of the river Gihon's golden waves."

A river that watered the Garden of Eden divided into four rivers. According to Genesis 2:13, the second river was Gihon: "*And the name of the second river is Gihon: the same compasseth the whole land of Cush*" (1599 Geneva Bible). Gihon is often identified with the Nile.

He continued, "I will not spare these proud Egyptians for the love of Venus, even if she would leave the angry god of arms and lie with me."

Venus, goddess of sexual passion, had had an affair with Mars, god of war.

Tamburlaine continued, "They have refused the offer of their lives and they know that my customary military practices are as peremptory and absolutely decided as are wrathful planets, death, or destiny."

Techelles returned.

Tamburlaine asked him, "Have your horsemen shown the virgins Death?"

"They have, my lord," Techelles answered, "and on Damascus' walls they have hoisted up the virgins' slaughtered carcasses."

Tamburlaine said, "That is a sight as toxic to their souls, I think, as are Thessalian drugs or mithridate."

Drugs can be used to cure people, and mithridate is a poison antidote. These things are hateful to the people of Damascus because the sight of the slaughtered virgins makes them wish not to prolong life because they know that they will die just like the virgins did. Some citizens are likely thinking that suicide by poison is a better and more honorable death than being slaughtered by Tamburlaine's warriors. The Median lord Agydas and the ancient Roman Cato the Younger considered suicide to be an honorable death in their situations.

Thessalian women are medicine women. A tradition states that Medea threw away her basket of medicinal plants, and the plants sprouted on Thessalian soil. According to a myth, Medea restored the health of Aeson, Jason's father, by withdrawing his blood, adding medicine to it, and then infusing it back into his body. Tamburlaine would withdraw the blood from the bodies of the citizens of Damascus, but the blood would not be infused back into their bodies.

Tamburlaine ordered, "But go, my lords, put the rest of the citizens of Damascus to the sword."

Everyone except Tamburlaine exited. He began a meditation on beauty and mercy and honor:

"Ah, fair Zenocrate! Divine Zenocrate! Fair is too foul an epithet for you, who feel extreme sorrow out of love for your country and feel fear that you will see harm come to your kingly father.

"You wipe your watery cheeks with your disheveled hair; and, like Flora, goddess of flowers, in her morning's pride, shaking her silver tresses in the air, you rain on the earth dissolved pearls — tears — in showers, and sprinkle blue sapphires — tears that catch the blue color of the sky — on your shining face, where Beauty, the mother of the Muses, sits, and writes with her ivory pen a commentary on the beauty of you, Zenocrate, taking instructions from your flowing eyes — eyes that when Ebena, personification of Night, steps to Heaven, in the silence of your solemn evening's walk, making the mantle of the richest night, the Moon, the planets, and the meteors, light. The Moon, the planets, and the meteors all receive their light from your eyes.

"There in your beautiful, sorrowful face angels in their crystal armors fight a divisive battle with my thoughts that are tempted to show mercy for Egypt's freedom and the Sultan's life, his life that so consumes Zenocrate with anxiety, whose sorrows lay more siege to my soul than all my army to Damascus' walls.

"Neither Persia's sovereign nor the Turk troubled my senses with thoughts of defeat as much as does Zenocrate. Zenocrate's beauty threatens to defeat me by making me merciful.

"What is beauty, ask my sufferings, then?

"If all the pens that poets ever held had fed the feeling of their masters' thoughts, and every sweetness that inspired their hearts, their minds, and their meditations on admired themes ...

"If all the heavenly quintessence — the most essential part — they distill from their immortal flowers of poetry, wherein, as in a mirror, we perceive the highest reaches of a human poetic intelligence ...

"If all of these had achieved the poets' goal of describing perfect beauty in one poem and if all of these had combined in describing beauty's worthiness ...

"Yet there would hover in the poets' restless heads one thought, one grace, one wonder, at the least, which no creative power can distill into words and express."

That one thought, one grace, one wonder is a paradox. One ought to pursue virtue, and virtue ought to encourage virtue. Virtue is excellence, and many kinds of excellence exist. One virtue is bodily excellence, or beauty. Another virtue is military excellence, which Tamburlaine believed in his case means having a code, and sticking to that code. To Tamburlaine, it is honorable to keep his word, and if he has sworn to kill all the citizens of a city that surrenders on the third day, then that is what he should do.

Zenocrate possesses the virtue of beauty, and that virtue ought to encourage Tamburlaine's virtue, he believes, but paradoxically it does not, instead encouraging him to be merciful and do the dishonor of breaking his sworn oath.

Tamburlaine continued:

"How unseemly it is for my sex, my discipline of arms and chivalry, my nature, and the terror of my name, to harbor effeminate and faint and weak thoughts!"

Zenocrate's beauty tempts Tamburlaine to show mercy to her father and at least some Egyptians. Indeed, his meditation now is evidence that he is tempted to show mercy to the virgins of Damascus. To Tamburlaine, to show mercy is to break his word. To Tamburlaine, no poet can explain how virtue can lead to lack of virtue.

The virtue is appreciating beauty, and the lack of virtue is not doing what he said he would do — not following his military code. For Tamburlaine to be true to himself, he has to kill the people he said he would kill.

Tamburlaine continued:

"But we must admit that beauty merits applause, and we must admit that the soul of man is touched instinctively by beauty, and we must admit that every warrior who is rapt and smitten with love of fame, of valor, and of victory, must necessarily have beauty beat on his thoughts.

"I thus both conceiving of and responding to beauty and subduing and controlling that response, shall cause the world to believe, for all my low birth, that virtue — excellence, which in my case is excellence as a military commander — solely is the high point of glory, and forms men with true nobility."

Tamburlaine believed that he could be a man of true nobility if he could both appreciate and respond to beauty and yet resist the temptations that beauty led him to — such as the temptation of showing mercy when he had sworn he would not show mercy.

He continued:

"What is it that I must conceive of and respond to and that I must subdue and control?

"It is that which has stooped the topmost of the gods and stopped the tempest of the gods who have come even from the fiery star-spangled veil of Heaven, to feel the lovely and lowly warmth of shepherds' flames and enter cottages strewn with reeds."

The classical gods often fell in love with and slept with mortals. In order to sleep with the mortal woman Mnemosyne, Jupiter, the King of the gods, disguised himself as a humble shepherd, and so the topmost of the gods stooped.

Jupiter is the god of *xenia*, which is often translated as hospitality. He grew angry at mortals in a certain region because of their lack of hospitality, and he and Mercury went in disguise to that region and knocked on doors and asked for hospitality. Ancient Greece had no inns, and so this was the accepted way of getting a meal and a place to stay. All of the heads of households in the region refused them hospitality except for an elderly couple named Baucis and Philemon, who invited them into their humble cottage. In gratitude, Jupiter and Mercury destroyed all the homes in the region except for the home of Baucis and Philemon. Here, the beauty of hospitality had stopped the tempest — anger — of the gods and caused them to be merciful.

Tamburlaine continued:

"Let me repeat: I thus both conceiving of and responding to beauty and subduing and controlling that response, shall cause the world to believe, for all my low birth, that virtue — excellence, in my case excellence as a military commander — solely is the high point of glory, and forms men with true nobility."

Tamburlaine was as good as his word: While meditating on Zenocrate's beauty, he had allowed his soldiers to slaughter all the inhabitants — men, women, and children — of Damascus. He knew that this would cause Zenocrate anguish because Damascus was in the territory controlled by her father, the Sultan of Egypt.

He stopped, and then he asked, "Who's within there?"

Two or three attendants entered the tent.

Tamburlaine asked, "Has Bajazeth been fed today?"

"Yes, my lord," an attendant replied.

"Bring him forth," Tamburlaine ordered, "and let us know if Damascus has been ransacked."

The attendants exited.

Theridamas, Techelles, Usumcasane, and others arrived.

Techelles said, "The town is ours, my lord, and a fresh supply of conquest and of spoil is offered to us."

"That's well, Techelles," Tamburlaine said. "What's the news?"

"The Sultan of Egypt and the King of Arabia together march on us with such eager violence that it is as if there were no way but one with us."

For the Egyptians, this is the "no way but one with us": "The Egyptians and Arabians are going to take the lives of Tamburlaine and his soldiers."

Tamburlaine replied, "No more than one there's not, I promise you, Techelles."

For Tamburlaine, this is the "no way but one with us": "We are going to take the lives of the Egyptians and Arabians."

The Moors brought in the Turk, Bajazeth, in his cage. Zabina followed them.

"We know the victory is ours, my lord," Theridamas said, referring to a future victory, "but let us save the reverend Sultan of Egypt's life for fair Zenocrate who so laments his state."

Using the majestic plural, Tamburlaine said, "That we will chiefly see to, Theridamas. We will do it for sweet Zenocrate, whose worthiness deserves a conquest over every heart."

He then said to Bajazeth, "And now, my footstool, if I lose the battle, do you hope for liberty and restitution?"

Then he ordered, "Here let him stay, my good sirs, away from the tents, until we have made us ready to fight on the battlefield."

Then he said, "Pray for us, Bajazeth; we are going."

Everyone exited except Bajazeth and Zabina.

"Go, never to return with victory!" Bajazeth said as Tamburlaine and the others exited. "May millions of men surround thee about, and gore thy body with as many wounds! May sharp barbed arrows light upon thy horse! May Furies from the lake of the black Cocytus break up the earth, and with their firebrands force you to run upon the life-destroying pikes! May volleys of shot pierce through thy charmed skin, and may every projectile be dipped in poisoned drugs! Or may roaring cannons sever all thy joints, blasting them high in the sky and making thee mount as high as eagles soar!"

Zabina said, "Let all the swords and lances in the battlefield stick in Tamburlaine's breast just as they fit in their proper rooms — their sheaths! At every pore of his body let blood come dropping forth, so that lingering pains may massacre his heart and madness send his damned soul to Hell!"

"Ah, fair Zabina," Bajazeth said, "we may curse his power, the heavens may frown, the earth may quake for anger, but such a favorable astrological star has influence in his sword as rules the skies and overrules the gods more than Cimmerian Styx or destiny."

The ancient gods were not omnipotent; they sometimes were forced to do what they didn't want to do. Phaëthon, the mortal son of the Sun-god, asked for a gift, which his father swore an inviolable oath to give to him. The gift was to be allowed to drive the Sun-chariot across the sky. Because his father had sworn an inviolable oath, he had to grant it.

The ancient gods were not omniscient; they did not know everything and so could be tricked. In Book 14 of Homer's *Iliad*, Hera wants to trick Zeus. To do so, she needs the god of Sleep to put Zeus to sleep so that the Greeks, whom she supports, can rally against the Trojans. To get the god of Sleep's help, she tells him that she will give him Pasithea, one of the Graces, to marry. This makes him happy, but he makes her swear an oath on the inviolable waters of the Styx that she will keep her word. Hera's trick works: Sleep puts Zeus to sleep, and the Greek troops rally.

The gods also cannot alter destiny, aka fate. Zeus' mortal son Sarpedon is fated to die in the Trojan War, In Book 16 of the *Iliad*, Sarpedon fights Patroclus, and Zeus knows that Sarpedon will die. Zeus is tempted to go against fate and save Sarpedon's life, but Hera tells him that if he does, the other gods and goddesses will want to save the lives of their mortal children. This apparently would have very bad effects on the universe. Saving Sarpedon's life would have such bad consequences that Zeus is forced to allow his son to die.

Zeus' Roman name is Jupiter, and Hera's Roman name is Juno.

According to Bajazeth, Tamburlaine has more power over the gods than do inviolable oaths and destiny.

Bajazeth continued, "And then shall we in this detested manner remain" — he could not bring himself to say "live" — "with shame, with hunger, and with horror, clutching our bowels with thoughts bending back to our former glory, and have no hope to end our frenzied fears and anguish."

Zabina said, "Then is there left no Mahomet, no god, no fiend from Hell to pray to, is there no Lady Fortune, and is there no hope of an end to our infamous, monstrous slaveries?

"Gape open, earth, and let the infernal fiends below view up here a Hell as hopeless and as full of fear as are the withered blasted banks of Erebus — the dark passage leading to Hell — where the shaking ghosts of the dead with ever-howling groans hover about the ugly ferryman Charon to get a passage to Elysium!"

Charon ferried spirits across the Styx into the Land of the Dead. Elysium is the part of the Land of the Dead that good souls go to. To Zabina, any part of the Land of the Dead would be Elysium in comparison to her present life.

"Why should we live" — Zabina gave a cry of distress — "as wretches, beggars, slaves!

"Why do we live, Bajazeth, and metaphorically build up nests so high within the region of the air, living on false hopes and building castles in the air, exposing ourselves by living long in this oppression, thereby ensuring that all the world will see us and laugh to scorn the former triumphs of our mightiness in this obscure infernal servitude we suffer?"

Bajazeth said, "Oh, life, more loathsome to my vexed and troubled thoughts than the foul vomit of the snakes of the Styx — vomit that fills the nooks of Hell with stagnant, unmoving air, infecting all the ghosts with cureless griefs!

"Oh, dreary instruments — eyes — of my loathed sight, that see my crown, my honor, and my name thrust under the yoke of a thief and see my captivity to a thief, why do you still feed on day's accursed beams, and not sink entirely into my tortured soul?

"You see my wife, my Queen, and my Empress, brought up and supported by the hand of Fame, Queen of fifteen tributory Queens, now thrown to employments of black degradation, smeared with blots of basest drudgery and menial work, and slave to shame, disdain, and misery.

"Accursed Bajazeth, whose words of pity that would with pity cheer Zabina's heart, and make our souls dissolve in ceaseless tears, sharp hunger bites upon and grips the root from whence the issue of my thoughts break."

Bajazeth's extreme hunger prevented him from thinking of and saying compassionate words to Zabina.

He continued, "Oh, poor Zabina! Oh, my Queen, my Queen! Fetch me some water for my burning breast, to cool and comfort me with longer life, so that in the shortened remainder of my life I may pour forth my soul into your arms with words of love whose moaning intercourse has hitherto been prevented with wrath and hate of our inexpressible cursed inflictions."

Zabina said, "Sweet Bajazeth, I will prolong your life as long as any blood or spark of breath can quench or cool the torments of my grief."

She exited.

Alone, Bajazeth said, "Now, Bajazeth, shorten your poisoned days, and beat the brains out of your conquered head, since all other means of suicide are forbidden me.

"Oh, Sun — highest lamp of ever-living, immortal Jove, accursed day, infected with my griefs — hide now your stained face in endless night, and shut the windows of the luminous, radiant heavens.

"Let ugly darkness with her rusty coach encircled with tempests, wrapped in pitch-black clouds, smother the earth with never fading mists, and let the horses pulling Darkness' coach breathe from their nostrils rebellious winds and dreadful thunderclaps, so that in this terror Tamburlaine may live, and my withering-away-from-sorrow soul, dissolved in the clear air, may still torture his tormented thoughts!

"Then let the stone-hearted spear of unfeeling cold pierce through the center of my withered heart, and make a passage for my loathed life!"

He brained himself against the cage.

Zabina returned and said, "What do my eyes see? My husband dead! His skull all split in two, his brains dashed out! The brains of Bajazeth, my lord and sovereign!

"Oh, Bajazeth, my husband and my lord!

"Oh, Bajazeth! Oh, Turk! Oh, Emperor!

"Give him his water? Not I. Bring milk and fire, and my blood I bring him again.

"Tear me in pieces.

"Give me the sword with a ball of incendiary wild-fire upon it.

"Down with him! Down with him!

"Go to, my child. Away! Away! Away!

"Ah, save that infant, save him, save him! I, even I, speak to her.

"The Sun was down. Streamers — pennons — white, red, black.

"Here, here, here! Fling the food in his face!

"Tamburlaine, Tamburlaine! Let the soldiers be buried. Hell, death, Tamburlaine, Hell!

"Make ready my coach, my chair, my jewels. I come! I come! I come!"

She ran against the cage and brained herself.

Zenocrate and Anippe arrived. Zenocrate was grieving so much over the deaths of the virgins and the other citizens of Damascus that at first she didn't notice the corpses of Bajazeth and Zabina.

Zenocrate said to herself, "Wretched Zenocrate, you have lived to see Damascus' walls dyed with Egyptian blood, the blood of your father's subjects and your countrymen. I have lived to see the streets strewn with the dissevered joints of men, I have lived to see the streets strewn with wounded bodies still gasping for life, and I have lived to see the most accursed sight of all: the Sun-bright troop of heavenly virgins and unspotted-by-sin maidens on horsemen's lances hoisted up and despite being guiltless forced to endure a cruel death.

"The looks of these virgins might make Mars, the angry god of arms, break his sword and mildly talk about love.

"When all their riders leveled their quivering spears for the charge against the virgins, then every deadly and formidable Tartarian steed that stamped on others with their thundering hooves, began to stop suddenly and stamp on the ground and rein themselves and pause, gazing upon the beauty of the virgins' looks.

"Ah, Tamburlaine, were you the cause of this, you who call me, Zenocrate, your dearest love?

"The virgins' lives were dearer to me, Zenocrate, than Zenocrate's own life, or anything except your own love."

Zenocrate now noticed the corpses of Bajazeth and Zabina and said, "But look, another bloody spectacle! Ah, wretched eyes, the enemies of my heart, how are you eyes of mine glutted with these grievous objects, and yet tell my soul more tales of bleeding suffering!

"Anippe, see whether they breathe or not."

Anippe examined the corpses of Bajazeth and Zabina and said, "No breath, nor sense, nor motion, in them both. Ah, madam, their slavery and the pitiless cruelty of Tamburlaine have forced them to do this!"

Zenocrate said, "Earth, cast up fountains of lava from your entrails, and wet your cheeks because of the untimely and too-early deaths of Bajazeth and Zabina.

"Shake with the weight of their corpses in an earthquake as a sign of fear and grief.

"Blush with shame, Heaven, you that gave them honor at their birth and let them die a death so barbarous.

"You people who are proud of treacherous imperial rule and place your chiefest good in earthly pomp, behold the Turk and his great Empress!

"Ah, Tamburlaine my love, sweet Tamburlaine, who fights for scepters and for slippery, hard-to-hold-on-to crowns, behold the Turk and his great Empress!

"You, Tamburlaine, under the guidance of your happy, fortunate stars, sleep every night with conquest and victory on your brows and yet you would shun the fortune-changing turns of war out of fear if you could feel the distress that Bajazeth and Zabina felt, behold the Turk and his great Empress!

"Ah, mighty Jove and holy Mahomet, forgive my love for Tamburlaine!

"Oh, pardon his contempt of earthly fortune and his contempt of regard for pity."

Tamburlaine did not show pity because he held in contempt the turn of the Wheel of Fortune. He believed that he would stay at the top of the wheel and therefore he felt no empathy and no pity for those who had fallen.

Zenocrate continued, "And let not conquest, ruthlessly pursued, be equally incensed against his life as it was against the lives of this great Turk and unlucky Empress!"

"And pardon me who was not moved with pity to see Bajazeth and Zabina live so long in misery!

"Ah, what may chance to happen to you, Zenocrate?"

Anippe said, "Madam, calm yourself, and know that your love — Tamburlaine — has Lady Fortune so much at his command that she shall stay her hand and turn her wheel no more, as long as life maintains the mighty arm of him who fights for honor so that he can adorn your head with a crown."

Philemus, a messenger, arrived.

Zenocrate asked, "What other sad, heavy news now brings Philemus?"

He replied, "Madam, your father, and the Arabian King, the first man who loved your excellence, comes now, as Turnus against Aeneas did, armed with lances into the Egyptian battlefields, ready to do battle against my lord, King Tamburlaine."

When Aeneas landed in Italy after the Trojan War, he fought a war against Turnus, leader of the Rutulian soldiers. He killed Turnus in single combat and won the right to marry the Italian Princess Lavinia.

Zenocrate said, "Now shame and duty, love and fear present a thousand sorrows to my martyred soul.

"Whom should I wish to achieve the fatal victory, when my poor pleasures are divided thus, and racked by duty from my cursed heart?

"My father and my first-betrothed love must fight against my life and present love.

"The change in allegiance I have made condemns my faith and makes my deeds infamous through the world."

She had, in fact, made a change in allegiance: She would support her beloved Tamburlaine instead of her beloved father and her first-betrothed love in the battle. But no matter whom she supported, people would blame her.

If Zenocrate supported her beloved father instead of her beloved Tamburlaine in the battle, then that would show a lack of loyalty to Tamburlaine, and people in the world would regard her as disloyal to him.

If Zenocrate supported her beloved Tamburlaine instead of her beloved father in the battle, then that would show a lack of loyalty to her beloved father, and people in the world would regard her as disloyal to him.

If Zenocrate supported her first-betrothed love instead of her beloved Tamburlaine in the battle, then that would show a lack of loyalty to her beloved Tamburlaine, and people in the world would regard her as disloyal to him.

If Zenocrate supported her beloved Tamburlaine instead of her first-betrothed love in the battle, then that would show a lack of loyalty to her first-betrothed love, and people in the world would regard her as disloyal to him.

Zenocrate continued:

"But as the gods, to end the Trojans' toil, deprived Turnus of Lavinia and fatally enriched Aeneas' love, so, for a final end to my griefs, to pacify both my country and my love, Tamburlaine must by the gods' resistless powers, by virtue of a gentle victory, conclude a treaty of honor in accordance with my hope. Then, as the divine Powers have preordained, Tamburlaine will provide happy safety for my father's life and send the same happy safety for the life of the fair King of Arabia."

Zenocrate was hoping that Tamburlaine would win a victory with little loss of life and the divine Powers would ensure that he spare the lives of her father and the man she had first been engaged to.

The battle took place, and Tamburlaine won the victory. Alcidamas, the King of Arabia, mortally wounded, walked near Zenocrate.

Not seeing Zenocrate, King Alcidamas of Arabia said to himself, "What cursed power guides the murdering hands of this infamous tyrant's soldiers, ensuring that no escape may save their enemies, and that fortune will not keep themselves from victory?"

As he lay down, he added, "Lie down, you King of Arabia, wounded to the death, and let Zenocrate's fair eyes behold that, as for her you bore these wretched weapons, these wretched arms, even so for her you die in these arms, leaving your blood for witness of your love."

Zenocrate went to him, cradled his head, and said, "I am too dear a witness for such love, my lord. Behold Zenocrate, the cursed object whose fortune in life has never conquered her sorrows and griefs.

"Behold her wounded in conceit for you as much as your fair body is wounded for me!"

Zenocrate's words were ambiguous:

1) "Behold her wounded in her mind for you as much as your fair body is wounded for me!"

This meant that she really did mourn his death. Indeed, the sights of the dead and wounded hurt her mind.

2) "Behold her wounded in your mind as much as your fair body is wounded for me!"

This meant that he should pretend that she really did mourn his death.

Zenocrate meant the first meaning, but Alcidamas thought she meant the second meaning. He, nevertheless, was a good man and he was happy if she was happy. Apparently, Zenocrate loved Tamburlaine despite being — Alcidamas thought — his captive. This victory would make the man she loved much more famous and powerful, although it would kill the man who first loved her.

King Alcidamas of Arabia said, "Then I shall die with a fully contented heart, having beheld divine Zenocrate, whose sight would take away my life with joy, as now it brings sweetness to my wound, if I had not been wounded as I am. Simply seeing you kills with joy, even without this wound.

"Ah, if only the deadly pangs I suffer now would lend another hour's license to my tongue, so that we could talk about some sweet occurrences of good fortune that have happened to you, you whose merits make you deserve them, in this bondage that is unworthy of you, and that I might know the secret of the state of your deserved contentment and your love.

"But, making now a virtue of my seeing you, to drive all sorrow from my fainting soul, since death denies me any further cause of joy, deprived of care, my heart with comfort dies, since your desired hand shall close my eyes."

He died.

Tamburlaine arrived, leading Zenocrate's father: the Sultan of Egypt. Theridamas, Techelles, Usumcasane, and others also arrived.

Tamburlaine said to the Sultan of Egypt, "Come, fortunate father of Zenocrate, a title higher than your Sultan's name. Although my right hand has thus enslaved you, your princely daughter here shall set you free. She has calmed the fury of my sword, which before this time has been bathed in streams of blood as vast and deep as the Euphrates or the Nile."

Zenocrate said, "Oh, sight thrice welcome to my joyful soul: To see the King, my father, come out safe from a dangerous battle against my conquering love!"

"We are well met, my only-dear Zenocrate, although with the loss of Egypt and my crown," the Sultan of Egypt said.

"It was I, my lord, who got the victory," Tamburlaine said to him, "and therefore don't grieve at your overthrow, since I shall render all into your hands, and add more strength to your dominions than has ever yet sustained the Egyptian crown.

"Mars, the god of war, resigns his position to me, intending to make me general of the world.

"Jove, viewing me in arms, looks pale and wan, fearing my power should pull him from his throne just like he pulled his father from the throne.

"Wherever I come the Fatal Sisters — the Three Fates — sweat, and so does grisly Death, because of running to-and-fro to do their ceaseless homage to my sword. I keep the Fates busy with cutting the threads of life, and I keep Death busy collecting the newly made ghosts of the dead.

"And here in Africa, where it seldom rains, since I arrived with my triumphant army, swelling clouds, drawn from wide-gasping wounds, have been often dissolved in bloody purple showers."

The spurts of blood caused by his soldiers' swords fell like rain in Egypt; in addition, people in this culture believed that the Sun could cause pools of blood to evaporate, form clouds, and become red rain.

Tamburlaine continued, "This is an evil omen that might terrify the earth, and make it quake at every drop of blood it drinks. Millions of souls sit on the banks of the Styx, waiting the return of Charon's boat, which is kept busy ferrying souls to the Land of the Dead.

"Hell and Elysium swarm with men whom I have sent from several battlefields to spread my fame through Hell and up to Heaven.

"And look, my lord, at a sight of unusual importance, Emperors and Kings lie breathless at my feet. The Turk and his great Empress, as it seems, left to themselves while we were at the battle, have desperately dispatched their slavish lives. With them the King of Arabia, too, has left his life.

"These are all sights of power that grace my victory, and as such they are fit for Tamburlaine to see.

"By looking at these sights, as if looking in a mirror, I may see my honor, which consists of shedding blood when men presume to wage war against me."

The Sultan of Egypt said, "Mighty has God and Mahomet made your hand, renowned Tamburlaine, to whom all Kings by force of necessity must yield their crowns and empires, and I am pleased with this my overthrow, if, as befits a person of your state, you have treated Zenocrate with honor."

Tamburlaine said, "Her state and person lack no pomp, as you can see, and as for all blot of foul lack of chastity, I call on Heaven to witness that her heavenly self is clear.

"Now then let me seek no more distant time to grace her princely temples with the Persian crown. Instead, here these Kings who attend on my fortunes, and have been crowned for proven worthiness, even by this hand that shall establish them, shall now, adjoining all their hands with mine, invest her here as my Queen of Persia. She and I shall be married.

"What do the noble Sultan of Egypt and Zenocrate say to that?"

The Sultan of Egypt said, "I yield with thanks and professions of endless honor to you because of her love of you and because of your love of her."

Tamburlaine said, "Then I don't doubt that fair Zenocrate will soon consent to satisfy us both."

"Otherwise I should much forget myself, my lord," Zenocrate said.

Theridamas said, "Then let us set the crown upon her head; the crown has long awaited so high a seat."

"My hand is ready to perform the deed," Techelles said, "for now her marriage time shall give us a time for rest."

Holding the crown, Usumcasane said to Tamburlaine, "And here's the crown, my lord; help set it on her head."

"So then sit down, divine Zenocrate," Tamburlaine said.

She sat on a throne.

Tamburlaine said, "Here we crown you Queen of Persia and of all the Kingdoms and dominions that recently the power of Tamburlaine has subdued."

He set the crown on her head.

Tamburlaine continued:

"Just like Juno, when the Giants who threw mountains at her brother Jove were suppressed, so my love looks. In her brows she portrays triumphs and trophies for my victories, or she portrays Latona's daughter, Diana, who is devoted to arms, adding more courage to my conquering mind."

Actually, Diana was much more devoted to hunting with weapons than to battling with weapons.

Tamburlaine continued:

"To gratify you, sweet Zenocrate, Egyptians, Moors, and men of Asia, from Barbary on the north coast of Africa to the western India, shall pay a yearly tribute to thy father; and from the boundaries of Africa to the banks of the Ganges shall his mighty arm extend.

"And now, my lords and loving followers, who won Kingdoms by your martial deeds, cast off your armor, put on scarlet robes of peaceful lawmakers, mount and rise up to your royal places of estate and be Kings, surrounded with troops of noblemen, and there make laws to rule your provinces."

Theridamas, Techelles, and Usumcasane were now able to rule their Kingdoms.

Tamburlaine continued:

"Hang up your weapons on Alcides' post — the doorpost of the temple dedicated to Hercules, another name for whom is Alcides — for Tamburlaine takes a truce with all the world."

He said to Zenocrate, "Your first-betrothed love, the King of Arabia, we shall with honor, as is fitting, entomb with this great Turk and his fair Empress. Then, after all these solemn funeral rites, we will perform our celebrated rites of marriage."

NOTES (Part 1)

— 4.2 —

The quotation in Act 4, Scene 2, comes from a footnote in W.R.M. Lamb's translation of *Timaeus* 39d:

Plato. *Plato in Twelve Volumes, Vol. 9* translated by W.R.M. Lamb. Cambridge, MA, Harvard University Press; London, William Heinemann Ltd. 1925.

http://www.perseus.tufts.edu/hopper/
text?doc=Perseus%3Atext%3A1999.01.0180%3Atext%3DTim.%3Asection%3D

One source that states that these two stories — Cephalus and the wolf, and Cephalus and Procris — are about two different Cephaluses is this:

https://www.britannica.com/topic/Cephalus

— 5.1 —

"Draw down the moon, hide it in a mirror: On Thessalian medicine women." 5 April 2018.

"'Thessalian woman': refers to medicine women, since the Thessalians are accused of being sorcerers. Even to the present day, Thessalian women are called medicine women (*pharmakides*). They say it's because when Medea fled, she tossed her basket of medicines (*pharmaka*) and there they sprouted."

https://www.ancientmedicine.org/home/2018/4/5/bring-down-the-moon-hide-it-in-a-mirror-on-thessalian-medicine-women

TAMBURLAINE, PART 2

97

CAST OF CHARACTERS (Part 2)

The Prologue.

Male Characters

Tamburlaine, King of Persia.

Tamburlaine's Sons:

• Calyphas, Tamburlaine's oldest son.

• Amyras, Tamburlaine's middle son.

• Celebinus, Tamburlaine's youngest son.

Tamburlaine's Kings:

• Theridamas, King of Algiers.

• Techelles, King of Fez.

• Usumcasane, King of Morocco (nicknamed Casane).

Other Kings:

Orcanes, King of Natolia. (Natolia is bigger than modern Anatolia; it includes all of the promontory of Asia Minor; approximately Turkey.)

• King of Trebizond.

• King of Syria.

• King of Jerusalem.

• King of Amasia.

• Gazellus, Viceroy of Byron, which is located near Babylon.

• Uribassa, Viceroy of a region that is not named.

• Sigismund, King of Hungary.

Lords of Hungary

• Frederick, Lord of Buda.

• Baldwin, Lord of Bohemia.

Callapine, son to Bajazeth and prisoner to Tamburlaine.

Almeda, his keeper.

The Captain of Balsera.

His Son.

Governor of Babylon.

Maximus.

Perdicas.

A Captain.

A Messenger.

Female Characters

Zenocrate, wife to Tamburlaine.

Olympia, wife to the Captain of Balsera.

Minor Characters

Lords, Citizens, Physicians, Soldiers, Pioneers (army ditch diggers and laborers), Turkish Concubines, Attendants.

Nota Bene

At the end of *Tamburlaine the Great, Part 1*, Tamburlaine and Zenocrate married. They now have three mostly grown sons.

In *Tamburlaine the Great, Part 1*, Tamburlaine made Kings of his generals: He made Theridamas the King of Algiers, Techelles the King of Fez, and Usumcasane the King of Morocco. At that time, they were Kings in name only, but since the end of *Tamburlaine the Great, Part 1*, they have been fighting successfully to establish themselves as Kings in reality.

The Ottoman Turks have recovered from their defeat in *Tamburlaine the Great, Part 1*, and they have grown powerful again. Tamburlaine is building an army to fight them. He has as a prisoner Callapine, the son to Bajazeth, the Turkish Emperor who died in *Tamburlaine the Great, Part 1*.

Barbary is the part of North Africa that is west of Egypt.

Cynthia is the personification of the Moon; sometimes, her name is used to refer to the Moon.

Apollo is the personification of the Sun; sometimes, his name is used to refer to the Sun.

THE PROLOGUE (Part 2)

The universal acclaim Tamburlaine received,
  When he arrived last upon our stage,
  Has made our poet — Christopher Marlowe — pen his second part,
  Where death cuts off the progress of Tamburlaine's pomp
  And the three murderous Fates — Clotho, who spins the thread of life;
Lachesis, who measures the thread of life; and Atropos, who cuts the thread of
life — throw all his triumphs down.
  But what became of fair Zenocrate,
  And with how many cities' sacrifice
  He celebrated her sad funeral,
  Tamburlaine himself in his own presence shall unfold at large.

CHAPTER 1 (Part 2)
— 1.1 —

With the death of Bajazeth, the Turkish Emperor, the new Turkish Emperor should be Callapine, his son. Callapine, however, was a prisoner of Tamburlaine in Egypt, and so Deputy Kings, aka Viceroys, were ruling his territories. Orcanes, King of Natolia, was the most powerful and ruled the greatest amount of territory among these Kings.

On the southern bank of the Danube River in Hungary in Europe, he was meeting with two other Deputy Kings. One King was Gazellus, Viceroy of Byron, and the other was Uribassa. With them were their train of attendants, with drummers and trumpeters.

As far as King Orcanes of Natolia was concerned, the meeting was necessary because of Tamburlaine, who was raising an army to fight the Turks. King Orcanes of Natolia was considering making a truce with the Europeans, whose territory in southeast Europe the Turks had been encroaching on. This would free troops to fight Tamburlaine. On the other hand, the Turks could fight the Europeans and try to win more territory. Both sides — the Turks and the Europeans — had armies ready to fight each other.

Soon King Sigismund of Hungary and two Hungarian lords named Frederick and Baldwin would arrive and join the meeting.

King Sigismund of Hungary and the two Hungarian lords were Christians. King Orcanes of Natolia and his fellow Viceroys and Deputy Kings were Muslims.

King Orcanes of Natolia said, "Distinguished Viceroys and Deputy Kings of these eastern parts, all of you — and me — were appointed to your positions by the son of great Bajazeth and sacred lord the mighty Callapine, who lives in Egypt as prisoner to that evil 'slave' Tamburlaine, who kept Callapine's father in an iron cage.

"Now we have marched from fair Natolia two hundred leagues, and our warlike army in complete armor rests on the Danube's banks, where Sigismund, the King of Hungary, is scheduled to meet our person to conclude a truce."

By "our person," he meant "me": He was using the majestic plural.

He continued, "Pay attention! Shall we parley and negotiate with the Christian, or cross the stream and meet him in the battlefield?"

Gazellus, Viceroy of Byron, said, "King of Natolia, let us talk of peace. We are all glutted with the Christians' blood, and we have a greater foe to fight against. That great foe is proud Tamburlaine, who now in Asia, near Guiron, is setting his conquering feet and intends to burn Turkey as he goes."

Guiron is a city on the upper Euphrates River; the city is located near the head of the Giulap River.

Actually, Tamburlaine was gathering his forces at Larissa, a seacoast town located close to Egypt's border with Syria.

Gazellus, Viceroy of Byron, continued, "Against Tamburlaine, my lord, you must prepare your army to fight."

Uribassa said, "Besides, King Sigismund of Hungary has brought from Christendom more than his military camp of stout Hungarians. The soldiers he leads include Slavs, Germans, cavalry, Swiss, and Danes, who with the halberd, lance, and murdering axe will put at risk that which we might otherwise with certainty hold."

King Orcanes of Natolia said, "Even if from the farthest north, vast Greenland, which is encircled by the frozen Arctic Sea and inhabited with tall and sturdy men who are giants as big as the huge one-eyed Cyclops Polyphemus, millions of soldiers cut through and cross the Arctic Circle southward, bringing the strength of Europe to these arms, our Turkish blades shall glide through all their throats, and make this open grassland a bloody swamp."

Orcanes now talked about the Danube River, which empties into the Black Sea. He believed that it formed a current that went across the Black Sea to the Turkish city of Trebizond. From there the current went from the Black Sea through the Bosporus into the Sea of Marmara and then through the Dardanelles into the Mediterranean Sea and through the area of the Mediterranean frequented by Italian sailors.

King Orcanes of Natolia continued, "The Danube River, which empties into the Black Sea and then runs to Trebizond in Natolia, shall carry, wrapped within its scarlet-with-blood waves, as martial presents to our friends at home the slaughtered bodies of these Christians. The bodies of those Christians will be proof to the Turks of our victory.

"The Mediterranean Sea, wherein the Danube River falls, shall by this battle of our Muslim army against the Christians be the Bloody Sea. The wandering sailors of proud Italy shall meet the bodies of those Christians, floating with the tide, beating in heaps against their argosies — their large merchant-ships — and make fair Europe, mounted on her bull, adorned with the wealth and riches of the world, alight from the bull and wear a woeful mourning robe. The slaughtered bodies of these Christians will make Italian sailors afraid."

According to mythology, Jupiter fell in love with a mortal woman named Europa, who was the daughter of King Agenor of Phoenicia. He took the form of a white bull, coaxed her onto his back, and swam with her to the island of Crete. Europe is named after her.

Gazellus said, "Yet, brave Orcanes, Viceroy of the World and leader of the Turks as long as Callapine is imprisoned, since Tamburlaine has mustered all his men, marching from Cairo northward with his camp to Alexandria and the frontier towns, meaning to make a conquest of our land, it is necessary to parley and negotiate for a peace with King Sigismund of Hungary and save our forces for the hot assaults proud Tamburlaine intends to make against Natolia."

King Orcanes of Natolia replied, "Viceroy of the city of Byron, you have spoken wisely. If my realm, the center of our empire, were once lost, all Turkey would be overthrown, and for that reason the Christians shall have peace."

Referring to himself in the third person, he said, "Orcanes does not fear Slavs, Germans, cavalry, Swiss, and Danes, but great Tamburlaine — nor does Orcanes fear him, but he does fear Lady Fortune, who has made Tamburlaine great."

Lady Fortune has a Wheel of Fortune that she turns, and as she turns it, a man's fortune rises and becomes better or his fortune falls and becomes worse. For Tamburlaine, it appeared that she had stopped the Wheel of Fortune with Tamburlaine at the top.

King Orcanes of Natolia said, "We have insurgent renegade Grecians, Albanians, Sicilians, Jews, Arabians, Turks, and Moors, Natolians, Syrians, black Egyptians, Illyrians, Thracians, and Bithynians, enough to swallow forceless, weak King Sigismund of Hungary, yet scarcely enough to encounter Tamburlaine in battle.

"Tamburlaine brings a world of people to the battlefield.

"From Scythia to the oriental — eastern — border of India, where the raging Lantchidol Sea — part of the Indian Ocean — beats with its boisterous blows on the regions that a seaman has never yet discovered, all Asia is in arms with Tamburlaine.

"Even from the Canary Islands in the midst of the fiery Tropic of Cancer to Amazonia in the south of Africa under the Tropic of Capricorn, and from there northward as far as the Archipelago — the Aegean islands above north Africa between Greece and Turkey — all Africa is in arms with Tamburlaine."

The Canary Islands can be thought of as being in the midst of the Tropic of Cancer because they are so close to the intersection of the Tropic of Cancer and the Prime Meridian.

King Orcanes of Natolia continued, "Therefore, Viceroys, the Christians must have peace."

Tamburlaine's army came from a large area: from the countries of the Barbary Coast in north Africa and from Persia and from Egypt and from India and from Scythia and from many areas in between with the main exception of Turkey. Indeed, much of Africa and Asia provided soldiers for Tamburlaine's armies.

Drums and trumpets were heard, and now the Christians arrived for the parley: King Sigismund of Hungary, the Hungarian lords Frederick and Baldwin, and a train of many attendants, including drummers and trumpeters.

King Sigismund of Hungary said, "Orcanes, as our ambassadors promised thee, we, with our peers, have crossed the Danube's stream to talk of friendly peace or deadly war. Take whichever thou will, for as the Romans used to do, I here present thee with a naked sword. If you choose to have war, then shake this blade at me. If peace, restore it to my hands again, and I will sheathe it to confirm the same."

King Sigismund of Hungary referred to King Orcanes of Natolia using "thee" and "thou," which were words a man of a higher social status used to refer to a man of a lower social status. He also did not call him by the title "King." These were insults, and King Orcanes of Natolia would respond in kind.

"Wait, Sigismund," King Orcanes of Natolia said. "Have thou forgotten that I am the man who with the cannon shook the walls of Vienna and made it dance upon the solid land as when an earthquake causes the massive foundation of the Earth to quiver about the axletree of Heaven?"

The axletree of Heaven is the axle or axis through the Earth around which the heavenly spheres revolve, according to the Ptolemaic theory of the universe.

King Orcanes of Natolia continued, "Have thou forgotten that I sent a shower of spears, mingled with powdered shot and feathered arrows with steel heads, so thick upon the blinking-with-fear-eyed burghers' heads, that thou thyself, who were then only a Count Palatine with autonomy over a region granted to you by the Holy Roman Emperor, the King of Bohemia, and the Austrian Duke, sent heralds out, who servilely on their knees, in all your names desired a truce of me?

"Have thou forgotten that to have me raise my siege, wagons of gold were set before my tent, stamped with the princely fowl — the eagle — that in her wings carries the fearful thunderbolts of Jove?

"How can thou think of this and offer war to me?"

"Vienna was besieged, and I was there," King Sigismund of Hungary replied. "Then I was a Count Palatine, but now I am a King and what we did was done out of extreme necessity.

"But now, Orcanes, view my royal army that covers and hides these plains and seems as vast and wide as does the desert of Arabia to those who stand on Baghdad's lofty tower, or as does the ocean to the traveller who rests upon the snowy Apennine Mountains, and tell me whether I should stoop so low, or talk of peace with the Natolian King."

The Turkish lord Gazellus said, "Kings of Natolia and of Hungary, we came from Turkey to confirm an alliance, and not to dare each other to go to the battlefield and fight. A friendly parley might befit both of you."

The Hungarian lord Frederick said, "And we came from Europe with the same intention, which if your general Orcanes refuses or scorns, our tents are pitched and our men stand in military array, ready to charge you before you stir your feet."

King Orcanes of Natolia said, "So ready are we, but yet, if Sigismund speaks as a friend, and does not insist upon terms that would wreak the treaty, here is his sword; let peace be ratified on these conditions that have been specified before and drawn with the advice of our ambassadors."

He gave the sword to King Sigismund of Hungary, who said, "Then here I sheathe it and give thee my hand. I will never draw the sword out or conduct war against thyself or thy confederates, but while I live I will be at truce with thee."

The words "thee" and "thy" could also be used among close friends — but were these two Kings friends?

King Orcanes of Natolia said, "But, Sigismund, confirm it with an oath, and swear in the sight of Heaven and by thy Christ."

King Sigismund of Hungary said, "By Him Who made the world and saved my soul, the Son of God and a virgin maiden, sweet Jesus Christ, I solemnly swear and vow to keep this peace inviolable."

King Orcanes of Natolia said, "By sacred Mahomet, the friend of God, whose holy Koran remains with us, whose glorious body, when he left the world, closed in a coffin mounted up in the air and hung on stately Mecca's temple roof, I swear to keep this truce inviolable.

"As memorable witness of our league, each of us shall retain a scroll on which is written this treaty's conditions and our solemn oaths, signed with our own hands.

"Now, Sigismund, if any Christian King should encroach upon the borders of thy realm, send word to that King that Orcanes of Natolia has confirmed this league beyond the Danube's stream, and they will, trembling, sound a quick retreat because I am so feared among all nations."

The treaty established peace between King Orcanes of Natolia and King Sigismund of Hungary, but it also required each of them to come to the aid of the other if a foreign army attacked one of them.

King Sigismund of Hungary said, "If any heathen potentate or King should invade Natolia, Sigismund will send a hundred thousand cavalry trained to the war, and backed by brave lancers of Germany, the strength and sinews and support of the imperial throne and seat of power."

"I thank thee, Sigismund," Orcanes said, "but when I war, all Asia Minor, Africa, and Greece follow my standard and my thundering drums.

"Come, let us go and banquet in our tents. I will dispatch the greater part of my army from here to fair Natolia and to Trebizond, to await my coming against proud Tamburlaine.

"Friend Sigismund and peers of Hungary, come, banquet and carouse with us a while, and then we will depart to our territories."

Callapine talked with Almeda, his keeper. Tamburlaine kept Callapine prisoner in Egypt, south of Alexandria. Almeda's job was to prevent Callapine from escaping.

Callapine said, "Sweet Almeda, pity the ruthful, pitiful plight of Callapine, the son of Bajazeth. I was born to be monarch of the western world — the Turkish Empire — yet I am detained here by cruel Tamburlaine."

"My lord, I pity it, and with my heart I wish your release," Almeda said, "but he whose wrath is death, my sovereign lord, renowned Tamburlaine, forbids you further liberty than this."

Callapine was Almeda's "lord," but Tamburlaine, a much more powerful superior, was Almeda's "sovereign lord."

"Ah, if I were now but half so eloquent to paint in words what I'll perform in deeds," Callapine said, "I know you would depart from here with me."

"Not for all Africa; therefore, don't urge me to do that," Almeda replied.

"Yet hear me speak, my gentle Almeda."

"No speech to that end, if you please, sir."

Callapine began, "By Cairo runs —"

Almeda interrupted, "No talk of running, I tell you, sir."

"A little further, gentle Almeda."

"Well, sir, what about this?" Almeda asked.

"By Cairo runs to the bay of Alexandria the stream of Darote," Callapine said.

The Nile River runs from Cairo to the Mediterranean Sea, forming a delta close to the Mediterranean. Alexandria is in the western part of the delta, and Darote is a town in the delta on the part of the Nile leading to Alexandria. Callapine wanted to get to a ship at Darote and then sail to the Mediterranean and get into Turkish waters.

He continued, "In the stream of Darote, a Turkish galley of my royal fleet lies at anchor, awaiting my coming to the riverside, hoping by some means I shall be released. This galley, when I come aboard, will hoist up sail and soon put forth into the Mediterranean Sea, where we quickly may arrive in Turkish seas between the islands of Cyprus and of Crete.

"Then you shall see a hundred Kings and more, upon their knees, all bid me welcome home. Among so many crowns of burnished gold, choose which you want — all are at thy command.

"A thousand galleys, manned with Christian slaves, I freely give you, which shall cut the Straits of Gibraltar, and bring armadas — large war ships — from the coasts of Spain, laden with the gold of rich America.

"The Grecian virgins shall attend on you. They are skillful in music and in amorous songs, as fair as was Pygmalion's ivory girl or lovely Io, who was metamorphosed."

Pygmalion carved a statue of a beautiful woman out of ivory, fell in love with it, and prayed to the gods for a woman just like that. Venus heard his prayer, and she made the statue come alive, and Pygmalion and the woman, named Galatea, married.

Io was a mortal woman with whom Jupiter, King of the gods, had an affair. Jupiter's jealous wife, Juno, changed Io into a white cow. (Another version of the myth states that Jupiter turned Io into a white cow in order to hide her from Juno.)

Callapine continued, "With naked negroes shall your coach be drawn, and, as you ride in triumph through the streets, the pavement underneath your chariot wheels shall be covered with Turkish carpets, and tapestries made of rich arras cloth hung about the walls, fit sights for your princely eye to pierce.

"A hundred Pashas, clothed in crimson silk, shall ride before you on steeds from the Barbary. And, when you walk, a golden canopy inlaid with precious stones, which shine as brightly as that fair veil of stars that covers all the world, when Phoebus the Sun-god, leaping from this hemisphere, descends his Sun-chariot downward to the Antipodes, who live on the opposite side of the Earth.

"And I will give you more than this, for all I cannot tell."

"How far from here lies the galley, do you say?" Almeda asked.

"Sweet Almeda, it is scarcely half a league from here."

A league is three miles, or three kilometers.

Almeda said, "But we need to not be seen going aboard!"

Callapine said, "Between the hollow hanging of a hill and the crooked bending of a craggy rock, the sails wrapped up, the mast and tackling and rigging down, the galley lies so well hidden that no one can find her."

"I like that well," Almeda said. "But tell me, my lord, if I should let you go, will you be as good as your word? Shall I be made a King for my labor?"

"As I am Callapine the Emperor, and by the hand of Mahomet I swear, you shall be crowned a King and be my equal."

"Then here I swear, as I am Almeda, your keeper under Tamburlaine the Great — for keeper is the official designation and title I have as yet — even if Tamburlaine were to send a thousand armed men to intercept this aspiring enterprise, yet I will undertake the risk to conduct your grace away from here and I will die before I bring you back again!"

"Thanks, gentle Almeda. Then let us make haste, lest time be past and lingering hinder us both."

"Whenever you will, my lord, I am ready," Almeda said.

"I am ready even right now," Callapine said, "and farewell, cursed Tamburlaine. Now I go to revenge my father's death."

— 1.3 —

Tamburlaine talked with Zenocrate and their three sons: Calyphas, Amyras, and Celebinus. Drummers and trumpeters were present. They were at Larissa, a seacoast town located close to Egypt's border with Syria. (Larissa is the modern El Arish; it is a seacoast town located close to Egypt's border with Israel.) Tamburlaine had traveled from Cairo to Alexandria and then headed east to Larissa, intending to travel a land route to Turkey.

Tamburlaine said, "Now, bright Zenocrate, you are the world's fair eye, the Sun, whose beams light up and illuminate the lamps of Heaven. Your cheerful looks clear the cloudy air and clothe it in a crystal livery.

"Now rest here on fair Larissa plains where Egypt and the Turkish Empire are separated, between your sons who shall be Emperors, and every one commander of a world."

Zenocrate replied, "Sweet Tamburlaine, when will you leave these arms — these weapons — and save your sacred person free from harm and the dangerous chances of the wrathful war?"

Tamburlaine replied, "When Heaven shall cease to move on both poles of the axle-tree of the Earth, and when the ground, whereon my soldiers march, shall rise aloft and touch the horned crescent moon, and not before, my sweet Zenocrate. Sit up, and rest yourself like a lovely Queen.

"So, now Zenocrate sits in pomp and majesty, and these, my sons, more precious in my eyes than all the wealthy kingdoms I have subdued, placed by her side, look on their mother's face.

"But yet I think that their looks are gentle and affectionate, not martial as ought to be the sons of Tamburlaine. Water and air, being mixed in one, argue their lack of courage and lack of sharpness of intellect."

This society believed that four elements — water, air, earth, and fire — made up everything, including human bodies. Tamburlaine's sons, he complained, were made of lots of water and air, but they lacked earth and fire. Tamburlaine was afraid that this imbalance made his sons' temperaments too gentle and affectionate. He would have preferred more earth and fire in his sons so that they would have sharp intelligence and courage.

Tamburlaine continued, "Their hair, as white as milk, and as soft as down — which should be like the quills of porcupines, as black as jet-colored coal, and as hard as iron or steel — reveals the fact that they are too dainty for the wars.

"Their fingers that are made to quaver and play on a lute, their arms that are made to hang about a lady's neck, and their legs that are made to dance and leap in the air would make me think them bastards, not my sons, except that I know they issued from your womb, Zenocrate, who never looked on any other man but Tamburlaine."

Zenocrate replied, "My gracious lord, our sons have their mother's looks, but when they wish, they have their conquering father's heart.

"This lovely boy, Celebinus, the youngest of the three, not long ago rode a Scythian steed, trotting his horse in the training ring, and tilting at a glove, which when he touched it with his slender rod, he reined his steed straightaway, and made him so curvet that I cried out for fear he would have fallen."

The game of tilting at a glove involved riding on horseback and attempting to touch a glove with the tip of a lance. In a curvet, the rider suddenly reins the horse, causing the horse's forelegs to rise and its hind legs to leap forward.

"Well done, my boy!" Tamburlaine said. "You shall have shield and lance, armor of proven strength, horse, helmet, and sword, and I will teach you how to charge your foe and unharmed run among the deadly pikes.

"If you will love the wars and follow me, you shall be made a King and reign with me, keeping Emperors in iron cages."

Tamburlaine had kept Bajazeth, the conquered Turkish Emperor, in an iron cage until Bajazeth killed himself.

He continued, "If you exceed your elder brothers' worth, and shine in perfect manliness more than they, you shall be King before them, and your children shall issue crowned from their mother's womb."

If Tamburlaine's youngest son, Celebinus, were to show more manliness than his elder brothers, then Tamburlaine would name Celebinus and Celebinus' children as his heirs.

Celebinus said, "Yes, father; you shall see me, if I live, have under me as many Kings as you, and march with such a multitude of men that all the world shall tremble at seeing them."

"These words assure me, boy, that you are my son," Tamburlaine said. "When I am old and cannot wage war, then you be the scourge and terror of the world."

Amyras, his middle son, asked, "Why may not I, my lord, as well as he, be termed the scourge and terror to the world?"

Tamburlaine replied, "All of my sons shall be a scourge and terror to the world, or else you are not sons of Tamburlaine."

Calyphas, his oldest son, said, "But while my brothers follow arms and fight in battles, my lord, let me accompany my gracious mother. My two brothers are enough to conquer all the world, and you have won enough territory for me to keep."

This infuriated Tamburlaine, who said, "Bastardly boy, sprung from some coward's loins, and not the child of great Tamburlaine!

"You shall not have a foot of territory, unless you bear a courageous and invincible mind. For the man who shall wear the crown of Persia is he whose head has the deepest scars, whose breast has the most wounds, who when he is angry sends lightning from his eyes and in the furrows of his frowning brows harbors revenge, war, death, and cruelty.

"For in a battlefield, whose ground is covered with a liquid red veil of blood and sprinkled with the brains of slaughtered men, my royal chair of state — my throne — shall be advanced and lifted high, and he who means to place himself thereon must armed wade up to the chin in blood."

Zenocrate said, "My lord, such speeches to our princely sons dismay their minds before they come to experience for themselves the wounding troubles that angry war affords."

"No, madam, these are speeches fit for us," Celebinus said. "For even if Tamburlaine's chair of state were in a sea of blood, I would prepare a ship and sail to it, before I would lose the title of a King."

Amyras said, "And I would strive to swim through pools of blood or make a bridge of murdered carcasses whose arches should be framed with the bones of Turks, before I would lose the title of a King."

"Well, lovely boys, you shall be Emperors both, stretching your conquering arms from east to west," Tamburlaine said to Celebinus and Amyras.

He then said to Calyphas, his oldest son, "And, sirrah, if you mean to wear a crown, then when we shall meet the Turkish Deputy Kings Orcanes and all his Viceroys, snatch it from his head, and cleave his skull with your sword."

Fathers often referred to their sons as "sirrah."

Calyphas said, "If any man will hold him, I will strike and cleave him to the collarbone or throat with my sword."

Calyphas was willing to kill a man if someone else were to hold the man so he could not fight back.

"Hold him, and cleave him, too, or I'll cleave thee," Tamburlaine said, "for we will march against them shortly. Theridamas, Techelles, and Casane have promised to meet me on the plains of Larissa with each bringing armies to fight against this Turkish crew, for I have sworn by sacred Mahomet to make Natolia part of my empire."

Tamburlaine had made Theridamas, Techelles, and Casane Kings; they owed their crowns to him.

Trumpets sounded.

Tamburlaine said, "The trumpets sound, Zenocrate; they come."

Theridamas and his train of attendants arrived.

"Welcome, Theridamas, King of Algiers," Tamburlaine said.

"My lord, the great and mighty Tamburlaine, arch-monarch of the world, I offer here my crown, myself, and all the power I have, in all affection at your kingly feet," Theridamas said as he handed his crown to Tamburlaine.

"Thanks, good Theridamas," Tamburlaine replied.

Theridamas said, "Under my flags march ten thousand Greeks, and twice twenty thousand valiant men-at-arms from Algiers and Africa's frontier towns, all of whom have sworn to sack Natolia. Five hundred brigandines — small, light ships — are under sail, suitable for your service on the sea, my lord. These ships, launching from Algiers to Tripoli, will quickly ride before Natolia, and batter down the castles on the shore."

Tripoli is a city on the northern Levant's Mediterranean coast.

"Well said, King of Algiers," Tamburlaine said. "Receive your crown again."

Tamburlaine gave back Theridamas' crown.

Then Techelles and Usumcasane arrived together.

"Kings of Morocco and of Fez, welcome," Tamburlaine said.

"Magnificent and peerless Tamburlaine," King Usumcasane of Morocco said as he gave him his crown, "I and my neighbor, King Techelles of Fez, have brought to aid you in this Turkish expedition, a hundred thousand expert soldiers. From Azimor on the Atlantic coast of Morocco to Tunis near the sea, I have stripped Barbary of its men for your sake, and I gladly offer you all the men in armor under me, along with my crown."

"Thanks, King of Morocco," Tamburlaine said. He handed him the crown and said, "Take your crown again."

Techelles gave Tamburlaine his crown and said, "And, mighty Tamburlaine, our earthly God, whose looks make this inferior world quake under the heavens, I here present you with the crown of Fez, and with an army of Moors trained to the war, whose coal-black faces make their foes retire and quake for fear, as if the infernal Jove — Pluto, God of the Underworld — meaning to aid you in these Turkish arms, should pierce the black circumference of Hell and bring out ugly Furies bearing fiery flags and millions of Hell's strong tormenting spirits."

The Furies are avenging deities who often carry firebrands.

Techelles continued, "From strong Tesella to Biledull, all Barbary is unpeopled for your sake."

Tamburlaine handed Techelles his crown back and said, "Thanks, King of Fez; take here your crown again. Your presence, loving friends and fellow Kings, makes me overindulge in conceiving joy."

In addition to the pleasure he felt when seeing his tributary Kings again, he was thinking ahead to the joy he would have when he conquered Natolia.

Tamburlaine added, "If all the crystal gates of Jove's high court were opened wide, and I might enter in to see the state and majesty of Heaven, it could not more delight me than your sight.

"Now we will banquet on these plains a while, and afterwards march to Turkey with our army, in number more than are the drops that fall when Boreas, god of the North wind, rends a thousand swelling clouds.

"And proud Orcanes of Natolia with all his Viceroys shall be so afraid that even though the stones, as at Deucalion's flood, were turned to men, he should be overcome."

When Jupiter decided to cause a great flood, he allowed Deucalion and his wife, Pyrrha, to survive on an ark Deucalion built. Afterward, they prayed to

Jupiter to repopulate the Earth. Following a sacrifice to the goddess Themis, she told them to throw the bones of the mother behind them. Interpreting the "bones" to be the stones of Mother Earth, they threw stones over their backs. From those stones grew people. This story is told in Ovid's *Metamorphoses* 1.318ff.

Tamburlaine continued, "Such lavish profusion will I make of Turkish blood that Jove shall send Mercury, his winged messenger, to command me to sheathe my sword and leave the battlefield. The Sun, unable to sustain the sight, shall hide his head in Thetis' watery lap, and leave his steeds to fair Boötes' charge."

According to mythology, the Sun-god drives the Sun-chariot, which is pulled by immortal horses each day across the sky.

Thetis is a sea-nymph and the mother of Achilles, the greatest warrior of the Trojan War. To "hide his head in Thetis' watery lap" means that the Sun will set over the ocean.

The constellation Boötes is also known as the Herdsman or the Plowman or the Wagoner — in other words, a driver of oxen and horses. The brightest star in Boötes is Arcturus, which is known as the guardian of the constellation Ursa Major, the Big Bear, because Boötes is so close to it in the night sky. The Big Dipper is part of Ursa Major.

Tamburlaine was saying in poetic language that he would cause such bloodshed that the gods would be sickened and order him to stop shedding blood. Also, the Sun would be sickened and so would set early in the west over the Atlantic Ocean — the Sun-god would then have Boötes take care of the immortal horses.

In non-poetic and non-hyperbolic language, Tamburlaine was simply saying that he would cause enormous amounts of bloodshed until the Sun set.

He continued, "For half the world shall perish in this fight. But now, my friends, let me examine you: How have you spent your time while absent from me?"

Usumcasane now described how he and his army had conquered Barbary, northwest Africa:

"My lord, our men of Barbary have marched four hundred miles with armor on their backs, and lain in military camp fifteen months and more. For, since we left you at the Sultan of Egypt's court, we have subdued the southern

Guallatia in the Libyan desert and all the land to the coast of Spain. We took control of the narrow Strait of Gibraltar, and made the Canary Islands call us Kings and lords.

"Yet never did my army enjoy recreations, or cease one day from war and hot alarms and calls to arms, and therefore let them rest a while, my lord."

"They shall, Casane, and it is time they rested, in faith," Tamburlaine said.

Techelles now described how he and his army had explored and conquered much of Africa. From Egypt, they went far south through the heart of Africa, following the Nile River and conquering Prester John in Machda, Abyssinia, and then they went west and then north along the south-west coast, and then west and north again. Finally they went north and east until they reached Damascus, where they stayed until receiving Tamburlaine's summons.

Techelles said, "And I have marched along the Nile River to Machda, where the mighty Christian priest-King, Prester John, called John the Great, sits in a milk-white robe. His triple miter — papal tiara — I took by force, and made him swear obedience to my crown.

"From thence unto Cazates — a town in the region where the Nile River finds its source in Lake Victoria — I marched, where Amazonians met me in the field, with whom (they being women), I made an alliance, and with my army I marched to Zanzibar on the western coast of Africa, where I viewed the Ethiopian sea — the South Atlantic — as well as rivers and lakes, but neither man nor child in all the land.

"Therefore I took my course to Manico, where, unresisted, I located my military camp. And, by the coast of Byather, at last I came to Cubar, where the negroes dwell, and, conquering that, made haste to Nubia, south of Egypt.

"There, having sacked Borno, the kingly seat, I took the King and led him bound in chains to Damascus, where I stayed before."

"Well done, Techelles," Tamburlaine said. "What does Theridamas say?"

Theridamas and his army had gone to Eastern Europe and conquered territory northwest of the Black Sea. Among the towns he subdued were Stoka, Codemia, and Oblia.

He replied, "I left the confines and the territory of Africa, and made a voyage into Europe, where, by the river Tyros, I subdued the towns of Stoka and Codemia and the province of Padalia.

"Then I crossed the sea and came to the town of Oblia and Nigra Silva —
the Black Forest — where the devils dance. In despite of the devils, I set Nigra
Silva on fire.

"From thence I crossed the gulf called the Mare Majore sea — the Black Sea
— by the inhabitants."

After Theridamas and his army sailed across the Black Sea, they marched
south to meet Tamburlaine.

Theridamas added, "Yet shall my soldiers make no pause; we shall not stop
moving until the King of Natolia kneels before your feet."

"Then we will triumph, banquet, and carouse," Tamburlaine said. "Cooks
shall have money to provide us delicacies and glut us with the dainties of the
world. Common soldiers shall drink bowls of *Lachryma Christi* — a sweet
red Italian wine — and Calabrian wines. Indeed, they shall drink liquid gold
mingled with coral and with orient pearl when we have conquered King
Orcanes of Natolia."

Lachryma Christi is Latin for "Christ's tears."

Pearls dissolve in vinegar, not wine — at least not quickly.

Tamburlaine then said, "Come, let us banquet and carouse the whiles —
until it is time to take action."

CHAPTER 2 (Part 2)

— 2.1 —

King Sigismund of Hungary and the Hungarian lords Frederick and Baldwin were talking in Hungary. Many attendants and followers were present.

Frederick was Lord of Buda, and Baldwin was Lord of Bohemia.

King Orcanes of Natolia had ordered much of his army out of Europe and back to Turkey so that he would be ready to resist Tamburlaine, who had raised an army to attack Natolia. King Orcanes had conquered territory in Europe, killing many Europeans in the process, and bad feelings remained despite the peace treaty and alliance that he had made with King Sigismund of Hungary.

Now Frederick and Baldwin were trying to persuade King Sigismund to break the peace treaty and to attack the Turkish troops that King Orcanes still had in Europe. In doing so, Frederick and Baldwin made use of religious differences: The Turks were Muslim, and the Europeans were Christian.

King Sigismund of Hungary said, "Now tell me, my Lords of Buda and Bohemia, what impulse is it that inflames your thoughts, and stirs your courage to such sudden arms?"

"Your majesty remembers, I am sure," Frederick said, "what cruel slaughter of our Christian bloods — our Christian people — these heathenish Turks and pagans lately made between the city of Zula and the Danube River and how they campaigned through the midst of Varna and Bulgaria, and almost to the very walls of Rome."

Rome is Constantinople, the capital of the Roman Byzantine Empire. The city was known as Byzantium before it became Constantinople, and now it is known as Istanbul. The Emperors of Constantinople were mainly Greek. Located on the Bosporus Strait, Constantinople straddles Europe and Asia.

Frederick continued, "They have, not long ago, massacred our army. It remains to be done now, then, that your majesty take all advantages of time and power, and work revenge upon these infidels.

"Your highness knows that in order to resist the return of Tamburlaine, who strikes a terror to all Turkish hearts, King Orcanes of Natolia has dismissed the greatest part of all his army pitched against our army between Cutheia and Mount Orminius, and sent them marching up to Belgasar in western Asia Minor, Acantha, Antioch, and Caesarea, to aid the Kings of Syria and Jerusalem."

The main part of King Orcanes' army was travelling to Natolia and nearby regions in preparation to fight Tamburlaine. King Orcanes was travelling with troops in the rear because he had been farthest from Natolia.

Frederick continued, "Now, then, my lord, take advantage of this and issue in battle suddenly upon the rest, so that in the good fortune of their defeat we may discourage all the pagan troops who dare attempt to war with Christians."

King Sigismund of Hungary replied, "But doesn't your grace remember the alliance we recently made with King Orcanes, confirmed by oath and articles of peace, and calling on Christ to witness our truths? We called on Christ to witness our good faith when we made the treaty.

"What you are advising me to do would be treachery and violence against the grace of our vow and religious beliefs."

"Not at all, my lord," Baldwin said, "for with such infidels, in whom no faith and no true religion rests, we are not bound to the fulfillment of those vows and sworn promises the holy laws of Christendom enjoin. Because the faith that they profanely pledge themselves to is by prudent statecraft not to be esteemed trustworthy by ourselves, so what we vow to them should not infringe our liberty of arms and victory."

In other words, King Orcanes of Natolia had made vows in the Muslim religion, which is something that Christians — according to Baldwin — necessarily do not regard as trustworthy. Because of that, Christians need not respect the vows that they made in the Christian religion and so they ought not to be prevented from seeking and obtaining a military victory against the Turks. In still other words, a Christian need not keep vows made with a Muslim — this is sometimes known as "no faith with heretics."

King Sigismund of Hungary said, "Though I confess the oaths that they undertake breed little strength to our sense of safety, yet those infirmities that thus defame their faiths, their honors, and their religion should not give us presumption to do the same thing they do.

"Our Christian pledges are sound and valid, and must be perfect, consummated and fulfilled, religious, righteous, and inviolate."

"Assure your grace," Frederick said, "that it is superstition to stand so strictly on dispensive faith — some oaths and vows can be broken with special dispensation from the church — and should we lose the opportunity that God has given to avenge our Christians' deaths and scourge the Turks' foul blasphemous paganism, as happened to Saul, to Balaam, and the rest, who would not kill and curse at God's command, so surely will the vengeance of the highest, and the jealous anger of his frightening arm, be poured with rigor on our sinful heads if we neglect this offered victory."

Saul, the first King of the Israelites, failed to carry out God's order to kill all living things following a victorious battle against the Amalekites; instead, he allowed King Agag of the Amalekites to live, as well as the sheep and the cattle. This story is told in 1 Samuel 15.

Frederick seemingly showed ignorance of the Bible while speaking about Balaam; actually, Balaam did what God told him to do. King Balak of Moab ordered Balaam to travel to the Israelites and curse them; instead, Balaam followed God's command and blessed them.

God, however, did get angry at Balaam for going with some men whom Balak sent, although God had given Balaam permission to go with those men (despite forbidding him earlier to go with them). Perhaps God knew that at that time Balaam was planning to curse the Israelites. (In Balaam's defense, he may have thought that God had changed His mind about the cursing of the Israelites; after all, God had given him permission to go with the men despite forbidding him to go with them earlier.) The story of Balaam (and his ass) is told in Numbers 22-24.

According to Frederick, God will punish King Sigismund of Hungary if he does not break the alliance he made with King Orcanes of Natolia.

Convinced by the Hungarian lords' arguments, King Sigismund of Hungary said, "Then arm, my lords, and issue suddenly, giving commandment to our general army, with haste to assail the pagan army and take the victory our God has given."

— 2.2 —

King Orcanes of Natolia and the Viceroys Gazellus and Uribassa talked together. Many of their attendants were present. Their location was the mountain Orminius in Transylvania, Romania. Because King Orcanes had sent most of his troops to Turkey following the peace treaty that he had made with King Sigismund of Hungary, his army in Eastern Europe was now much weaker.

King Orcanes of Natolia said, "Gazellus, Uribassa, and the rest, now we will march from proud Orminius mountain to fair Natolia, where our neighbor Kings await our army and our royal presence to do battle against the cruel Tamburlaine, who commands a mighty army near Larissa, and with the thunder of his martial weapons makes earthquakes in the hearts of men and Heaven."

Gazelles said, "And now we come to make his muscles shake with greater power than his pride has ever before felt. A hundred Kings, by scores — twenty at a time — will challenge him to combat, and a hundred thousand soldiers will be allotted to each score of Kings.

"These troops, even if a shower of wounding thunderbolts should break out of the interior of the clouds and fall as thick as hail upon our heads, favoring and giving aid to that proud Scythian, yet our courages and steeled helmets and more than infinite numbers of men would be able to withstand and conquer him."

Uribassa said, "I think I see how glad and joyful your granted truce made the Christian King, who could not but before be terrified by the unexampled power of our army."

A messenger entered and said, "Arm, dread sovereign, and my noble lords! The treacherous army of the Christians, taking advantage of your small, slender army, comes marching on us, and is determined to immediately bid us to battle for our dearest lives."

"Traitors, villains, damned Christians!" King Orcanes of Natolia said. "Haven't I here the articles of peace and solemn covenants we — King Sigismund of Hungary and I — have both confirmed, he by his Christ, and I by Mahomet? Both of us have sworn oaths by our prophets."

121

Gazelles said, "May Hell and ruin alight upon their heads, who with such treason seek our overthrow, and care so little for their prophet Christ!"

King Orcanes of Natolia asked, "Can there be such deceit in Christians, or treason in the soft heart of man, whose shape is the image of the highest God?"

Genesis 1:27: states, *So God created man in his own image* (King James Version).

He then said this:

"Then if there is a Christ, as Christians say, but in their deeds Christians deny him for their Christ,

"If their Christ is son to always-living Jove, and has the power of his outstretched arm,

"If their Christ is protective of his name and honor as is our holy prophet Mahomet,

"Then I say to their Christian Christ, 'Take here these papers as our sacrifice to You and as evidence of your servant Sigismund's perjury.'"

He tore up the articles of peace.

He added, "Open, you shining veil of the Moon goddess Cynthia. Open, you moonlit sky, and make a passage from the Empyreal Heaven, the dwelling place of God, so that He — God — Who sits on high and never sleeps, nor in one place is circumscribable — able to be contained, but everywhere fills every continent and space with strange infusion of his sacred vigor, may, in His endless power and purity, behold and avenge this traitor's perjury!

"You Christ Who are esteemed to be omnipotent, if You will prove Yourself a perfect God, worthy of the worship of all faithful hearts, be now revenged upon this traitor's soul, and make the troops I have left behind with us — who are too few to defend our guiltless and innocent lives — sufficient to defeat and destroy the treacherous, unable-to-be-trusted force of those false Christians."

In the Muslim religion, Jesus is a prophet, but Jesus is not divine.

"To arms, my lords!" King Orcanes of Natolia said. "On Christ let us continuously cry. If Christ exists, we shall have victory."

The sounds of the battle were heard, and a mortally wounded King Sigismund of Hungary appeared.

King Sigismund said, "All the Christian army has been routed, and God has thundered vengeance from on high, for my accursed and hateful perjury and breaking of my oath.

"Oh, just and dreadful Punisher of Sin, let the dishonor of the pains I feel in this my mortal well-deserved wound end all my penance in my sudden death! And let this death, which will make me incapable of sinning anymore, conceive a second life in endless mercy!"

King Sigismund of Hungary died.

King Orcanes of Natolia, Gazellus, Uribassa, and others arrived.

King Orcanes said, "Now lie the Christians bathing in their bloods, and Christ or Mahomet has been my friend."

Gazellus said, "See here the perjured traitor King Sigismund of Hungary, bloody and without breath and dead for his villainy."

King Orcanes of Natolia said, "Now shall his barbarous body be a prey to beasts and fowls, and all the winds through shady leaves of every senseless tree shall breathe murmurs and hisses for his heinous sin.

"Now his soul scalds in the Tartarian streams of Hell and feeds upon the baneful, deadly, poisonous tree of Hell, that Zoacum, that fruit of bitterness, that in the midst of fire is grafted."

Tartarus is where the worst sinners are punished in Hell.

According to Islam, the tree of Zoacum provides fruit that resembles the heads of devils for the damned in Hell, but it is fruit that causes the sinners to drink scalding water afterwards. The tree of Zoacum is described in 37:62-68 of the Koran.

He continued, "Yet the tree of Zoacum flourishes as does Flora, Roman goddess of flowers, in her pride. The tree of Zoacum bears apples like the heads of damned fiends.

"The devils there, in chains of quenchless flame, shall lead King Sigismund's soul through Hell's burning gulf, from pain to pain, whose torments will change but shall never end.

"What do you say yet, Gazellus, to his disgrace and defeat, which we appealed to the justice and power of his Christ? His disgrace and defeat here appears as fully as do the rays of Cynthia — the moonlight — to the clearest sight!"

"It is only the fortune of the wars, my lord," Gazellus said. "The power of the fortune of war is often offered as evidence of a miracle."

King Orcanes of Natolia said, "Yet in my thoughts shall Christ be honored, not doing Mahomet an injury, whose power had a share in this our victory. And since this miscreant misbeliever — King Sigismund — has disgraced his faith and died a traitor both to Heaven and Earth, we order that a continuous lookout and guard keep Sigismund's corpse amid these plains for fowls to prey upon.

"Go, Uribassa, give the order to do that immediately."

"I will, my lord," Uribassa said.

He exited to carry out the order.

King Orcanes of Natolia said, "And now, Gazellus, let us make haste and meet the main body of our army in Turkey, and our brothers — fellow Kings — of Jerusalem, Syria, Trebizond, and Amasia, and happily, with full Natolian bowls of Greek wine, now let us celebrate our happy conquest and Sigismund's stinging fate."

— 2.4 —

In the city of Larissa, Zenocrate, ill, was lying in her bed of state. Tamburlaine sat by her. Three physicians were around her bed, mixing potions. Theridamas, Techelles, Usumcasane, and the three sons of Tamburlaine and Zenocrate were present.

Tamburlaine said, "Black is the beauty of the brightest day. The Sun, that golden ball of Heaven's eternal fire, which danced with glory on the silver waves, now lacks the fuel that inflamed its beams, and all with faintness and for foul disgrace, the Sun binds its temples with a frowning cloud, ready to darken Earth with endless night.

"Zenocrate, who gave the Sun light and life, whose eyes shot fire from their ivory chambers, and refreshed every soul with lively heat, now by the malice of the angry pagan gods in the skies, whose jealousy admits no second mate, no rival, draws comfort from her last and final mortal breath, all overcome by the hellish mists of death.

"Now walk the angels on the walls of Heaven, as sentinels to warn the immortal souls to welcome divine Zenocrate.

"Apollo the Sun, Cynthia the Moon, and the ceaseless lamps that are the stars that gently looked upon this loathsome Earth, shine downwards now no more, but deck the heavens to welcome divine Zenocrate.

"The crystal springs, whose taste illuminates refined eyes with a clearer and eternal sight, like purified silver ore run through Paradise to welcome divine Zenocrate."

The crystal springs are perhaps similar to the Lethe and Eunoë streams that appear in the Forest of Eden in Dante's *Purgatory*. Drinking from the stream of Lethe takes away the sting of one's sins. Drinking from the stream of Eunoë revives the memory of one's good deeds.

Later, Tamburlaine says that the Lethe is a river in Hell, but people make mistakes. In Canto 14 of Dante's *Inferno*, Dante the Pilgrim believes that the Lethe is in the Inferno, but Virgil informs him that he will see the Lethe later in a place where souls wash themselves after they have purged their guilt with penitence. Indeed, Dante the Pilgrim sees the Lethe in the Forest of Eden at the top of the Mountain of Purgatory. In his *Aeneid*, Virgil placed Lethe in the

Land of the Dead, and so he had made a mistake, as he learned after he died, according to Dante's *Divine Comedy*.

Tamburlaine continued:

"The cherubim and holy seraphim, who sing and play before the King of Kings, use all their voices and their instruments to welcome divine Zenocrate.

"And in this sweet and elaborate and exquisite harmony, the God Who tunes this music to our souls holds out His hand in highest majesty to entertain divine Zenocrate.

"Then let some holy trance convey my prayerful thoughts up to the palace of the Empyreal Heaven, the dwelling place of God, requesting that this my life may be as short to me as are the days of sweet Zenocrate."

He then asked, "Physicians, will no medicine do her good?"

A physician replied, "My lord, your majesty shall soon know whether it will: If she survives this crisis, then the worst is past."

Tamburlaine then asked his wife, "Tell me, how fares my fair Zenocrate?"

She replied, "I fare, my lord, as do other Empresses, who, when this frail and transitory flesh has sucked the measure of that vital air that feeds the body with its allotted time of health, then diminish with enforced and necessary change."

Tamburlaine said, "May never such a change transform my love, in whose sweet being I repose my life, whose heavenly presence, beautified with health, gives light to Phoebus — the Sun — and the fixed stars.

"The absence of her — Zenocrate's — life makes the Sun and Moon as dark as when, opposed in one diameter — the Sun, Earth, and Moon cause an eclipse — their spheres are mounted on the Serpent's Head, or else descended to his winding train, the Serpent's Tail."

Tamburlaine was referring to two constellations: One was called the Serpent, and the other was called the Serpent Bearer. People in this society thought that the stars depicted a person holding a serpent: The Serpent's Head was on one side of the Serpent Bearer, and the Serpent's Tail was on the other side. The Sun, Earth, and Moon were also aligned when there was an eclipse, and so the Sun, Earth, and Moon were likened to the Serpent's Head, the Serpent Bearer, and the Serpent's Tail.

In a lunar eclipse, the Earth was the Serpent Bearer, and the Sun and Moon were the Serpent's Head and the Serpent's Tail. In a solar eclipse, the Sun and

Moon would be on the same side of the Earth, and so the Moon would be the Serpent Bearer.

When an eclipse occurs, the Moon must cross the ecliptic — the Sun's apparent path — at one of two points that are called nodes. The Moon crosses one node while going north, and two weeks later it crosses the other node while going south. Tamburlaine called the eclipse with the Moon crossing the node while going north the Serpent's Head, and he called the eclipse with the Moon crossing the node while going south the Serpent's Tail.

Tamburlaine continued, "Live still, my love, and so preserve my life, or, dying, be the author of my death."

"Continue to live, my lord!" Zenocrate said. "Oh, let my sovereign live! And sooner let the fiery element — the Sphere of Fire — dissolve so you can make your kingdom in the sky, than this base earth should shroud and cover your majesty."

Some people in this society believed that a Sphere of Fire existed between the Earth and the Moon. Because Zenocrate wanted Tamburlaine's glory to be widely seen and not hidden in his grave, she wanted the Sphere of Fire to be extinguished so that his glory could find a home in the heavens.

Zenocrate continued:

"For, should I but suspect your death would be caused by mine, the comfort of my future happiness in my second — immortal — life and my hope to meet your highness in the heavens, turned to despair, would break my wretched breast, and fury would ruin my present rest.

"But let me die, my love; yes, let me die; with love and patience let your true love die.

"Your grief and fury hurts my second life — my afterlife.

"Yet let me kiss my lord before I die, and let me die with kissing of my lord."

They kissed.

She continued, "But since my life is lengthened yet a while, let me take leave of these my loving sons, and of my lords, whose true nobility has merited my last act of remembering as I die.

"Sweet sons, farewell! In death resemble me and die with dignity, and in your lives resemble your father's excellence."

She then said to Tamburlaine, "Some music, and my crisis will cease, my lord."

People present called for music.

Tamburlaine said, "Proud fury and intolerable crisis, which dares torment the body of my love and scourge the scourge of the immortal God!

"Those spheres, her eyes, where Cupid, god of love, used to sit, wounding with his arrows the world with wonder and amazement and with love, now are instead sadly supplied with pale and ghastly Death, whose deadly arrows pierce the center of my soul.

"Zenocrates' sacred beauty has enchanted Heaven, and if she had lived before the siege of Troy, Helen, whose beauty summoned Greece to arms and drew a thousand ships to Tenedos, an island near Troy, would not have been named in Homer's *Iliad*; instead, Zenocrate's name would have been in every line he wrote.

"Or, if those wanton poets, writers of lewd verses, for whose birth old Rome was proud, had only gazed a while on her, neither Lesbia nor Corinna would have been named."

The Roman poet Catullus celebrated Lesbia, and Corinna appeared in a poem by Ovid in his *The Art of Love*, a seduction manual in verse.

Tamburlaine continued, "Zenocrate would have been the theme of every epigram or elegy."

Music sounded, and Zenocrate died.

Tamburlaine said, "Is she dead?

"Techelles, draw your sword and wound the earth, so that it may split in two halves and we may descend into the infernal vaults, to drag the Fatal Sisters — the Three Fates — by the hair and throw them in the triple moat of Hell, for taking away from here my fair Zenocrate."

According to Tamburlaine, as he will say later, the Fates live on an island surrounded by three rivers of Hell: Lethe, Styx, and Phlegethon.

Tamburlaine continued, "Casane and Theridamas, to arms! Raise cavalieros higher than the clouds, and with the cannon break the frame of Heaven."

Cavalieros are mounds on which cannons were placed.

Tamburlaine continued:

"Batter the shining palace of the Sun, and smash all the starry firmament — the sphere that holds the fixed stars — for amorous Jove has snatched my love away from here, meaning to make her stately Queen of Heaven.

"Whichever god holds you in his arms, giving you nectar and ambrosia, the food and drink of the gods, behold me here, divine Zenocrate, raving, impatient, desperate, and mad, breaking my steeled lance, with which I burst the rusty beams of Janus' temple doors, letting out death and tyrannizing war, to march with me under this bloody flag!"

The doors of the temple of Janus in the Roman Forum were open only during times of war. Tamburlaine was ready to go to war immediately and so metaphorically force open the rusty doors of the temple.

He continued, "And, if you pity Tamburlaine the Great, come down from Heaven, and live with me again!"

Theridamas said, "Ah, my good lord, be patient! She is dead, and all this raging cannot make her live.

"If words could be effective, our voices would have pierced the air.

"If tears could be effective, our eyes would have watered all the earth.

"If grief could be effective, our murdered hearts would have trickled forth blood.

"Nothing will be effective, for she is dead, my lord."

Tamburlaine said, "'For she is dead'! Your words pierce my soul! Ah, sweet Theridamas, say so no more. Though she is dead, yet let me think she lives and feed my mind that dies for want of her.

"Wherever her soul is —"

He turned to the late Zenocrate and addressed her:

"— you shall stay with me, embalmed with cassia, ambergris, and myrrh, not wrapped in lead, but in a sheet of gold, and until I die you shall not be interred.

"Then in as rich a tomb as that of King Mausolus of Caria we both will rest and have one epitaph written in as many different languages as I have conquered kingdoms with my sword."

After King Mausolus of Caria died, his widow made a magnificent tomb for him: It was one of the seven wonders of the world. We get our word "mausoleum" from King Mausolus' name.

Tamburlaine continued, "This cursed town — Larissa — I will consume with fire, because this place bereft me of my love. The houses, burnt, will look as if they mourned, and here I will set up her statue and march around it with my mourning army, drooping and mourning for Zenocrate."

CHAPTER 3 (Part 2)

— 3.1 —

The King of Trebizond and the King of Syria entered a room at the Turkish court. One King held a sword, and the other King held a scepter. Next Deputy King Orcanes of Natolia and the King of Jerusalem brought in the imperial crown. Next came in Callapine, and after him, Almeda and other lords. Orcanes and Jerusalem crowned him, and the others gave him the scepter. During processions, the sword of state was carried before the King.

Deputy King Orcanes said, "Callapinus Cyricelibes, otherwise Cybelius, son and successive heir to the late mighty Emperor Bajazeth, by the aid of God and his friend Mahomet, Emperor of Natolia, Jerusalem, Trebizond, Syria, Amasia, Thracia, Illyria, Carmonia, and all the hundred and thirty kingdoms recently tributory to his mighty father — long live Callapinus, Emperor of Turkey!"

Callapine, now the Turkish Emperor, said, "Thrice worthy Kings, of Natolia and the rest, I will repay your royal gratitudes with all the benefits my empire yields, and were the muscles — the strength — of the imperial seat as knit and strengthened as when Bajazeth, my royal lord and father, filled the throne, whose cursed fate has so dismembered the Turkish Empire and caused it to come apart, then you would see this thief of Scythia, this proud usurping King of Persia, do us such honor and supremacy, acknowledging me as his lord and suffering the vengeance of our father's wrongs, that all the world should blot our dignities out of the book of baseborn infamies.

"If only the Turkish Empire were as strong as it was when my father, Bajazeth, ruled, then it would crush Tamburlaine so badly that the indignities we have suffered from him would be forgotten by history.

"And now I don't doubt that your royal cares have so provided for this cursed foe, that, since I, the heir of mighty Bajazeth — an Emperor so honored for his virtues — revive the spirits of true Turkish hearts, in full-of-grief memory of my father's shame, we shall not need to nourish any doubt that proud Lady Fortune, who has long followed the martial sword of mighty Tamburlaine, will now return to her old inconstancy and raise our honors to as high an altitude, in this our strongly armed, many-soldiered, and favored-by-Lady-Fortune encounter in battle."

Callapine, Emperor of the Turks, was hoping that Lady Fortune would turn her wheel so that Tamburlaine's fortune would fall and the fortune of the Turkish Empire and Emperor would rise. Previously and currently, it seemed as if Lady Fortune had favored Tamburlaine so much that she had stopped turning her wheel once Tamburlaine reached the top.

Callapine continued, "For so has Heaven provided my escape from all the cruelty my soul sustained, by the happy means of Almeda, my friendly keeper, that Jove, overwhelmed with pity for our wrongs" — he was using the majestic plural — "will pour pity down in showers on our heads, scourging the pride of cursed Tamburlaine."

Deputy King Orcanes of Natolia said, "I have a hundred thousand men in arms. Some, who fought in the battle that conquered the perjured Christian King Sigismund of Hungary, although they were a handful of soldiers fighting King Sigismund's mighty army, think that they in themselves are in number yet sufficient to drink the Nile or the Euphrates, and as for their power, it is enough to win the world."

The army of the Persian King Cyrus the Great was so large that its soldiers drank rivers dry.

The King of Jerusalem said, "And I have as many soldiers from the territory of Jerusalem, Judaea, the city of Gaza, and the city of Scalonia that the soldiers on Mount Sinai, with their banners spread, look like the multi-colored clouds of Heaven that promise fair weather to the next morning."

The King of Trebizond said, "And I bring as many soldiers from Trebizond, Chio, Famastro, and Amasia, all of which border on the Mare Majore sea — the Black Sea. I also bring soldiers from Riso, Sancina, and the bordering towns that touch the end of the famous Euphrates River: These soldiers' courage and valor are kindled with the flames that the cursed Scythian — Tamburlaine — sets on all their towns, and these soldiers vow to burn the villain's cruel heart."

The King of Syria said, "From Syria with seventy thousand soldiers, taken from Aleppo, Soldino, Tripoli, and so on unto my city of Damascus, I march to meet and aid my neighbor Kings, all of whom will join together to fight against this Tamburlaine and bring him captive to your highness' feet."

Deputy King Orcanes of Natolia said, "Our army then, in martial manner arranged, as according to our ancient custom, shall bear the figure of the semi-circled Moon, whose horns shall sprinkle through the tainted air the poisoned brains of this proud Scythian."

In other words, the Turkish army will form in a crescent formation to fight Tamburlaine and his army.

The Turkish Emperor Callapine said, "Well, then, my noble lords, as for this my friend Almeda, who freed me from the bondage of my foe, I think it requisite and honorable to keep my promise and make him King. That man is a gentleman, I know, at least."

Almeda said, "That doesn't matter for being a King, sir, because Tamburlaine came up from nothing."

The King of Jerusalem said to the Turkish Emperor Callapine, "Your majesty may choose some appointed time, performing all you promised to the full. It is nothing for your majesty to give a kingdom."

"Then I will shortly keep my promise, Almeda," the Turkish Emperor Callapine said.

"Why, I thank your majesty," Almeda said.

Tamburlaine, Usumcasane, and his three sons stood together. Four men set down the bier of Zenocrate. Drums stopped sounding a doleful march, and the town of Larissa burned.

Tamburlaine said, "Burn the turrets of this cursed town — Larissa. Burn it so the flames reach to the highest region of the air, and kindle heaps of exhalations that, being fiery meteors, may presage death and destruction to the inhabitants!"

Meteors were ill omens. This society believed that very light vapors (exhalations) rose from the Earth, caught fire, and formed fiery meteors. Usually, perhaps, they would catch fire from the Sphere of Fire that separated the Earth from the Moon. In this case, however, they would catch fire from the burning flames of Larissa.

"Over my zenith, the highest point over my head, hangs a blazing star — a comet — that may endure until Heaven is dissolved, fed with the fresh supply of earthly dregs, threatening famine to this land!"

This society used the word "star" broadly. A star could be a planet, the Sun, a comet, a meteor, etc.

The blazing star over his head would be fed with the fires rising from the devastation Tamburlaine would cause on Earth. The smoke from the fires could also appear to form shapes such as dragons.

He continued, "May flying dragons, lightning, fearful thunderclaps singe these fair plains and make them seem as black as is the island where the Furies lurk unseen, surrounded by the Lethe, Styx, and Phlegethon, because my dear Zenocrate is dead."

Calyphas, Tamburlaine's oldest son, said, "On this pillar, placed in memory of her, in Arabian, Hebrew, and Greek is written, '*This town, being burnt by Tamburlaine the Great, forbids the world to build it up again.*'"

Amyras, Tamburlaine's middle son, said, "And here this mournful banner shall be placed, embroidered with the Persian and Egyptian coat-of-arms, to signify she was a Princess born and wife to the Monarch of the East."

Celebinus, Tamburlaine's youngest son, said, "And here we will set this memorial tablet as a record of all her virtues and perfections."

Tamburlaine said, "And here we will set this picture of Zenocrate, to show her beauty that the world admired. This sweet picture of divine Zenocrate, hanging here, will draw the gods from Heaven and cause the stars fixed in the southern hemisphere — southern stars whose lovely faces never has anyone in the northern hemisphere viewed who has not crossed the equator to the southern hemisphere. These stars will be like pilgrims as they travel to our hemisphere, just to gaze on Zenocrate."

People in the northern hemisphere above the equator cannot see the stars at the southern pole and the stars at the opposite end of the Earth. According to Tamburlaine, those southern stars would move of their own accord to the northern hemisphere to look at beautiful Zenocrate's picture.

Tamburlaine changed his mind about leaving the picture of Zenocrate at Larissa.

Speaking to the picture of Zenocrate, Tamburlaine said, "You shall not beautify Larissa's plains, but instead will stay within the circle of my arms. At every town and castle I besiege, you shall be set upon my royal tent, and when I meet an army in the field, your looks will shed such influence in my army, as if Bellona, goddess of the war, threw naked, unsheathed swords and sulphur-balls of fire upon the heads of all our enemies.

"And now, my lords, raise aloft your spears again.

"Sorrow no more, my sweet Casane, now.

"Boys, cease to mourn; this town shall always mourn, being burnt to cinders for your mother's death."

Calyphas, Tamburlaine's oldest son, said, "If I had wept a sea of tears for her, it would not ease the sorrows I endure."

Amyras, Tamburlaine's middle son, said, "As is that town, so is my heart consumed as if by fire with grief and sorrow for my mother's death."

Celebinus, Tamburlaine's youngest son, said, "My mother's death has mortified my mind, and sorrow stops the passage of my speech."

Tamburlaine said, "But now, my boys, stop mourning and listen to me. I intend to teach you the rudiments of war. I'll have you learn to sleep upon the ground, march in your armor through watery fens, endure the scorching heat and freezing cold, hunger, and thirst, all of which are fit adjuncts of the war.

"And after I teach you that, I will teach you this: how to scale a castle wall, how to besiege a fort, how to undermine a town and plant explosives to make whole cities leap up and dance in the air.

"Next I will teach you the way to build fortifications for your men.

"I will teach you what fortification lay-out serves you best on level, open ground.

"I will also teach you for which kind of ground — rough and uneven — the five-angled shape is best, because the corners there may fall more flat and form wider angles where the fort may fittest be assailed and sharpest where the assault is dangerous to make."

With the star-fortification, the flatter and sharper corners can be placed irregularly in the terrain where they are most advantageous for the defenders. The obtuse-angled corners can be placed on terrain that favors the attackers, and the acute-angled corners can be placed on terrain that favors the defenders. Obtuse-angled corners are easier to defend; acute-angled corners are harder to defend.

An obtuse angle is larger than a right angle and so is more than 90 degrees.

An acute angle is smaller than a right angle and so is less than 90 degrees.

Tamburlaine continued, "The ditches must be deep."

The ditches were dug around the fortification. Deep ditches made the attackers' job more difficult because they had to cross the ditch and also the earthen wall that was built from the earth dug to make the ditch.

Tamburlaine continued, "The counterscarps must be narrow and steep. The walls must made high and broad."

The scarp is the inner wall of the ditch; the counterscarp is the outer wall of the ditch. The ditch, if filled with water, becomes a moat. The counterscarps are the steep outer earthen walls of the ditch; these walls supported the covered ways — a protected path that the defenders could walk along. Sometimes the word "counterscarps" was used to refer to the covered ways and the glacis. The glacis is a wall of earth facing the attackers and protecting the defenders who are on the covered way. The walls of the counterscarp and the glacis must be built high. Apparently, Tamburlaine preferred that the covered ways be narrow.

Tamburlaine continued, "The bulwarks and the rampires must be large and strong, with cavalieros and thick counterforts, and room within to lodge six thousand men."

The bulwarks are substantial defensive positions, often made of earth, often placed at the corners of fortifications, and often made to provide stations for artillery; they are defensive walls. Sometimes the word "bulwark" is used to refer to the fortification itself. The rampiers are ramparts used to support the walls from behind. Both bulwarks and rampiers must be large and strong.

Cavalieros are mounds on which large cannon were placed.

Counterforts are extra buttresses to strengthen defensive walls.

Tamburlaine continued, "The fortification must have privy ditches, countermines, and secret issuings to defend the ditch."

A cunette is a deeper ditch dug in the middle of a defensive ditch. It is another obstacle for attackers to overcome, it serves as a drain, and it helps to prevent mining by the attackers.

A privy ditch is possibly a ditch built for sanitation. Or, possibly, a privy ditch is a cunette. The first citation for "cunette" in the *Oxford English Dictionary* is 1688. The word "privy" can mean "secret," and a cunette can be an obstacle for attackers.

Countermines are underground tunnels dug outward from the fortress in order to counteract mines, aka tunnels, dug by the enemy to either cause fortification walls to collapse by use of explosives or to gain entry into a fortification.

Secret issuings are hidden doors that allow defenders to get to the ditch area. In some cases, they can be used to surprise any attackers who are in that area.

Tamburlaine continued, "The fortification must have high *argins* and covered ways, to keep the bulwark fronts from battery."

A high glacis can deflect attackers' cannonballs. "*Argins*" is the French word for "glacis." The glacis is a high wall of earth placed in front of a covered way for protection; a covered way is a passageway protected by the high *argins*.

Tamburlaine continued, "The fortification must have parapets to hide the musketeers."

Parapets are protective walls; in particular, they are low walls that edge the wallwalk, aka walkway on top of the wall. Parapets are located on the scarp part of the ditch; that is, they are located on the inner side of the main defensive wall. The covered way and glacis are located on the other side of the ditch.

Tamburlaine continued, "The fortification must have casemates on which to place the great artillery."

A casemate is a protected chamber or room in which a cannon can be placed. A battery of cannon is different; it is a grouping of cannon.

Tamburlaine continued, "The fortification must have a store of ordnance that from every flank may scour the outward curtains of the fort, dismount the cannon of the enemy, murder the foe, and save the walls from being breached."

Curtains are the plain walls of a fortification; they connect the bulwarks, which are often located at corners.

A flank is a part of a fortification that allows defenders to protect with flanking fire another part of the fortification.

Bastions are defensive structures projecting outward from the curtains. They allow defenders to defend more area than if they were located on top of the curtains.

Cannon were sometimes placed on bastions, which were outward indentations on the outer wall; such cannon could be fired horizontally to the wall and so kill (Tamburlaine used the word "murder") enemy soldiers close to the wall.

Tamburlaine may have been making wordplay here by referring to a type of small cannon that was called the murderer.

Tamburlaine continued, "When this is learned for service on the land, by plain and easy demonstration I'll teach you how to make the water mount by holding it back with a dam, so that you may march with dry feet through lakes and pools, deep rivers, sheltered harbors, creeks, and little seas, and I'll teach you how to make a fortress in the raging waves, protected by the cavity of a monstrous rock, invincible by the nature of the place.

"When all this is done, then you are soldiers, and worthy sons of Tamburlaine the Great."

Calyphas, Tamburlaine's oldest son, said, "My lord, but this is dangerous to be done. We may be slain or wounded before we learn all this."

Angry, Tamburlaine said, "Villain, are you the son of Tamburlaine, and fear to die, or with a sword to hew your flesh, and make a gaping wound?

"Have you beheld a discharge of cannon strike a ring of soldiers wielding pikes, supported with musketeers and flanked by cavalry, whose shattered limbs, being tossed as high as Heaven, hang in the air as thick as sunny motes of dust, and can you, coward, stand in fear of death?

"Haven't you seen my horsemen charge the foe and get shot through the arms and cut across the hands, dyeing their lances with their streaming blood, and yet at night carouse within my tent, filling their empty veins with airy — hot and moist, like blood — wine that, being digested by the soldiers, turns to crimson blood, and will you shun the battlefield for fear of wounds?

"Look at me, your father, who has conquered Kings, and with his army marched round about the Earth. I am quite devoid of scars and clear from any wound. I have not lost a dram of blood by the wars.

"And now see your father lance his flesh to teach you all."

Tamburlaine cut his arm.

He then said, "A wound is nothing, be it never so deep. Blood is the god of war's rich uniform.

"Now I look like a soldier, and this wound is as great a grace — gift — and majesty to me, as if a chair of gold enameled, inlaid with diamonds, sapphires, rubies, and fairest pearl of wealthy India, were mounted here under a canopy, and I sat down, clothed with the large robe that lately adorned Bajazeth the African potentate, whom I brought bound to Damascus' walls.

"Come, boys, and with your fingers feel how deep is my wound, and in my blood wash all your hands at once, while I sit smiling to behold the sight.

"Now, my boys, what do you think about a wound?"

Calyphas, Tamburlaine's oldest son, said, "I don't know what I should think of it. I think it is a pitiful sight."

Celebinus, Tamburlaine's youngest son, said, "It is nothing. Give me a wound, father."

Amyras, Tamburlaine's middle son, said, "And give me another, my lord."

Tamburlaine said to Celebinus, "Come, sirrah, give me your arm."

"Here, father, cut it bravely and boldly, as you did your own," Celebinus said.

"It shall suffice that you dare to abide a wound," Tamburlaine said. "My boy, you shall not lose a drop of blood before we meet the army of the Turkish Emperor.

"But then, run desperate through the thickest throngs, now dreading blows, bloody wounds, and death. And let the burning of Larissa's walls, my speech of war, and this my wound you see, teach you, my boys, to bear courageous minds, fit for the successors of great Tamburlaine.

"Usumcasane, now come and let us march towards Techelles and Theridamas, whom we have sent before to set fire to the towns, the towers and cities of these hateful Turks, and hunt that coward faint-hearted runaway Callapine, with that accursed traitor, Almeda, until fire and sword have found them at bay. We will corner them and force them to fight us."

Usumcasane said, "I long to pierce with my sword the bowels of that man who has betrayed my gracious sovereign: that cursed and damned traitor, Almeda."

Tamburlaine said, "Then let us see if that coward Callapine dares to muster arms against our army, with the result that we may tread upon his captive neck, and triple all his father's slaveries."

Techelles and Theridamas talked together. Many soldiers and attendants were present.

Theridamas said, "Thus have we marched northward from Tamburlaine to the frontier point of Syria, and this is Balsera, their chiefest stronghold, wherein is all the treasure of the land."

Techelles said, "Then let us bring our light artillery, minions, falconets, and sakers — all our small cannon — to the trench, filling the ditches with the walls' wide breach. We will blast the wall with our small cannon, and the pieces of the wall will fill in the ditches. And then we will enter to seize upon the gold.

"What do you say, soldiers? Shall we do that?"

"Yes, my lord, yes," the soldiers said. "Come, let's set about it."

Theridamas said, "But wait a while.

"Summon a parley, drummer.

"It may be they will yield Balsera quietly, knowing that two Kings, friends to Tamburlaine, stand at the walls with such a mighty army."

The drummer played a rhythm that was recognized by both sides as a request to hold a meeting under a flag of truce.

The Captain of Balsera appeared on the wall of the stronghold. With him were his wife, who was named Olympia, and his son. The Captain was the Commander of the castle.

The Captain of Balsera asked, "What do you require, my masters?"

"My masters" meant "gentlemen."

Theridamas said, "Captain, we require that thou yield up thy stronghold to us."

"To you!" the Captain of Balsera replied. "Why, do you think that I am weary of it?

Techelles said, "No, Captain, thou are weary of thy life if thou withstand the friends of Tamburlaine."

Theridamas said, "These pioneers — diggers — of Algiers in Africa even in the cannon's face shall raise a hill of earth and bundles of sticks higher than thy fort, and over thy *argins* and covered ways shall play upon the bulwarks of thy fortress volleys of cannon, until the breach is made that with its ruin fills up all the trench. And, when we enter in, not Heaven itself shall ransom thee, thy wife, and thy family.”

Generally, a trench is deeper than it is wide; ditches tend to be wider than they are deep.

Techelles said, “Captain, these Moors shall cut the leaden pipes that bring fresh water to thy men and thee, and lay siege, protected by the trench, before thy castle walls, so that no supply of food shall come in, nor will any of your people issue forth but they shall die, and, therefore, Captain, yield your stronghold to us quietly.”

The Captain of Balsera replied, “Even if you, who are the friends of Tamburlaine, were brothers to holy Mahomet himself, I would not yield it; therefore, do your worst. Raise earthworks, batter the gates with a battering ram, build a trench around the fort, and undermine the fort’s walls, cut off the water and all supply convoys that can come to bring us provisions, yet I am resolute to defend the stronghold, and so, farewell.”

The Captain and his wife and son exited.

“Pioneers, away!” Theridamas said. “And where I stuck the stake, build a trench with those dimensions I prescribed. Cast up the earth towards the castle wall. Until the earth forms a wall to defend you, keep low while working and building the wall, and few or none of you shall perish by their shot.”

“We will, my lord,” the pioneers said as they exited.

Techelles said, “A hundred cavalry shall scout the plains to spy what force comes to relieve the stronghold.

“Both of us, Theridamas, will have our men build the trench that will protect them, and with the gunner’s quadrant called the Jacob’s staff, they will measure the height and distance of the castle from the trench so that we may know if our artillery will shoot cannonballs completely point-blank at their walls. We want the cannonballs to hit the wall horizontally with full force.”

This is why Theridamas had talked earlier about raising a hill of earth and bundles of sticks higher than the fort. Take away the hyperbole, and he was saying that he wanted the cannon to shoot horizontally over the lower outer walls so that the cannonballs would strike the main walls of the fortress with full force.

Theridamas said, "Then see the bringing of our ordnance along the trench into the battery — the platform on which the cannon are placed — where we will have gabions of six foot broad, to save our cannoneers from musket shot."

Gabions are containers filled with earth, used like sandbags to protect people in the battery and to steady cannon.

Theridamas continued, "Between the gabions our ordnance shall thunder forth, and with the breach's fall, smoke, fire, and dust, the crack, the echo, and the soldier's cry, our ordnance shall deafen the air and dim the crystal sky."

Techelles ordered, "Trumpeters and drummers, play a call to arms at once! And, soldiers, act like men; the hold is yours!"

The Captain of Balsera talked with his wife, Olympia. Their son was present.

Olympia said, "Come, my good lord, and let us quickly go away from here along the underground passage that leads beyond the foe. No hope is left to save this conquered fortress."

The Captain of Balsera replied, "A deadly bullet gliding through my side lies heavy on my heart; I cannot live. I feel my liver pierced, and all my veins, that there begin and nourish every part, mangled and torn, and all my entrails bathed in blood that oozes from their openings.

"Farewell, sweet wife! Sweet son, farewell! I die."

He died.

Olympia said, "Death, where have you gone, that both my son and I live? Come back again, sweet Death, and strike us both. Let one minute end our days, and one sepulcher contain our bodies! Death, why don't you come?"

She drew a dagger and said, "Well, this dagger must be the messenger for you.

"Now, ugly Death, stretch out your black, sable wings and carry both my and my son's souls to where my husband's soul resides."

She then asked her son, "Tell me, sweet boy, are you content to die? These barbarous Scythians, full of cruelty, and Moors, in whom pity was never found, will hew us into pieces, or tie us to a torture-wheel and break our bones with clubs, or else invent some torture worse than that; therefore, die by the hand of your loving mother, who gently now will lance your ivory throat, and quickly rid you both of pain and life."

"Mother, dispatch me, or I'll kill myself," her son said. "For do you think I can live and see my father dead? Give me your knife, good mother, or strike home. The Scythians shall not cruelly tyrannize me. Sweet mother, strike, so that I may meet my father."

She stabbed him, and he died.

Olympia said, "Ah, sacred Mahomet, if this is sin, entreat a pardon of the God of Heaven, and purge my soul and free it from sin before it comes to you."

She burned the bodies of her husband and son and then prepared to kill herself.

Theridamas and Techelles and many soldiers entered the room.

Theridamas forcibly took the dagger away from Olympia and said, "What is this, madam! What are you doing?"

Olympia replied, "Killing myself, as I have killed my son, whose body, with his father's, I have burnt, lest cruel Scythians should dismember him."

"It was bravely done, and like a soldier's wife," Techelles said. "You shall go with us to Tamburlaine the Great, who, when he hears how resolute you were, will match you with and marry you to a Viceroy or a King."

"My deceased lord was dearer to me than any Viceroy, King, or Emperor," Olympia said. "And for his sake I will end my days here."

Theridamas said, "But, lady, go with us to Tamburlaine, and you shall see a man greater than Mahomet, in whose high looks is much more majesty than exists from the curved surface of Jove's vast palace, the empyreal sphere, to the shining dwellings where Cynthia the Moon sits, like the lovely sea-nymph Thetis, in a crystal robe."

In other words, Tamburlaine looks much more majestic than does anything in the universe from the highest sphere — the empyreal heaven — to the Moon. Cynthia is the Moon-goddess, but sometimes her name was used to refer to the Moon.

Theridamas continued, "Tamburlaine treads Lady Fortune underneath his feet and makes the mighty Mars — god of arms and war — his slave.

"Death and the Fatal Sisters — the three Fates — wait on Tamburlaine with naked swords and scarlet, blood-red uniforms.

"Before Tamburlaine, mounted on a lion's back, Rhamnusia — Nemesis, the goddess of vengeance, who has a temple at Rhamnus — bears a helmet full of blood and strews the way with the brains of slaughtered men.

"By Tamburlaine's side the ugly, horror-causing Furies run, listening carefully for when he shall order them to plague the world.

"Over Tamburlaine's zenith, clothed in windy air and with eagle's wings joined to her feathered breast, Fame hovers, sounding her golden trumpet, so that to the opposite poles of that straight line — the axle-tree of the heavens — which measures the glorious frame of Heaven, the name of mighty Tamburlaine is spread. His name is known throughout the world from north pole to south pole.

"And, fair lady, your eyes shall behold Tamburlaine.

"Come."

Olympia replied, "Take pity on a lady's pitiful tears, a lady who humbly begs upon her knees to stay and cast her body in the burning flame that feeds upon her son's and husband's flesh."

Techelles said, "Madam, sooner shall fire consume us both than scorch a face as beautiful as yours, in fashioning which Nature has showed more skill than when she gave eternal chaos form, drawing from it the shining lamps of Heaven."

Theridamas said, "Madam, I am so far in love with you, that you must go with us — you must."

Olympia said, "Then carry me, I care not, where you will, and let the end of this my fated, fatal journey be likewise the end to my accursed life."

"No, madam," Techelles said, "it will be the beginning of your joy. Come willingly, therefore."

Theridamas said, "Soldiers, now let us meet the general, Tamburlaine, who by this time is at Natolia, ready to charge the army of the Turkish Emperor. The gold, the silver, and the pearl you got, plundering this fort, divide in equal shares. This lady shall have twice as much again out of the coffers of our treasury."

The Turkish Emperor Callapine, Deputy King Orcanes of Natolia, the King of Jerusalem, the King of Trebizond, the King of Syria, and Almeda were meeting. Many soldiers and attendants were present, as was a messenger.

The Turkish Emperor Callapine and his army had traveled from Asia Minor to battle Tamburlaine. Tamburlaine's army was at Aleppo in northern Syria.

The messenger said, "Renowned Emperor, mighty Callapine, God's great lieutenant over all the world, here at Aleppo, with an army of men, camps Tamburlaine, this King of Persia — in number they are more than are the quivering leaves of Mount Ida's forest near Troy in western Natolia, where your highness' hounds with open cry pursue the wounded stag. Tamburlaine intends to encircle the walls of Natolia with siege, set fire to the town, and overrun the land."

The messenger referred to Natolia as a town: He meant the military camp of Natolia's royal army. Tamburlaine intended to utterly defeat the Turkish Emperor's royal army. According to the messenger, Tamburlaine had so many soldiers that he could surround Natolia's royal army as if he were besieging a city.

The Turkish Emperor Callapine said, "My royal army is as great as Tamburlaine's army. My royal army, from the bounds of Phrygia in western Asia Minor to the Mediterranean Sea that washes the island of Cyprus with its brinish waves, covers the hills, the valleys, and the plains.

"Viceroys and peers of Turkey, be valiant. Sharpen all your swords to mangle Tamburlaine, his sons, his captains, and his followers.

"By Mahomet, not one of them shall live. Forever call the field on which this battle shall be fought the Persians' sepulcher, in memory of this our victory."

Deputy King Orcanes of Natolia said, "Now he who calls himself the scourge of Jove, the Emperor of the World, and earthly god shall end the warlike progress he intends and travel headlong to the lake of Hell, where legions of devils — knowing he must die here in Natolia's military camp by your highness' hands — all brandishing their flaming torches of quenchless fire, stretching their monstrous paws, grin with their teeth, and guard the gates to receive his soul."

The Turkish Emperor Callapine said, "Tell me, Viceroys, the number of your men in your armies, and the total number of men we have when all your armies are combined in our royal army."

The King of Jerusalem said, "From Palestine and Jerusalem, of Hebrews three score thousand fighting men have come, since last we showed the numbers to your majesty."

Deputy King Orcanes of Natolia said, "From Arabia's desert, and the territory of that sweet land whose brave metropolis — Babylon — the fair Semiramis rebuilt, have come forty thousand warlike foot soldiers and horsemen, since last we showed the numbers to your majesty."

The King of Trebizond said, "From Trebizond in Asia Minor, naturalized Turks — people who became Turks after living a long time in Asia Minor — and valiant Bithynians have come to my bands of soldiers, full fifty thousand more, who, when fighting, know not what retreat means, nor will ever return but with the victory, since last we showed the numbers to your majesty."

The King of Syria said, "Syrians from Halla and neighbor cities of your highness' land have travelled here, ten thousand horsemen and thirty thousand soldiers on foot, since last we showed the numbers to your majesty.

"And so the royal army is estimated to number six hundred thousand valiant fighting men."

In an apostrophe, Callapine spoke to Tamburlaine, who was not present: "Then welcome, Tamburlaine, to your death."

He then said, "Come, powerful Viceroys, let us go to the battlefield — the Persians' sepulcher — and sacrifice mountains of breathless men to Mahomet, who now, with Jove, opens the heavens to see the slaughter of our enemies."

Tamburlaine arrived with his three sons, Usumcasane, and some soldiers.

Tamburlaine said, "Hey, Casane! Look, a gang of Kings, sitting as if they were a-telling riddles."

"My lord, your presence makes them pale and wan," Usumcasane said. "Poor souls, they look as if their deaths were near."

"Why, it is true that Death is near, Casane, because I am here," Tamburlaine said. "But still I'll save their lives and make them slaves.

"You petty Kings of Turkey, I have come, as Hector did into the Grecian camp, to outdare and daunt the pride of Greece, aka the Greek army, and set his — Hector's — warlike person to the view of fierce Achilles, rival of his fame. I do you honor in the simile."

This is true. In the simile, Tamburlaine compared the petty Kings of Turkey to Achilles, while Tamburlaine compared himself to Hector. Achilles was the superior warrior; in fact, he was the greatest warrior in the Trojan War. Tamburlaine, of course, expects to defeat the petty Kings of Turkey — and the Turkish Emperor Callapine.

In William Shakespeare's *Troilus and Cressida*, Hector visits the Greek camp. Post-Homeric accounts of the Trojan War sometimes included this episode, which is not in Homer's *Iliad*.

Tamburlaine continued, "For, if I should, as Hector did Achilles, the worthiest knight who ever brandished sword, challenge in combat any of you, I see how fearfully you would refuse, and flee from my glove that I throw down in challenge as you would flee from a scorpion."

Orcanes, the main "petty King" of Turkey, replied, "Now that thou are afraid that thy army's strength will be insufficient to achieve victory, thou would prefer to overmatch a person in single combat."

An overmatch is a contest in which one person is clearly superior.

Orcanes continued, "But, shepherd's son, baseborn Tamburlaine, think of thy end; this sword shall slash thy throat."

Tamburlaine, who was the son of a shepherd, replied, "Villain, the shepherd's son, at whose birth Heaven gave me a gracious astrological aspect of good fortune and joined those stars that shall be astrologically opposite even until the dissolution to the world — the astrological aspect of good fortune given to me shall never be seen again — and never meant to make a conqueror as famous as is mighty Tamburlaine, shall so torment thee and that Callapine, who, like a roguish runaway, bribed that villain Almeda there, that slave, that Turkish dog, to act falsely and betray his service to his sovereign, that you shall curse the birth of Tamburlaine."

"Don't rant, proud Scythian," the Turkish Emperor Callapine said. "I shall now revenge the vile ill treatment that first my father and then I suffered at your hands."

The King of Jerusalem said, "By Mahomet, Tamburlaine shall be tied in chains, rowing with Christians in a brigandine — a small pirate vessel — about the Grecian isles to rob and plunder, and turn back to his ancient trade of banditry again. I think the slave will make a vigorous thief."

"No," the Turkish Emperor Callapine said, "when the battle ends, we all will meet and sit in council to invent some pain that most may afflict his body and his soul."

"Sirrah Callapine, I'll hang a heavy clog of wood about your neck to keep you from running away again," Tamburlaine said. "You shall not trouble me thus to come and fetch you."

"Sirrah" was a word that people of higher class used to refer to a man of lower class.

"But as for you, Viceroys, you shall have bits thrust in your mouths like horses, and, harnessed like my horses, draw my coach. And, when you don't move quickly enough, you will be lashed with whips of wire. I'll have you learn to feed on horse fodder and lie upon the planks in a stable."

Deputy King Orcanes of Natolia said, "But, Tamburlaine, first thou shall kneel to us and humbly crave a pardon for thy life."

The King of Trebizond said, "The common soldiers of our mighty army shall bring thee bound to the General Callapine's tent."

The King of Syria said, "And all have jointly sworn to cause thy cruel death, or to bind thee in eternal torments' wrath."

Tamburlaine said, "Well, sirs, feed yourselves well; you know I shall have occasion shortly to make you take me on a journey by drawing my coach."

Celebinus, Tamburlaine's youngest son, said, "Look, father, how Almeda the jailor looks at us."

Tamburlaine said to Almeda, "Villain, traitor, damned fugitive, I'll make thee wish the earth had swallowed thee. Don't thou see death within my wrathful looks? Go, villain, cast theeself headlong from a rock, or rip thy bowels and tear out thy heart to appease my wrath; or else I'll torture thee, searing thy hateful flesh with burning irons and drops of scalding lead, while all thy joints are torn apart on the rack and beat to pieces with the torture-wheel, for if thou live, no element — not earth, not air, not fire, and not water — shall shroud and hide thee from the wrath of Tamburlaine."

The Turkish Emperor Callapine said, "Well, in despite of thee, he shall be made a King.

"Come, Almeda, receive this crown from me. I here invest thee King of Ariadan, which borders Mare Rosso — the Red Sea — near Mecca."

Ariadan was an unimportant town. Almeda was a petty King, indeed.

Callapine held out a crown to Almeda, who, afraid of Tamburlaine, hesitated to take the crown.

Deputy King Orcanes of Natolia said, "What! Take it, man!"

Trembling, Almeda said to Tamburlaine, "My good lord, let me take it."

The Turkish Emperor Callapine said, "Do thou ask him for permission? Here! Take it!"

Tamburlaine said, "Bah, sirrah, take your crown, and make up the half dozen."

Almeda took the crown.

The half-dozen Kings were Deputy King Orcanes of Natolia, the King of Jerusalem, the King of Trebizond, the King of Syria, the King of Amasia, and now King Almeda of Ariadan.

"So, sirrah," Tamburlaine said, "now you are a King, you must give arms."

"To give arms" meant "to wear a coat of arms." It also meant that Almeda, as a King, had the right to grant a coat of arms to other people, and it meant that Almeda, as a tributary King, would have to supply soldiers to the Turkish Emperor.

Orcanes said, "So he shall, and wear thy head in his escutcheon."

An escutcheon is a shield that displays a coat of arms.

"No," Tamburlaine said, "let him hang a bunch of keys on his military banner, to remind himself that he was a jailor, so that when I capture him, I may knock out his brains with them, and lock you in the stable, when you shall come sweating from my chariot."

"Let's leave," the King of Trebizond said, "so that the villain Tamburlaine may be slain."

He meant that Tamburlaine would be slain in the upcoming battle.

"Sirrah, prepare whips, and bring my chariot to my tent," Tamburlaine said, "for, as soon as the battle is done, I'll ride in triumph through the camp."

Theridamas, Techelles, and some of their soldiers and attendants arrived.

Tamburlaine said to Callapine's Kings, "Hey, you petty Kings! Look, here are bug-bears — my generals — who will make the hair stand upright on your heads, and cast your crowns in slavery at their feet."

He then said, "Welcome, Theridamas and Techelles, both. Do you see this mob of Kings?"

Pointing to Almeda, he added, "And do you know this King?"

"Yes, my lord," Theridamas said. "He was Callapine's keeper."

"Well, now you see he is a King," Tamburlaine said. "Look to him, Theridamas, when we are fighting, lest he hides his crown as the foolish King of Persia did."

King Mycetes of Persia had attempted to hide his crown when his army was fighting Tamburlaine's army. Tamburlaine, victorious, became the new King of Persia.

The King of Syria said, "No, Tamburlaine; he shall not be put to that exigent, I warrant thee."

Tamburlaine replied, "You don't know that, sir."

He then said, "But now, my followers and my loving friends, fight as you always have, like conquerors. The glory of this happy day is yours. My stern aspect shall make the fair goddess Victory, hovering between our armies, alight on me, laden with laurel wreaths — symbols of victory — to crown us all."

The stern aspect was both Tamburlaine's stern facial expression and the astrological aspect — the way the heavenly bodies look to a person on Earth. Tamburlaine believed that the astrological aspect indicated a defeat for the royal Turkish army.

Techelles said, "I smile to think how when this battle is fought and rich Natolia is ours, our men shall sweat with carrying pearl and treasure on their backs."

Tamburlaine said to his men, "You shall be princes all, immediately."

He then said, "Come, fight, you Turks, or yield us victory."

Deputy King Orcanes of Natolia replied, "No, we will meet thee on the battlefield, slavish Tamburlaine."

CHAPTER 4 (Part 2)

— 4.1 —

A trumpeter blew a call to arms.

Amyras, Tamburlaine's middle son, and Celebinus, Tamburlaine's youngest son, came out of a tent. Calyphas, Tamburlaine's oldest son, stayed in the tent, asleep.

Amyras said to Celebinus, "Now the golden crowns of these proud Turks shine in their glories, much like so many suns that half dismay the majesty of Heaven. Now, brother, we follow our father's sword, which flies with fury swifter than our thoughts and cuts down armies with its conquering wings."

Celebinus said, "Call forth our lazy brother from the tent, for if my father should miss him on the battlefield, wrath, kindled in the furnace of his breast, will send a deadly lightning to his heart."

Amyras called to Calyphas, "Brother, ho! Do you like to sleep so much that you cannot leave it when our enemies' drums and rattling cannon thunder in our ears our own destruction and our father's disgrace?"

Calyphas said, "Go away, you fools! My father doesn't need me, nor does he need you, truly, but you want to fight because you prefer to be thought more childish-valorous than manly wise.

"If half our camp of soldiers should sit and sleep with me, my father would be enough to scare and scar the foe.

"You do dishonor to his majesty by thinking our helps will do him any good."

Amyras said, "What, do thou dare, then, to be absent from the fight, knowing my father hates thy cowardice, and often has warned thee to be always in the field of battle, when he himself amidst the thickest troops beats down our foes, to flesh our taintless swords?"

The swords of Tamburlaine's sons were taintless: The sons had not yet wounded or killed an enemy soldier. To flesh one's sword meant to get it bloody in battle. In the sport of hawking, hawks were fleshed when they were given a portion of the animal they had killed.

Calyphas said, "I know, sir, what it is to kill a man; it works a remorse of conscience in me. I take no pleasure in being murderous, nor do I care for blood when wine will quench my thirst."

"Oh, cowardly boy!" Celebinus said. "Bah, for shame, come out of the tent and go to the battle! Thou dishonor manhood and thy family."

"Go, go, brave stripling," Calyphas said. "You fight for us both, and take my other eager, promising brother here as a person likely to prove a second Mars, god of war. It will please my mind as well to hear that you both have won a heap of honor in the battlefield and left your slender carcasses behind, as it would if I lay dead with you for company on the battlefield."

"You will not go, then?" Amyras asked.

"You say the truth," Calyphas said.

Amyras said, "Were all the lofty mountains of *Zona Mundi* — the Zone of the World — that fill the midst of farthest Tartary on northwest Asia turned into pearl and offered the pearl to me if I would stay out of the battle, I would not abide the fury of my father, when he, made a victor in these proud conquests, comes and finds his sons have had no shares in all the honors he proposed for us."

"You take the honor," Calyphas said. "I will take my ease. My wisdom shall excuse my cowardice. Should I go to the battlefield before I have to?"

The battle trumpets sounded, and Amyras and Celebinus ran to the battlefield.

Calyphas said to himself, "The bullets fly at random where they please, and if I would go and kill a thousand men, I would be at the earliest moment rewarded with a shot, and far sooner than he who never fights. And if I should go and do neither harm nor good, I might receive harm, which all the wealth I have, joined with my father's crown, would never cure.

"I'll play cards, not go to the battlefield."

He called, "Perdicas!"

Perdicas, Calyphas' servant, walked over to him and said, "Here I am, my lord."

"Come, you and I will play cards to drive away the time," Calyphas said.

"I am happy to, my lord," Perdicas said, "but what shall we play for?"

"Shall we play to see who shall kiss the fairest of the Turks' concubines first, when my father has conquered the Turks?" Calyphas asked.

"Agreed, indeed," Perdicas replied.

They began to play cards.

Calyphas said, "They say I am a coward, Perdicas, and I fear as little their taratantaras — bugle calls — their swords, or their cannon as I do a naked lady in a net — veil — of fine gold mesh, and who out of fear that I should be afraid, would put it off and come to bed with me."

"Such a fear, my lord, would never make you retire from 'battle' with such a woman," Perdicas said.

Calyphas said, "I wish that my father would let me be put in the front of such a battle once, to try my valor."

Battle noises sounded.

"What a noisy tumult they make!" Calyphas said. "I believe there will be some hurt done soon amongst them."

Tamburlaine, Theridamas, Techelles, Usumcasane, Amyras, and Celebinus returned to the camp, leading some of the Turkish petty Kings: Deputy King Orcanes of Natolia, the King of Jerusalem, the King of Trebizond, and the King of Syria. Soldiers were present.

Tamburlaine said to the petty Kings, "See now, you slaves, my children humiliate your pride and lead your glories sheeplike to the sword."

He then said, "Bring them, my boys, and tell me if the wars aren't a life that may shed luster on gods? Don't the wars tickle your spirits with desire continually to be trained in arms and chivalry?"

"Shall we let go these Kings again, my lord," Amyras said, "to gather greater numbers against our power, so that they may say it is not luck that gave us this victory, but unmatched strength and great courage?"

"No, no, Amyras," Tamburlaine said. "Don't tempt Lady Fortune that way. Nourish your valor continually with fresh supplies of Kings to conquer elsewhere, and don't glut it with stale and daunted foes.

"But where's this coward villain, who is not my son, but is instead a traitor to my name and majesty?"

Tamburlaine went into the tent and brought Calyphas, his oldest son, out.

Tamburlaine said to Calyphas, "Image of sloth, and picture of a slave, the disgrace and scorn of my renown! How may my heart, thus inflamed with what my eyes see, wounded with shame and killed with discontent, shroud and conceal any thought that may stop my striving hands from executing martial justice on thy wretched soul?"

Theridamas said, "Yet pardon him, I beg your majesty."

Techelles and Usumcasane said, "Let all of us entreat and beg for your highness' pardon."

Theridamas, Techelles, and Usumcasane knelt.

Tamburlaine said, "Stand up, you base, unworthy soldiers! Don't you know yet the argument of arms? Don't you know the code of military conduct?"

Theridamas, Techelles, and Usumcasane stood up, but Amyras and Celebinus knelt.

Amyras said, "My good lord, let him be forgiven for once, and we will force him to go to the battlefield hereafter."

Tamburlaine said, "Stand up, my boys, and I will teach you arms, and what the zeal for military values must do."

Amyras and Celebinus stood up.

"Oh, Samarkand, where first I breathed and first enjoyed the fire of this martial flesh, blush, blush, fair city, at your honor's dishonor and shame of nature, which the stream of Jaertis, embracing you, Samarkand, with its deepest love, can never wash off from your dishonored brows!

"Here, Jove, receive my oldest son's faint-hearted soul again. Calyphas' soul is not worthy of being the immortal part of a body that comes from the seed of Tamburlaine.

"In Tamburlaine, an incorporeal spirit moves. This incorporeal spirit is made of the same mold of which thou yourself, Jove, and thy incorporeal spirit consist. Our incorporeal spirits are the same, and my incorporeal spirit makes me valiant, proud, ambitious, and ready to levy power against thy throne. I am willing to challenge thee so that I might be the one to move the turning Spheres of Heaven, for Earth and all this airy region cannot contain the state of Tamburlaine."

Tamburlaine was not using the respectful "you" and "your" when referring to Jove.

Although Tamburlaine referred to Jove, what he said can be applied to the Judeo-Christian-Muslim God.

1 Kings 8:27 states, "*But will God indeed dwell on the earth? behold, the heaven and heaven of heavens cannot contain thee; how much less this house that I have builded?*" (King James Version).

Tamburlaine believed that like God, Earth and the heavens could not bound him.

Genesis 1:26 states, "*And God said, Let us make man in our image, after our likeness: and let them have dominion over the fish of the sea, and over the fowl of the air, and over the cattle, and over all the earth, and over every creeping thing that creepeth upon the earth*" (King James Version).

Tamburlaine was made in God's image; he believed, apparently, that in his case he was made in the image of God as a vengeful God Who causes the death of those who displease Him.

Tamburlaine stabbed and killed Calyphas, his oldest son, and then he said, "By Mahomet, thy — Jove's — mighty friend I swear, in sending to my son such a soul, created of the densest dregs of earth, the scum and tartar of the four elements, a soul in which was found neither courage nor strength nor wit, but only folly, sloth, and damned idleness, thou have procured a greater enemy than the mythological being who darted mountains at thy head, shaking the burden — the sky — mighty Atlas bears. Confronted with this mountain-throwing enemy, thou trembling hid thyself in the air, covered with a pitch-black cloud to prevent thy being seen."

Tamburlaine was wrong. Jove had not hidden; he had won the battle.

Tamburlaine had just declared himself to be a powerful enemy and rival to God.

He then said to the petty Kings, "And now, you cankered curs — worm-infested dogs — of Asia, who will not see and acknowledge and recognize the strength of Tamburlaine, although it shines as brightly as the Sun, now you shall feel the strength of Tamburlaine and learn the state of his supremacy by experiencing the difference between himself and you."

Orcanes said to Tamburlaine, "Thou show the difference between ourselves and thee, in this thy barbarous damned tyranny."

The conquered King of Jerusalem said to Tamburlaine, "Thy victories are grown so violently destructive, that shortly Heaven, filled with the meteors of blood and fire thy tyrannies have made, will pour down blood and fire on thy head, whose scalding drops will pierce thy seething brains, and, with our bloods, revenge our bloods on thee."

The conquered King of Jerusalem was saying that the pools of blood that Tamburlaine and his army had caused to be shed by the Turks would be evaporated and form a scalding bloody rain that would fall on Tamburlaine and avenge the Turks and their blood that Tamburlaine had spilled.

Tamburlaine replied, "Villains, these terrors, and these tyrannies — if you consider war's justice to be tyrannies — that I execute and carry out were given to me from the gods above to scourge the pride of such people as Heaven abhors, nor am I made Arch-Monarch — the greatest King — of the world, crowned and invested by the hand of Jove, for deeds of generosity or nobility.

"But since I wield a greater name — 'the scourge of God and terror of the world' — I must apply myself to make my actions fit those terms, in war, in blood, in death, and in cruelty, and plague such peasants as resist the power of Heaven's eternal majesty in me."

Tamburlaine then ordered, "Theridamas, Techelles, and Casane, ransack the tents and the pavilions of these proud Turks, and take their concubines. Make the concubines then bury this effeminate brat, my oldest son, for not a common soldier shall defile his manly fingers with so faint-hearted a boy. Then bring those Turkish harlots to my tent, and I'll dispose of them as pleases me best. Meanwhile, take the corpse of this effeminate brat in."

Some soldiers replied, "We will, my lord."

Theridamas, Techelles, Usumcasane, and some soldiers exited with the body of Calyphas.

"Oh, damned monster!" the conquered King of Jerusalem said to Tamburlaine. "Nay, a fiend of Hell, whose cruelties are not so harsh as thine, nor yet imposed with such a bitter hate!"

The conquered Deputy King Orcanes of Natolia prayed, "Revenge it, Rhadamanth and Aeacus, and let your hates, made more fierce because of Tamburlaine's cruelties, expel the hate wherewith he pains our souls!"

Rhadamanth and Aeacus were wise and just while alive, and after death, along with Minos, they became judges in the Land of the Dead. Rhadamanth tutored Hercules, and Aeacus ruled the Greek island of Aegina. One good way for them to expel from Tamburlaine the hate with which he torments the captured petty Kings of the Turkish Empire would be to kill him.

The conquered King of Trebizond prayed, "May never day give power to his eyes, whose sight, composed of fury and of fire, sends such severe passions to his heart!"

The conquered King of Syria prayed, "May never spirit, vein, or artery feed the cursed substance of that cruel heart; but, lacking moisture and compassionate blood, may it dry up with anger, and be consumed with heat!"

Tamburlaine said, "Well, bark, you dogs. I'll bridle all your tongues and bind them tightly with bits of burnished steel, down to the channels of your hateful throats, and with the pains my rigor shall inflict, I'll make you roar so that the earth may echo forth the far resounding torments you endure, as when a herd of lusty Cimbrian bulls runs around mourning because of the loss of the females, and stung with the fury of their chasing after and trying to find the females, fill all the air with sorrowful bellowing.

"I will, with war machines never yet used, conquer, sack, and utterly burn your cities and your golden palaces, and with the flames that beat against the clouds, I will burn the heavens and make the stars melt as if they were the tears of Mahomet for the hot destruction of his country's pride.

"And, until by vision or by speech I hear immortal Jove say 'Cease, my Tamburlaine,' I will persist as a terror to the world, making the meteors (that, personified, seem like armed men marching upon the towers of Heaven) run jousting round about the sky and break their burning lances in the air, all for the honor of my wondrous victories."

He then ordered his soldiers, "Come, bring the conquered petty Kings into our pavilion."

In Tamburlaine's military camp and outside the tent she had been staying in, Olympia, alone and holding a bowl filled with an ointment, said to herself, "Distressed Olympia, whose weeping eyes since your arrival here have beheld no Sun, but instead, enclosed within the confines of a tent, have stained your cheeks with tears and made you look like Death.

"Devise some means to rid yourself of your life rather than yield to Theridamas' detested wooing. His intention is only to dishonor you, and since this earth, dewed with your brinish tears, provides no herbs whose taste may poison you, and this air, beat often with your sighs, provides no contagious smells and vapors to infect you, and your stuffy cave — this tent — provides no sword to murder yourself with, let this idea I have come up with be the instrument of my death."

Theridamas arrived.

"We are well met, Olympia," Theridamas said. "I sought you in my tent, but when I saw the place dim and dark, the place that with your beauty you were accustomed to light up, I enraged ran about the fields for you, supposing that amorous Jove had sent his son, the winged messenger-god Hermes, to convey you away from here. But now I find you, and that fear is past.

"Tell me, Olympia, will you grant my suit?"

She replied, "My lord and husband's death, with my sweet son's, with whom I buried all emotions except grief and sorrow, which torment my heart, forbids my mind to entertain a thought that tends to love, but to instead meditate on death, which is a fitter subject for a pensive soul."

Theridamas replied, "Olympia, pity him in whom your looks have greater efficacy and more force than Cynthia the Moon's ability to cause tides in the watery wilderness, for with my seeing you my joys are at the full, and ebb again as you depart from me."

"Ah, pity me, my lord," Olympia said, "and draw your sword and make a passage for my troubled soul, which beats against this prison — my body — to get out and meet my husband and my loving son."

"You still speak of nothing except your husband and your son?" Theridamas said. "Leave this talk, my love, and listen more to me. You shall be the stately

Queen of fair Algiers, and clothed in costly cloth of weighty gold, upon the marble turrets of my court you shall sit similar to Venus in her chair of state — her throne — commanding all that your princely eye desires, and I will set aside my military endeavors to sit with you, spending my life in sweet discourse of love."

Olympia said, "No such discourse is pleasant in my ears, except that where every period ends with death, and every line begins with death again. I cannot love to be an Empress."

She meant both 1) I cannot love simply in order to be an Empress, and 2) I don't want to be an Empress.

Theridamas said, "Lady, if nothing will prevail, then I'll use some other means to make you yield. Such is the sudden fury of my love that I must and will be pleased, and you shall yield.

"Come to the tent again."

"Wait, my good lord," Olympia said, "and if you will save my honor and respect my chastity, I'll give your grace a present of such price as all the world cannot afford the like."

"What is it?"

"An ointment that a cunning alchemist distilled from the purest balsam and the purest extracts of all minerals, in which is the essential property — the hardness — of marble stone, tempered and brought to the proper consistency by metaphysical, supernatural knowledge, and spells of magic from the mouths of spirits, with which if you only anoint your tender skin, neither pistol, nor sword, nor lance can pierce your flesh."

"Why, madam, do you think to mock me thus so obviously?" Theridamas asked.

"To prove it, I will anoint my naked throat, which when you stab it, look at your weapon's point, and you shall see it blunted with the blow," Olympia said.

"Why didn't you give your husband some of it, if you loved him, and if it is so precious?"

"My intention was, my lord, to use it for that purpose, but his sudden death prevented that, and for an immediate easy proof that it works and that I am not lying, try it on me."

"I will, Olympia, and I will keep it for the richest present of this eastern world."

Olympia anointed her throat with the ointment, and then said, "Now stab, my lord, and observe your weapon's point that will be blunted even if the blow is great."

"Here, then, Olympia," Theridamas said as he stabbed her.

She leaned into the blow to ensure the cut was mortal.

Her throat cut, she bled and fell and died.

"Have I slain her!" Theridamas said. "Villain, stab yourself! Cut off this arm that has murdered my love, in whom the learned Rabbis and sages of this age might find as many wondrous miracles as they find in the contemplation of the world.

"Now Hell is fairer than Elysium. A greater lamp than that bright eye of Heaven, the Sun, from whence the stars borrow all their light, wanders about the black circumference of Hell, and now the damned souls are free from pain, for every Fury gazes on her looks.

"Infernal Dis — Pluto, god of the Land of the Dead — is courting my love, inventing masques and stately shows for her, opening the doors of his rich treasury to welcome this Queen of Chastity, whose body shall be entombed with all the pomp the treasure of my kingdom may afford."

Tamburlaine arrived, drawn in his chariot by the conquered petty Kings of Trebizond and Syria, who had bits in their mouths. Tamburlaine held in his left hand the reins, and he held in his right hand a whip with which he scourged them.

Techelles, Theridamas, and Usumcasane were present, as were Tamburlaine's surviving sons Amyras and Celebinus. Also present were the conquered Deputy King Orcanes of Natolia and the conquered King of Jerusalem, led roughly by five or six common soldiers.

Tamburlaine and his army were heading east toward Babylon. They were now a short distance north of the Persian Gulf at the city of Byron, which was near Babylon.

Tamburlaine said to the conquered Kings pulling his chariot, "Holla, you pampered jades — worn-out horses — of Asia! Can you draw a chariot only twenty miles a day, although you have so proud a chariot at your heels and such a coachman as great Tamburlaine, from the plains of Asphaltis, where I conquered you, to Byron here, where thus I honor you by being your charioteer?"

"Pulling me in my chariot is a greater honor than pulling the Sun-god in his chariot. The horses that guide the golden eye of Heaven by pulling the Sun-chariot across the sky and that blow the morning from their nostrils, making their fiery gait above the clouds, are not so honored in their charioteer, the god Apollo, as you, you slaves, are in mighty Tamburlaine.

"Hercules tamed the headstrong jades of Thrace that King Aegeus fed with human flesh and made so unmanageable that they knew their strengths; those horses were not subdued with valor more divine than you by this unconquered arm of mine."

In most versions of the myth, it is King Diomedes of Thrace who owned the man-eating horses.

Tamburlaine continued, "To make you fierce and fit my appetite, you shall be fed with flesh as raw as blood and drink the strongest sweet muscatel wine in pails.

"If you can live with it, then live, and draw my chariot swifter than the wind-driven clouds. If not, then die like beasts, and be fit for nothing but perches for the black and deadly and ominous ravens.

"Thus am I rightly the scourge of highest Jove. See the very emblem of my dignity — my whip — by which I hold my name and majesty!"

The "scourge of highest Jove" is ambiguous and can mean 1) the person whom Jove uses to scourge people, or 2) the person who scourges Jove. Right now, Tamburlaine was scourging the petty Kings, but he wished to scourge Jove.

Amyras, Tamburlaine's oldest surviving son, said, "Let me have a coach, my lord, so that I may ride, and thus be drawn by these two idle Kings."

The conquered Deputy King Orcanes of Natolia and the conquered King of Jerusalem were not currently drawing a chariot.

"Your youth forbids such ease, my kingly boy," Tamburlaine said. "They shall tomorrow draw my chariot, while these their fellow Kings may be rested."

Orcanes prayed to Pluto, god of the Land of the Dead, "Oh, you who rule the region under the earth, and in your own realm are a King as absolute as Jove, come as you did in fruitful Sicily, surveying all the glories of the land, and come just as you took the fair Proserpina as she enjoyed the fruit of Ceres' garden plot, for love, for honor, and to make her Queen."

Ceres was the mother of Proserpina, who was kidnapped by Hades. Ceres mourned, and since she was the goddess of agriculture, nothing would grow when she mourned. Fortunately, an arrangement was made in which her daughter would spend six months of the year with her and be Queen of the Land of the Dead the other six months.

Proserpina and Ceres are Roman names. Proserpina's Greek name is Persephone, and Ceres' Greek name is Demeter.

Orcanes continued, "So, for just hate, for shame, and to subdue this proud scorner of thy dread-inspiring power, come once and for all in fury and survey his pride and then hale him headlong to the lowest Hell."

Theridamas said to Tamburlaine, "Your majesty must get some bits for these, to bridle their contemptuous cursing tongues that, like unruly never broken jades, break through the hedges — teeth — of their hateful mouths and pass their fixed bounds exceedingly."

Techelles said, "No, we will break the hedges of their mouths, and pull their kicking colts — unruly tongues — out of their pastures."

Usumcasane said, "Your majesty already has devised a means, as fit as may be, to restrain these coltish coach horse tongues from blasphemy."

Celebinus bridled Orcanes and asked, "How do you like that, sir King? Why don't you speak?"

The King of Jerusalem said, "Ah, cruel brat, sprung from a tyrant's loins! How like his cursed father he begins to practice taunts and bitter tyrannies!"

Smiling, Celebinus unbridled Orcanes.

"Aye, Turk, I tell thee," Tamburlaine said, "this same boy is he who must — advanced in higher pomp than this — plunder the kingdoms I shall leave unsacked, if Jove, esteeming me to be too good for Earth, should raise me to match the fair Aldebaran — known as the Eye of Taurus and the brightest star in the constellation of Taurus — above the threefold astracism of Heaven, before I conquer all the triple world of Europe, Asia, and Africa."

Tamburlaine wanted to become a star after his death, as happened to some mythological heroes.

The threefold astracism of Heaven is a grouping of three constellations: the Corvus (Raven), the Hydra (Water-Snake), and the Crater (Cup). A myth told the story of how the god Apollo sent a Raven to fetch him a Cup of water. The Raven was late returning because it saw some unripe figs and waited a few days for them to ripen so it could eat them. Returning to Apollo, the Raven lied and said that it had been delayed by a Water-Snake. As "proof" of its tale, the Raven showed Apollo a Water-Snake that it had brought with him. Seeing through the lie, Apollo made the Raven, Cup, and Water-Snake constellations. Apollo also ordered the Water-Snake to never allow the Raven to drink from the Cup and so the Water-Snake constellation separates the other two constellations.

The constellation Taurus is located in the northern celestial hemisphere while the constellations Corvus (Raven), Hydra (Water-Snake), and Crater (Cup) are located in the southern celestial hemisphere, and so Aldebaran is located above the threefold astracism of Heaven.

In addition to animals, the gods often stellified (made into stars or constellations) ancient heroes.

Stellification, therefore, can be done for noble beings such as Perseus, who slew the snake-haired Medusa, but it can also be done for ignoble beings such as the Raven.

Tamburlaine ordered, "Now fetch me out the Turkish concubines. I will 'promote' them for the funeral they have bestowed on my abortive son — that monster of nature."

Some soldiers brought the Turkish concubines.

Tamburlaine asked, "Where are my common soldiers now, who fought so like lions upon the plains of Asphaltis?"

"Here, my lord," the soldiers answered.

Tamburlaine said, "Control yourselves, brave soldiers. Take you Queens for each of you — I mean such Queens as were Kings' concubines."

He was punning on "queans," which means "whores."

He continued, "Take them; divide them, and their jewels, too, and let them equally serve all your turns."

Tamburlaine was ordering his soldiers to rape the Turkish concubines as much as they wanted.

"We thank your majesty," the soldiers replied.

"Don't brawl, I warn you, on account of your lechery," Tamburlaine said, "for every man who so offends shall die."

Orcanes said, "Injurious tyrant, will thou so bring disrepute on the hateful fortunes of thy victory, to exercise upon such guiltless dames the violence of thy common soldiers' lust?"

Speaking to all the conquered Turkish petty Kings, and amused at their defending the chastity of concubines, Tamburlaine replied, "Live chastely, then, you slaves, and don't meet me in battle with troops of harlots at your lazy heels."

The concubines pleaded, "Oh, pity us, my lord, and save our honors by keeping us from being raped."

Tamburlaine said to his common soldiers, "Aren't you gone, you villains, with your spoils?"

The soldiers ran away with the Turkish concubines.

"Oh, merciless, infernal cruelty!" the conquered King of Jerusalem said.

Thinking about the words of the concubines, Tamburlaine said, "Save your honors! It's about time you spoke up about honor indeed, since your honors were lost long before you knew what honor meant."

Theridamas said, "It seems that the Turks meant to conquer us, my lord, and make us laughable spectacles for their whores."

That would explain why the Turks had brought their concubines.

"And now they themselves shall make our laughable spectacles," Tamburlaine said, "and common soldiers will 'jest' with all their trulls — their whores.

"Let the common soldiers take pleasure soundly in their spoils, until we prepare our march to Babylon, to which we will next make a quick journey."

"Let us not be idle, then, my lord," Techelles said, "but soon be ready to conquer it."

Tamburlaine said, "We will, Techelles."

He then said to the Turkish petty Kings harnessed to his chariot, "Forward, then, you jades. Move, you poor-quality horses."

He then addressed in an apostrophe Kings he intended to conquer in the future: "Now crouch, you so-far-unconquered Kings of greatest Asia, and tremble when you hear that this scourge will come who whips down cities and controls crowned Kings, adding their wealth and treasure to my store.

"The Euxine — Black — Sea, north of Natolia; the Mediterranean Sea, to the west of Natolia; the Caspian Sea, to the north northeast of Natolia; and the Sinus Arabicus — the Red Sea — to the south of Natolia shall all be laden with the martial spoils we will convey with us to Persia.

"Then shall my native city, Samarkand, and the crystal waves of fresh Jaertis' stream, the pride and beauty of her princely seat, be famous through the furthest continents, for there my royal palace shall be placed, whose shining turrets — towers — shall dismay the heavens and cast the fame of Ilion's — Troy's — tower to Hell.

"Through the streets, with troops of conquered Kings, I'll ride in golden armor like the Sun, and in my helmet a triple plume shall spring, spangled with diamonds, dancing in the air, to note me Emperor of the threefold world — Asia, Europe, and Africa — like an almond tree mounted high upon the lofty and celestial mountain of the evergreen Sicilian city Selinus, location of a temple to Jupiter, quaintly decked with blooms whiter than the brows of Erycina — Venus, who has a shrine at Mount Eryx in Sicily — whose tender blossoms tremble every one at every little breath through Heaven blown.

"Then in my coach, like Jupiter, Saturn's royal son, mounted in his shining chariot made golden with fire, and drawn by princely eagles through the path paved with bright crystal and inlaid with stars, when all the gods stand gazing at his pomp, so will I ride through Samarkand's streets, until my soul, dissevered from this flesh, shall mount the milky-white way — the Milky Way — and meet him there.

"To Babylon, my lords, to Babylon!"

CHAPTER 5 (Part 2)

— 5.1 —

Tamburlaine was besieging the city of Babylon. This was the third day of the siege, and so Tamburlaine's tents, banners, and armor were all in black, indicating that he would show no mercy to the inhabitants — men, women, and children — of Babylon.

The Governor of Babylon stood on the city walls, looking at Tamburlaine's camp. With the Governor of Babylon were his advisor Maximus and other people.

"What do you think, Maximus?" the Governor of Babylon asked.

Maximus replied, "My lord, the breach the enemy has made in our walls gives such assurance of our being conquered that little hope is left to save our lives or hold our city from the conqueror's hands.

"So then hang out flags, my lord, of humble truce, and satisfy the people's general prayers, so that Tamburlaine's intolerable wrath may be suppressed by our submission."

"Villain, do thou respect more thy slavish life than the honor of thy country or thy name?" the Governor of Babylon asked. "Is not my life and state, the city and my native country's welfare, as dear to me as anything of value that you can imagine?

"Don't we have hope, despite all our battered walls, to live safely and keep his forces out, when this our famous lake of Limnasphaltis makes walls afresh with everything that falls into the liquid substance of its stream, stronger than are the Gates of Death or Hell?"

The bituminous lake of Limnasphaltis petrified anything that fell into it, making defenses for Babylon. Using the bituminous, aka asphaltic, water of Asphaltis, the people of Babylon had created a moat around their city. In this culture, the word "lake" meant "channel" as well as its usual meaning. Asphaltis' lake was a usual lake, while Limnasphaltis' lake was a moat.

The Governor of Babylon continued, "What faintness should dismay our courages, when we are thus defended against our foe, and have no terror but his threatening looks?"

A Babylonian citizen came over to the Governor and knelt before him.

The citizen said, "My lord, if ever you did a deed of pity and mercy, and now will work to create a refuge for our lives, offer submission to Tamburlaine, and hang up flags of truce so that Tamburlaine may pity our distress and treat us like a loving conqueror.

"Although this is supposed to be the last day of his dreadful siege, on which he spares neither man nor child, yet there are Christians of Georgia here, whose condition in life he has always pitied and relieved: They will get his pardon, if your grace would send notification of surrender to Tamburlaine."

Because Tamburlaine had soundly defeated the Ottoman Turks at a time when they seemed unstoppable as they defeated Christian territory, many people viewed him as sympathetic to Christians.

The Governor of Babylon said, "How my soul is environed with cares! And how this eternally famous city of Babylon is filled with a pack of fainthearted fugitives who thus beg for their own shame and servitude!"

A second citizen arrived and said, "My lord, if ever you will win our hearts, surrender the town, and save our wives and children, for I will cast myself from off these walls or die some death of quickest violence before I endure the wrath of Tamburlaine."

"Villains, cowards, traitors to our state," the Governor of Babylon said. "Fall to the earth, and pierce the pit of Hell, so that legions of tormenting spirits may vex your slavish bosoms with continual pains — I don't care! Babylon will never yield as long as any life is in my breast."

Theridamas and Techelles, with other soldiers, arrived outside the walls of Babylon.

Theridamas said, "Thou desperate Governor of Babylon, to save thy life, and save us a little labor, yield speedily the city to our hands, or else be sure thou shall be forced to do so with pains more excruciating than ever traitor felt."

Theridamas was apparently telling the Governor of Babylon that if he surrendered the city, he would not be killed. This offer was an exception to Tamburlaine's usual rules regarding sieges:

• If the city surrendered on the first day, Tamburlaine would kill no one. On the first day of the siege, Tamburlaine's tents, pennants, and clothes were white.

• If the city surrendered on the second day, Tamburlaine would kill only those who were capable of fighting in battle. On the second day of the siege, Tamburlaine's tents, pennants, and clothes were red.

• If the city surrendered on the third day, Tamburlaine would kill everyone without respect of sex, social status, or age: He would raze all his foes with fire and sword. On the third day of the siege, Tamburlaine's tents, pennants, and clothes were black.

The Governor of Babylon replied, "Tyrant, I return the charge of 'traitor' down thy throat, and I will defend the city in despite of thee."

He then ordered, "Call up the soldiers to defend these walls."

"Yield, foolish Governor," Techelles said. "We offer more than ever yet we did to such proud slaves as dared resist us until our third day's siege. Thou see us ready to give the last assault, and we shall abide no more negotiations."

"Assault and spare not," the Governor of Babylon said. "We will never yield."

Trumpets sounded the call to arms, and Tamburlaine's soldiers climbed the walls of Babylon and took the city.

Tamburlaine arrived, drawn in his chariot by the conquered Kings of Trebizond and Syria, with two spare conquered Kings, Orcanes and Jerusalem, not in harness. With Tamburlaine were Usumcasane, Amyras, and Celebinus. Because this was the third day of the siege, Tamburlaine was dressed in black.

Tamburlaine said, "The stately buildings of fair Babylon, whose lofty pillars, higher than the clouds, were accustomed to guide the seaman in the deep, being carried thither by the cannon's force, now fill the mouth of the lake of Limnasphaltis and make a bridge to the battered walls."

The towers of Babylon had fallen into Limnasphaltis — the moat whose water came from the lake of Asphaltis — and in the moat the broken towers now formed a bridge to the battered walls of Babylon. The mouth of the lake of Limnasphaltis is the place where the water of Asphaltis and the water of Limnasphaltis met.

Tamburlaine was vastly exaggerating when he said that Babylonian buildings "were accustomed to guide the seaman in the deep." Babylon was located in the center of Iraq, approximately 150 miles northwest of the Persian Gulf.

Tamburlaine added, "Where Belus, Ninus, and Alexander the Great have ridden in triumph, Tamburlaine triumphs."

Belus was the founder of Babylon.

Ninus, the son of Belus, founded Nineveh, the capital of the ancient Assyrian Empire; he founded the first Assyrian Empire by conquering much of western Asia.

In 331 B.C.E., Babylon surrendered to Alexander the Great.

Tamburlaine continued, referring to himself in the third person, "Tamburlaine's chariot wheels, drawn by these Kings on heaps of carcasses, have broken the Assyrians' bones.

"Now in the place where fair Semiramis, widow of Ninus, courted by Kings and peers of Asia, danced stately dances, do my soldiers march, and in the streets, where richly dressed Assyrian dames have ridden in pomp like Juno, the rich daughter of Saturn, my horsemen brandish their unruly blades with furious words and frowning faces."

Theridamas and Techelles arrived, bringing the Governor of Babylon.

Tamburlaine asked, "Who do you have there, my lords?"

Theridamas answered, "The defiant, refractory Governor of Babylon, who made us all labor for the town and made such slender reckoning of your majesty."

"Go and bind the villain," Tamburlaine said. "He shall hang in chains upon the ruins of this conquered town."

He then said to the Governor of Babylon, "Sirrah, the view yesterday of our red tents, which threatened more than if the region next underneath the Sphere of Fire that separates the Moon from the Earth were full of comets and of blazing stars — meteors — whose flaming comet tails and meteor trails should reach down to the Earth, could not frighten you; no, nor I myself, mighty Jove's wrathful messenger, who with his sword have caused all earthly Kings to tremble, could not persuade you to surrender Babylon, but still you kept the city gates shut.

"Villain, I say, should I but touch the rusty gates of Hell, the triple-headed dog Cerberus that guards the Underworld would howl and make black Jove — Pluto, god of the Land of the Dead — crouch and kneel to me. But I have sent volleys of shot to you, yet I could not enter until the breach was made."

The Governor of Babylon replied, "Nor if my body could have stopped the breach, should thou have entered, cruel Tamburlaine. It is not thy bloody-red tents that can make me yield, nor indeed thyself, thou who embodied the anger of the Highest. For although thy cannon shook the city walls, my heart never quaked nor did my courage faint."

"Well, now I'll make it quake," Tamburlaine said.

He ordered, "Go, raise him up. Hang him in chains upon the city walls, and let my soldiers shoot the slave to death."

The Governor of Babylon said, "Vile monster, born of some infernal hag, and sent from Hell to tyrannize on the surface of the Earth, do all thy worst; neither death, nor Tamburlaine, nor torture, nor pain can daunt my fearless mind."

"Up with him, then," Tamburlaine said. "Hang him on the wall. His body shall be scared and scarred."

In an attempt to save his life, the Governor of Babylon said, "But, Tamburlaine, in Limnasphaltis' lake lies more gold than Babylon is worth. This gold, when the city was besieged, I hid. Just save my life, and I will give it to thee."

"Then, despite all your 'valor,' you would save your life?" Tamburlaine said. "Whereabouts does it lie?"

"Under a hollow bank, right opposite against the western gate of Babylon," the Governor of Babylon said.

Tamburlaine ordered, "Go there, some of you, and seize his gold."

Some soldiers exited.

Tamburlaine said to some other soldiers, "Take the Governor of Babylon away from here; let him speak no more."

He then said to the Governor of Babylon, "I think I am making your courage somewhat quail."

The soldiers exited with the Governor of Babylon.

Tamburlaine said, "When this is done, we'll march from Babylon and make our greatest haste to Persia. These jades — the conquered Kings of Trebizond and Syria — are broken winded and half tired. Unharness them, and let me have fresh horses."

Some attendants unharnessed the conquered Kings of Trebizond and Syria.

Tamburlaine then ordered, "So, now that their best is done to honor me, take them and hang them both up presently."

He meant to hang them up on the walls of Babylon, just like the Governor of Babylon.

"Vile tyrant!" the conquered King of Trebizond shouted. "Barbarous bloody Tamburlaine!"

Tamburlaine ordered, "Take them away, Theridamas; see them dispatched."

"I will, my lord," Theridamas said.

Theridamas exited with the conquered Kings of Trebizond and Syria.

Tamburlaine said to the conquered Kings who were acting as his spare horses, "Come, Asian Viceroys, work your tasks for a while, and take such fortune as your fellows felt. They have drawn my chariot, and now it's your turn."

The conquered Deputy King Orcanes of Natolia replied, "First let thy Scythian horses tear apart my limbs and the limbs of the King of Jerusalem rather than we should draw thy chariot, and, like base slaves, degrade our princely minds by performing vile and ignominious servitude."

"Rather lend me thy weapon, Tamburlaine," the conquered King of Jerusalem said, "so that I may sheathe it in this breast of mine. A thousand deaths could not torment our hearts more than the thought of this vexes our souls."

Amyras, Tamburlaine's oldest surviving son, said, "They will continue to always talk, my lord, if you don't bridle them."

"Bridle them," Tamburlaine ordered, "and let me go to my coach."

Some attendants bridled the conquered Deputy King Orcanes of Natolia and the conquered King of Jerusalem.

While that was happening, the Governor of Babylon was hung in chains on the walls of Babylon.

Theridamas returned.

Amyras said to his father, Tamburlaine, "See, now, my lord, how bravely the captain — the Governor of Babylon — hangs."

"It is bravely — splendidly — done, indeed, my boy," Tamburlaine said.

He then said to Theridamas, "Well done! Shoot first, my lord, and then the rest shall follow."

Theridamas replied, "Then I'll have at him — shoot him — for a beginning."

Theridamas shot the Governor of Babylon, who said to Tamburlaine, "Yet save my life, and let this wound appease the mortal fury of great Tamburlaine."

"No," Tamburlaine replied, "even though Asphaltis' water were liquid gold, and it was offered to me as ransom for thy life, you still would die."

He ordered, "All of you shoot at him all at once."

They shot and killed the Governor of Babylon.

Tamburlaine was very good at ordering other people to kill and having them obey his orders.

Tamburlaine said, "So, now he hangs like Baghdad's Governor, having as many bullets in his flesh as there are breaches in her battered wall."

Did Tamburlaine mistakenly call Babylon Baghdad? Or had the Governor of Baghdad suffered the same fate as the Governor of Babylon?

"Go now and bind the burghers hand and foot, and cast them headlong in the city's lake. Tartars and Persians shall inhabit there, and to command the city, I will build a citadel in Babylon for which all Africa, which has been subject to the Persian King, shall pay me tribute."

Techelles asked, "What shall be done with the burghers' wives and children, my lord?"

"Techelles, drown them all — man, woman, and child," Tamburlaine said. "Leave not a Babylonian in the town."

"I will set about it immediately," Techelles said. "Come, soldiers."

Later, he would say that he had drowned thousands of men in the lake of Asphaltis. Possibly, the lake of Limnasphaltis was not big enough to drown thousands of people.

He and the soldiers exited.

"Now, Casane, where's the Turkish Koran and all the heaps of superstitious books found in the temples of that Mahomet whom I have thought to be a god?" Tamburlaine said. "They shall be burnt."

"Here they are, my lord," Usumcasane replied.

"Well done," Tamburlaine said. "Let a fire be made immediately.

"In vain, I see, men worship Mahomet. My sword has sent millions of Turks to Hell and slew all his priests, his kinsmen, and his friends, and yet I live untouched by Mahomet.

"There is a God, full of revenging wrath, from whom the thunder and the lightning break, whose scourge I am, and him I will obey."

Tamburlaine believed in a vengeful God, but not in the people who are widely regarded as God's prophets.

He continued, "So, Casane; fling them in the fire."

Usumcasane burned the religious books.

Tamburlaine said, "Now Mahomet, if thou have any power, come down thyself and work a miracle. Thou are not worthy to be worshipped if thou allow flames of fire to burn the scripture wherein the sum of thy religion rests.

"Why don't thou send a furious whirlwind down to blow thy Koran up to thy throne, where men report that thou sit by God himself?

"Or why don't thou take vengeance on the head of Tamburlaine, who shakes his sword against thy majesty and kicks the epitome of thy foolish laws?

"Well, soldiers, Mahomet remains in Hell. He cannot hear the voice of Tamburlaine.

"Seek out another godhead to adore — adore the God who sits in Heaven, if you adore any god, for he alone is God, and none but he."

Techelles returned and said, "I have fulfilled your highness' will, my lord. Thousands of men, drowned in the lake of Asphaltis, have made the water swell above the banks, and fishes, fed by human carcasses, dazed, swim up and down upon the waves, as when they swallow the bitter plant resin called asafoetida, which makes them float on the surface and gasp for air."

Fish are unlikely to live or survive in asphaltic water.

"Well, then, my friendly lords, what now remains," Tamburlaine said, "but that we leave a sufficient garrison of soldiers behind here in Babylon and immediately depart to Persia, to triumph after all our victories?"

"Aye, my good lord, let us hasten to Persia," Theridamas said, "and let this deceased captain — the Governor of Babylon — be removed from the walls to some high hill about the city here."

"Let it be so," Tamburlaine said. "Set about it, soldiers. But hold on; I suddenly feel ill."

"What is it that dares make Tamburlaine ill?" Techelles asked.

"Something, Techelles," Tamburlaine said, "but I don't know what.

"But, go forth, you vassals! Whatsoever it may be, neither sickness nor death can ever conquer me."

The Turkish Emperor Callapine and the King of Amasia talked together. A captain, soldiers, drummers, and trumpeters were present. They were within sight of Babylon and talking about attacking Tamburlaine's army, which they regarded as not fully recovered from the effort of attacking Babylon.

The Turkish Emperor Callapine said, "King of Amasia, now our mighty army marches in Asia Major, where the streams of Euphrates and Tigris swiftly run, and here may we behold great Babylon, circled about with Limnasphaltis' lake, where Tamburlaine with all his army lies. Since his army is faint and weary with the siege, we may lie ready to encounter Tamburlaine in battle before his army returns to full strength and is fully recovered from the siege of Babylon, and so revenge our latest grievous loss, if God or Mahomet should send any aid."

The King of Amasia said, "Don't doubt, my lord, that we shall conquer him. Our Turkish swords shall headlong send to Hell the monster that has drunk a sea of blood and yet opens his maw for still more to quench his thirst, and that vile carcass, drawn by warlike Kings, the fowls shall eat, for never shall a sepulcher grace this baseborn tyrant Tamburlaine."

"When I remember my parents' slavish life, their cruel death, my own captivity, and my Viceroys' bondage under Tamburlaine," the Turkish Emperor Callapine said, "I think I could sustain a thousand deaths in order to be revenged on all his villainy.

"Ah, sacred Mahomet, you who have seen millions of Turks perish because of Tamburlaine, kingdoms made waste, brave cities sacked and burnt, and now only one army is left to honor you, aid your obedient servant Callapine and make him, after all these defeats, triumph over cursed Tamburlaine."

"Fear not, my lord," the King of Amasia said. "I see great Mahomet, clothed in purple clouds, and on his head wearing a wreath brighter than Apollo's crown, marching about the air with armed men, to join with you against this Tamburlaine."

The Captain said, "Renowned General, mighty Callapine, even if God himself and holy Mahomet were to come in person to resist your power, yet might your mighty army encounter all, and pull proud Tamburlaine upon his knees to beg for mercy at your highness' feet."

"Captain," the Turkish Emperor Callapine said, "the force of Tamburlaine is great, his good fortune greater, and the victories with which he has so sorely paralyzed with fear the world are greatest to discourage all our intentions. Yet when the pride of Cynthia the Moon is at full, she wanes again, and so shall his fortune, I hope, for we have here the chief especially selected men of twenty different kingdoms at the least.

"Neither plowman, nor priest, nor merchant stays at home. All Turkey is in arms and fighting beside me, Callapine, and never will we break down the military camps and discharge the army before either Tamburlaine himself or his army is conquered.

"This is the time that must eternally make me famous for conquering the tyrant of the world.

"Come, soldiers, let us lie in wait for him, and if we find him absent from his military camp, before his soldiers are reassembled again at full strength, we will assail it and be sure of victory."

Theridamas, Techelles, and Usumcasane talked together. They were mourning Tamburlaine's severe illness.

Theridamas said, "Weep, heavens, and vanish into liquid tears! Fall, stars that govern Tamburlaine's birth and summon all the shining lamps — the stars — of Heaven to cast their useless fires to the Earth and shed their feeble influence in the air. Hide your beauties with eternal clouds, for Hell and Darkness pitch their pitch-black tents, and Death, with armies of Cimmerian spirits, gives battle against the heart of Tamburlaine."

The Cimmerians were believed to never see daylight because they lived in caves and came out only to rob travelers at night.

Theridamas continued, "Now in defiance of that customary love your sacred virtues poured upon his throne, and made his state an honor to the heavens, these cowards invisibly assail his soul and threaten conquest on our sovereign. But if he dies, your glories are disgraced, and Earth droops and says that Hell is placed in Heaven."

Techelles said, "Oh, then, you powers who rule eternally and guide this massive substance of the Earth, if you still are deserving of holiness and religious worship, as your supreme estates instruct our thoughts, don't be unfaithful, don't be unconcerned about your reputation, don't bear the burden of your enemies' joys, and don't join the chorus as your enemies sing about their joys as they triumph in the fall of Tamburlaine, whom you advanced, but as his birth, life, health, and majesty were exceptionally blest and cared for by Heaven, so may Heaven — until Heaven is dissolved — honor his birth, his life, his health, and his majesty!"

Usumcasane said, "Blush, Heaven, to lose the honor of your name, to see your footstool set upon your head. Only a foolish god would wear a footstool on his head! And let no baseness in your haughty breast sustain a shame of such inexcellence and indignity as to see the devils mount in angels' thrones, and angels dive into the pools of Hell — the universe will turn upside-down if Tamburlaine dies!

"And though the devils think their painful period of suffering has ended, and that their power is as mighty as Jove's, which makes them conduct war against your — Heaven's — state, yet make them feel that the strength of Tamburlaine, your instrument and note — distinguishing mark — of majesty, is greater far than they can thus subdue. For, if he dies, then your glory is disgraced, and Earth droops and says that Hell is placed in Heaven."

Tamburlaine arrived in his chariot, drawn by the conquered Deputy King Orcanes of Natolia and the conquered King of Jerusalem. Tamburlaine's surviving sons Amyras and Celebinus and some physicians also arrived.

Tamburlaine said, "What daring god torments my body thus and seeks to conquer mighty Tamburlaine? Shall sickness prove me now to be a mortal man — me who has been called the terror of the world?

"Techelles and the rest, come, take your swords, and threaten him whose hand afflicts my soul. Come, let us march against the powers of Heaven and set black banners in the sky to signify the slaughter of the gods."

As if it were the third day of a siege — the day on which he would show no mercy — Tamburlaine wanted to use the color black to announce his intention — or wish — to slaughter all the gods who opposed him.

He continued, "Ah, friends, what shall I do? I cannot stand. Come, carry me to war against the gods, who thus envy the health of Tamburlaine."

Theridamas said, "Ah, my good lord, stop saying these impatient words that add much danger to your already dangerous malady."

"Why, shall I sit and languish in this pain?" Tamburlaine said. "No, strike the drums, and, in revenge of this, come, let us level our spears, charge, and pierce the breast of Atlas, whose shoulders bear the axis of the world."

Tamburlaine was wrong. Atlas holds up the sky and stars, not the axis of the world, which is the axis that passes through the center of the Earth. To it are affixed the Ptolemaic spheres that revolve around the Earth. If Atlas were to attempt to hold up the axis of the world, he would be attempting to hold up the Earth and the rest of the universe, with nowhere to stand: He would be attempting to exceed what he is capable of doing, much like Tamburlaine.

Tamburlaine continued, "Let's do this so that if I perish, Heaven and Earth may fade and perish with me.

"Theridamas, hasten to the court of Jove. Command him to send Apollo, the god of medicine and healing, here straightaway to cure me, or I'll fetch him down myself."

Techelles said, "Sit still, my gracious lord; this suffering will cease and cannot last — it is so violent and extreme."

"Cannot last, Techelles?" Tamburlaine said. "No, for I shall die. See where my slave, the ugly monster Death, shaking and quivering, pale and sickly because of fear, stands aiming at me with his murdering arrow. Death flies away at every glance I give, and when I look away, comes stealing near me.

"Villainous Death, leave, and hasten to go to the battlefield! I and my army come to load thy — and Charon's — boat with the souls of a thousand mangled carcasses.

"Look, where he goes! But see, he comes again because I stay here.

"Techelles, let us march and weary Death by making him bear many souls to Hell."

A physician asked, "May it please your majesty to drink this potion, which will lessen the fury of your fit and cause some milder spirits to govern you."

"Tell me," Tamburlaine asked, "what do you think about my sickness now?"

"I viewed your urine," the physician said, "and the hypostasis — sediment in the urine — thick and obscure, shows that your danger is great.

"Your veins are full of abnormally excessive heat, whereby the moisture of your blood is dried."

The physician continued, "The humidum and calor — moisture and heat — that some believe is not a part of the natural elements, but of a more divine and pure substance, is almost completely extinguished and spent, which, since moisture and heat are the cause of life, signifies your death.

"Besides, my lord, this day is astrologically critical and dangerous to those whose crisis is like yours.

"Your arteries, which parallel to the veins convey the lively spirits that the heart engenders, are parched and void of those spirits, with the result that the soul, lacking those organons by which it moves — the material parts that interact with the soul — cannot endure, as far as the medical knowledge can tell."

This society regarded blood as half spiritual and half physical, and Tamburlaine's blood was losing its spiritual part (lively spirits) and its material parts (organons).

Tamburlaine lacked organons — the material parts that interact with the soul. In another person who had a sufficient number of organons, their presence would manifest itself in things of the soul. These things may include compassion, empathy, sympathy, morality, and mercy. Apparently, Tamburlaine had been losing his organons throughout his military career.

Blood is the sanguine humor, and one definition of "sanguine" is "causing bloodshed and delighting in bloodshed." As Tamburlaine was dying, he was losing his ability (but not his desire) to cause bloodshed, and so he was losing what made Tamburlaine Tamburlaine.

Earlier, the conquered King of Syria had prayed about Tamburlaine, "May never spirit, vein, or artery feed the cursed substance of that cruel heart; but, lacking moisture and compassionate blood, may it dry up with anger, and be consumed with heat!"

The physician continued, "Yet, if your majesty may escape this day, no doubt you shall soon recover all."

Tamburlaine replied, "Then I will husband all my vital parts, and live, to spite death, longer than one day."

Noises sounded, and a messenger arrived and said, "My lord, young Callapine, who lately fled from your majesty, has now gathered a fresh army, and hearing about your absence in the field, acts as if he will set upon us immediately."

"See, my physicians, now, how Jove has sent a ready medicine to cure my pain," Tamburlaine said. "Sight of me shall make them fly, and if I can follow them, not one of all the villain's army shall live to give the offer of another fight."

Usumcasane said, "I take joy, my lord, because your highness is so strong that you can so well make your royal presence continue to exist, which alone will dismay the enemy. Your fighting off death and showing yourself to the enemy will dismay the enemy."

Tamburlaine said, "I know it will, Casane.

"Pull my chariot, you slaves! To spite death, I will go show my face."

Tamburlaine was not healthy enough to fight, but he could show himself to the enemy. Tamburlaine was such a cruel military leader that the mere sight of him dismayed the enemy.

In Homer's *Iliad*, after Hector has killed Patroclus and has stripped Achilles' armor, which Patroclus had been wearing, from his corpse, Achilles, who was unable to fight because he lacked armor big enough to fit him, showed himself to the Trojans and shouted; this dismayed the Trojans enough that the Greeks were able to recover Patroclus' corpse.

The two armies fought, and Tamburlaine's army won the victory.

"Thus are the villains," Tamburlaine said. "They are cowards who fled out of fear, like summer's mist vanished by the Sun. And if I could for just awhile pursue the cowards in the field, then that Callapine would be my slave again.

"But I perceive that my martial strength is spent. In vain I strive and rail against those powers that mean to invest me in a higher throne by killing me, whom they regard as much too high for this disdainful Earth.

"Give me a map; then let me see how much is left for me to conquer all the world, so that these, my boys, may conquer every place that I have not."

An attendant brought him a map.

Holding the map and pointing to various places on it, Tamburlaine said, "Here I began to march towards Persia, along Armenia and the Caspian Sea, and thence into Bithynia, where I took the Turkish Emperor Bajazeth and his great Empress prisoners.

"Then I marched into Egypt and Arabia, and here, not far from Alexandria, where the Mediterranean Sea and the Red Sea meet, being distant less than a full hundred leagues, I meant to cut a channel — a canal — to them both, so that men might quickly sail to India.

"From thence to Nubia near Borno lake, and so along the Ethiopian Sea, aka the south Atlantic Ocean, cutting across the Tropic of Capricorn, I conquered all as far as the province of Zanzibar, which is part of the west coast.

"Then, by the northern part of Africa, I came at last to Graecia, and from thence to Asia, where I stay against my will.

"The length of my travels from Scythia, where I first began, backward and forwards, totals nearly five thousand leagues, or fifteen thousand miles.

"Look here, my boys; see what a world of ground lies westward from the midst of the Tropic of Cancer's line to the rising of this earthly globe, where the Sun, declining from our sight and setting in the west, begins the day with our Antipodes — the opposite side of the Earth.

"And shall I die, and leave all this unconquered?

"Look! Here, my sons, are all the golden mines, inestimable drugs, and precious stones — more of worth than Asia and the world beside.

"And from the Antarctic Pole eastward, behold as much more land, which never was charted, wherein are rocks of pearl that shine as bright as all the lamps that beautify the sky.

"And shall I die, and leave all this unconquered?

"Here, lovely boys, is my command to you: That which death forbids my life, let your lives command that to spite death."

Amyras said, "Alas, my lord, how should our bleeding hearts, wounded and broken with your highness' grief, retain a thought of joy or spark of life? Your soul gives living essence to our wretched bodies, whose flesh comes from and is embodied by your flesh."

Tamburlaine, as Amyras' and Celebinus' father, gave them their bodies. Amyras also believed that Tamburlaine's soul gave his sons a living essence, aka an animating spirit.

Celebinus said, "Your pains pierce our souls; no hope survives, for by your life we maintain our lives."

Tamburlaine said, "But, sons, this subject — my body — that lacks enough force to continue to hold the fiery spirit it contains, must depart, but when this subject departs, it will impart its fiery spirit in equal portions into both your breasts.

"My flesh, divided in your precious shapes, shall still retain my spirit, although I die, and live in all your descendants immortally.

"So then now remove me from my chariot so that I may resign my position and my title to my son.

"Amyras, first take my scourge — my chariot whip — and my imperial crown, and then mount into my royal chariot of estate, so that I may see you crowned before I die.

"Help me, my lords, to make my last move."

They moved him from the chariot and put him in a chair.

Theridamas said, "This is a woeful change, my lord, that daunts our thoughts more than the ruin of our own souls."

"Sit up, my son," Tamburlaine said. "Let me see how well you will befit your father's majesty."

Amyras, Tamburlaine's oldest living son, would become the next King of Persia.

They crowned Amyras, who because he was mourning his father's quickly coming death, would not climb into the chariot.

Amyras said, "I would have such a flinty bosom if I were to enjoy the breath of life and the burden of my soul if this pain of losing my father were not dissolved into relieved pain by the recovery of my father.

"If my father does not recover, then my body's deadened parts will exercise the beating of my heart, which will be pierced if I should take any joy in having the titles of my father!"

Amyras was thinking of committing suicide by stabbing his heart with a knife if he found that he was capable of enjoying becoming a King solely due to the death of his father.

He continued, "Oh, father, if the unrelenting ears of Death and Hell are shut against my prayers, and if the spiteful influence of Heaven denies my soul the possession of any joy, how should I step or stir my hateful feet against the inward powers of my heart, leading a life that strives only to die, and plead in vain against unpleasing sovereignty?"

Amyras was different from his father. Tamburlaine would place being a King above being a father; after all, he had killed his oldest son because he felt dishonored by him. If Amyras were to be like his father, he would have to enjoy being a King although his father's death had given him the crown.

Tamburlaine said, "Let not your love exceed your devotion to honor, son, nor bar from your mind that greatness of soul that nobly must admit necessity."

In other words, he was saying this: Amyras, enjoy being a King although my death gave you the crown. "Devotion to honor" — being a King — comes before devotion to your father.

Tamburlaine continued, "Sit up, my boy, and with these silken reins bridle the steeled stomachs — the proud and obstinate spirits — of those jades, the conquered Kings."

Theridamas said to Amyras, "My lord, you must obey his majesty, since fate and proud necessity command you to."

Amyras climbed into the chariot, saying, "May the heavens witness with what a broken heart and sorrowful spirit I ascend this seat.

"And may the heavens send to my soul, before my father dies, his anguish and his burning agony! May the heavens allow me to suffer my father's pain so that he doesn't have to!"

Tamburlaine said, "Now fetch the hearse of fair Zenocrate. Let it be placed by this chair in which I will die, and let it serve as part of my funeral."

Usumcasane said, "So then your majesty feels no sovereign ease? Our hearts, all drowned in tears of blood, may not enjoy any hope of your recovery?"

Tamburlaine replied, "Casane, there is no hope of my recovery. The Monarch of the Earth and the eyeless monster that torments my soul cannot behold the tears you shed for me, and therefore continually augments and increases his cruelty."

The Monarch of the Earth is most likely Death, which is often depicted as a skeleton without flesh or eyes. The eyeless monster is most likely the illness that is killing Tamburlaine.

War, or perhaps the vengeful God of the Old Testament, appears to be the god whom Tamburlaine worships.

Techelles said, "Then let some god use his holy power to oppose the wrath and tyranny of Death, so that his tear-thirsty and unquenched hate may be turned upon himself!"

Some attendants brought in Zenocrate's hearse.

Tamburlaine said, "Now, eyes, enjoy your last benefit, and when after my death my soul, freed from my body, has the virtue of your sight, my soul's sight will pierce through the coffin and the sheet of gold, and glut your — my eyes' — longings to see Zenocrate, resulting in a Heaven of joy.

"So, reign, my son; guiding your chariot with your father's hand, scourge and control those slaves.

"As precious is the responsibility you undertake as that which Phaëthon, Clymene's brainsick son, did when he guided the Sun-chariot, when wandering Phoebe the Moon's ivory cheeks were scorched, and all the Earth, like the volcano Mount Etna, was breathing fire."

Phoebe is another name for the Moon goddess.

Amyras' responsibility is as great as that of Phaëthon, but Phaëthon was unable to handle that responsibility. He could not control the Sun-chariot and almost burned up the Earth. Jupiter saved the Earth by killing Phaëthon with a thunderbolt.

Tamburlaine said, "Be warned by him, then learn with eyes filled with awe to wield authority as dangerous as his, for if your body thrives not full of thoughts as pure and fiery as Pythias' — Apollo the Sun-god's — beams, the nature of these proud rebelling jades — the conquered Deputy King Orcanes of Natolia and the conquered King of Jerusalem — will take opportunity by the slenderest hair of its forelock and tear you to pieces by dragging you, like Hippolytus, through rocks steeper and sharper than the Caspian cliffs."

Hippolytus was one of Theseus' sons, and Theseus' second wife, Phaedra, fell in love with him, but he rejected her advances. She told Theseus that Hippolytus had raped her, and Theseus prayed to the sea-god Poseidon to kill his son. A bull came out of the sea, scaring Hippolytus' horses so badly that they upset his chariot and dragged him to his death.

Tamburlaine wanted Amyras to be on his guard lest Orcanes and the King of Jerusalem kill him just as Phaedra got Hippolytus killed.

Tamburlaine continued, "The nature of your chariot will not bear a guide of baser temperament than myself, more than Heaven's coach the pride of Phaëthon."

It takes a great being such as Apollo to drive the Sun-chariot, and Tamburlaine was saying that it takes a great being such as himself to drive his chariot. No doubt, he also thought that he could control Hippolytus' horses.

Tamburlaine continued, "Farewell, my boys! My dearest friends, farewell! My body feels, my soul weeps to see your sweet desires deprived my company, for Tamburlaine, the scourge of God, must die."

He died.

Amyras said, "Let Heaven and Earth collide into one another, and here let all things end, for Earth has spent the pride of all her fruit, and Heaven has consumed its choicest living fire.

"Let Earth and Heaven deplore Tamburlaine's untimely death, for both their worths will equal him no more."

NOTES (Part 2)

Unless otherwise noted, line numbers are those of this edition:

Marlowe, Christopher. *Tamburlaine*. Edited by J.S. Cunningham. The Revels Plays. Manchester and New York: Manchester University Press, 1999.

— 1.2 —

Almeda says this:

"*But need we not be spied going aboard?*"

(1.2.56)

Possible meanings:

- But will we not inevitably be spied going aboard!
- But don't we need to avoid being spied going aboard!
- But won't we necessarily be seen going aboard!
- But we need to not be seen going aboard!
- But we need to not be seen going aboard!

— 1.3 —

Usumcasane says this:

> *My lord, our men of Barbary have marched*
> *Four hundred miles with armour on their backs,*
> *And lain in leaguer fifteen months and more.*

(1.3.174-176*)*

Usumcasane says that he and his soldiers have "lain in leaguer" fifteen months and more since leaving Tamburlaine at the court of the Sultan of Egypt, apparently a little after the events of *Tamburlaine the Great, Part 1.*

"Leaguer" means a military camp, especially one engaged in a siege. Some critics think that "lain in league" refers to a military campaign rather than a siege that is part of a longer military campaign, but this conflicts with Tamburlaine and Zenocrate having three mostly grown sons (but chances are that Marlowe's audience would not notice or care). It is most likely, in my opinion, that "lain in leaguer fifteen months and more" (1.6.49) refers to a siege that lasted that long, and so Usumcasane and his army could have spent years traveling and fighting.

<h1 style="text-align:center">— 2.1 —</h1>

Frederick says this:

And almost to the very walls of Rome,

(2.1.9)

David Fuller writes this about the word "Rome":

The name was applied to Constantinople as the capital of the eastern Roman Empire, and the centre of eastern Christiandom (Rome itself being the centre of the western Church). It is so used by Richard Knolles in his version of Bonfinius in The General History of the Turks *(1603), which Marlowe may have read in manuscript: Hugh G. Dick,* Studies in Philology, *46 (1949), 154-66.*

Source: *The Complete Works of Christopher Marlowe. Volume V. Tamburlaine Parts 1 and 2.* Edited by David Fuller. *The Massacre at Paris.* Edited by Edward J. Esche. Oxford: Clarendon Press, 1998. Page 240.

— 2.4 —

Tamburlaine says this:

May never such a change transform my love,
In whose sweet being I repose my life,
Whose heavenly presence, beautified with health,
Gives light to Phoebus and the fixèd stars; (line 50)
Whose absence makes the sun and moon as dark
As when, opposed in one diameter,
Their spheres are mounted on the serpent's head,
Or else descended to his winding train.
(2.4.47-54)

The note below appears in the Everyman edition of *The Complete Plays of Christopher Marlowe*:

Tamburlaine describes a lunar eclipse. Eclipses took place at northward and southward points, the caput draconis *(serpent's head and the* caudra draconis *(serpent's tail) respectively. On opposite sides of the earth, the sun and moon are in diametric positions.*

Source: *The Complete Plays of Christopher Marlowe.* Edited by Mark Thornton Burnett. London: Everyman, 1999. Page 550.

The information below comes from Michael A. Seeds, *Foundations of Astronomy*, 9th Edition (Chapter 3: Cycles of the Moon):

The orbit of the moon is tipped 5°8'43" to the plane of Earth's orbit, so you see the moon follow a path tipped by that angle to the ecliptic. Each month, the moon crosses the ecliptic at two points called nodes. It crosses at one node going southward, and two weeks later it crosses at the other node going northward.

Eclipses can only occur when the sun is near one of the nodes of the moon's orbit. A solar eclipse happens at new moon if the moon passes in front of the sun. Most new moons pass too far north or too far south of the sun to cause an eclipse. Only when the sun is near a node in the moon's orbit can the moon cross in front of the sun, as shown in Figure 3-12a. A lunar eclipse doesn't happen at every full moon because most full moons pass too far north or too far south of the ecliptic and miss Earth's shadow. The moon can enter Earth's shadow only when the shadow is near

191

a node in the moon's orbit, and that means the sun must be near the other node. This is shown in Figure 3-12b.

So there are two conditions for an eclipse: The sun must be crossing a node, and the moon must be crossing either the same node (solar eclipse) or the other node (lunar eclipse). That means, of course, that solar eclipses can occur only when the moon is new, and lunar eclipses can occur only when the moon is full.

Source (You can see the Figures here):

https://www.webassign.net/seedfoundations/ebook/CH03-4.html

The Penguin edition of Christopher Marlowe's *The Complete Plays* has this note:

[...] as during a lunar eclipse (occurring at points in the celestial map at which the moon's orbit intersects with the ecliptic, known as the serpent's head and tail).

Source: Christopher Marlowe. *The Complete Plays*. Edited by Frank Romany and Robert Lindsey. London: Penguin Books, 2003. Page 603.

The *Oxford American Dictionary* defines *ecliptic* in this way:

a great circle on the celestial sphere representing the sun's apparent path during the year, so called because lunar and solar eclipses can occur only when the moon crosses it.

4.3 and 5.1 and 5.2
Asphaltis and Limnasphaltis

Marlowe's geography is sometimes odd. He seems to locate Babylon on the coast, which it isn't. He also may perhaps locate the Dead Sea much nearer Babylon than it was.

Marlowe makes Babylon a great city in the Middle Ages. (The real Tamburlaine was named Timur, and his dates are 9 April 1336 – 18 February 1405.) Actually, Babylon was a great ancient city, but it was abandoned around 1,000 C.E.

As always, we read the historical plays of the Elizabethan era as literature, not as history. Sometimes Marlowe seems to be deliberately vague about locations because he knows that what he is writing is not historical.

Idea #1:

We may want to regard Asphaltis and Limnasphaltis as referring to the same body of water: the Dead Sea. If so, I would write in *Tamburlaine, Part 2*, something like this:

Asphaltis, sometimes called Limnasphaltis, is near Jerusalem and is better known as the Dead Sea. The Governor of Babylon regarded the lake as being close enough to Babylon to be part of its defenses. [In actual fact, it is not.]

A mapmaker of the time named Abraham Ortelius created a map of Palestine and labeled the Dead Sea as Asphaltis.

The actual battlefield where Tamburlaine had conquered the petty Kings was far from Asphaltis, but he was playing with words. He was calling the battlefield where he had won his victory the Dead Plains.

I reject this: See Ideas #2 and #3.

Idea #2:

We may want to regard Asphaltis and Limnasphaltis as referring to the same body of water, but that body of water is not the Dead Sea; instead, it is a lake near enough to Babylon to be part of its defenses.

When Tamburlaine refers to Asphaltis as a battlefield (4.3.5), he is referring to the plains of Asphaltis; he mentions "Asphaltis' plains" specifically a little later (4.3.68). Perhaps by doing that, he is emphasizing how important he thinks Babylon is. He could have referred to the plains of Jerusalem but chose to refer to the plains of Babylon instead.

Plains can extend far. This information about the Great Plains of North America comes from Wikipedia:

Length: 3,200 km, or 1,988 miles

Width: 800 km, or 497 miles

Area: 1,300,000 square km, or 501,933 square miles

Source: "Great Plains." Wikipedia. Accessed 5 September 2018 <https://en.wikipedia.org/wiki/Great_Plains>.

I accept this, but see Idea #3.

Idea #3:

And here may we behold great Babylon,

Circled about with Limnasphaltis' lake,

(5.2.4-5)

My best guess is that Asphaltis and Limnasphaltis are basically the same body of water (or at least share water), and that the battle in which Tamburlaine defeated the Turkish Emperor Callapine and Deputy King Orcanes of Natolia was fought on the plains of Asphaltis.

According to Act 5, Scene 2, Lines 4-5, Babylon is surrounded by Limnasphaltis. Unless Babylon is built on an island, which we aren't told it is, it would not be surrounded by what we call a lake today. Therefore, I conclude that Babylon has a moat whose water comes from Asphaltis. When referring to the moat, Marlowe used the word "Limnasphaltis."

"Lim" comes from Latin and means boundary, edge, line. The moat around the city of Babylon would be the boundary of the city.

According to the *Oxford English Dictionary*, an obsolete meaning of "Lake" is "A small stream of running water; also, a channel for water." Also according to the *Oxford English Dictionary*, one definition of "Moat" is "A pond or lake; esp. a fish pond."

In Act 5, Scene 1, the Governor of Babylon tells Tamburlaine that gold is hidden "in Limnasphaltis' lake" (5.1.115) "Under a hollow bank, right opposite / Against the western gate of Babylon" (5.1.121-122). The gold is hidden in the moat. This also means that the Governor of Babylon and probably others call the moat a lake that encircles Babylon.

In Act 5, Scene 1, men, women, and children are drowned in Asphaltis (line 203). That means that they are drowned in the lake proper, not in the moat whose water comes from Lake Asphaltis.

Two Lines:

Tamburlaine says this:

And cast them headlong in the city's lake.

(5.1.161)

In the line above, Tamburlaine is ordering Techelles to drown the burghers in the city's lake. A few lines later, Techelles asks about the burghers' wives and children, and Tamburlaine tells him to drown them all. We may think that "city's lake" refers to Limnasphaltis, which is probably correct, but we find out that Techelles drowned the people of Babylon in Asphaltis. My guess is that the citizens of Babylon were too numerous to be drowned in Limnasphaltis and so Techelles drowned them in Asphaltis.

Tamburlaine says this:

Now fill the mouth of Limnasphaltis' lake

(5.1.67)

The mouth of a river is where a river flows into a lake. A moat is unlikely to be running water, so my guess is that "the mouth of Limnasphaltis' lake" is where the water of Limnasphaltis and the water of Asphaltis meet.

Note:

In any case, Asphaltis / Limnasphaltis is an asphaltic lake.

Here is some information on Liquid Asphalt:

First of all, it's not "tar." Asphalt is a natural substance that has some amazing physical properties. It's sticky (adhesive) and it's elastic, able to stretch, bend and flex without breaking (cohesive). This material does an excellent job of waterproofing. At air temperatures, asphalt cement is a very, very thick liquid (highly viscous). When heated, it becomes thinner and easier to use. Asphalt has been used since before Roman times as a glue and for water proofing. In a few places in the world, it's naturally occurring, such as in a lake on the island of Trinidad and in the LaBrea "tar pits" in downtown Los Angeles. Almost all of the asphalt used today for paving comes from petroleum crude oil. Liquid asphalt is the heaviest part of the crude — what's left after all the volatile, light fractions are distilled off for products such as gasoline. In Europe and Canada it is commonly called bitumen.

Source: "What is Liquid Asphalt (Asphalt Cement)?" My AsphaltPavingProject.com. 2017. Accessed 2018. https://tinyurl.com/y7wewx5h

Amyras says this:

With what a flinty bosom should I joy (line 185)
The breath of life and burthen of my soul,
If not resolv'd into resolved pains,
My body's mortified lineaments
Should exercise the motions of my heart,
Pierced with the joy of any dignity! (line 190)

— From the U.M. Ellis-Fermor edition.

This is a difficult passage. In my retelling, I treat the passage as if a period were at the end of line 185:

"I would have such a flinty bosom if I were to enjoy the breath of life and the burden of my soul if this pain of losing my father were not dissolved into relieved pain by the recovery of my father.

"If my father does not recover, then my body's deadened parts will exercise the beating of my heart, which will be pierced if I should take any joy in having the titles of my father!"

Amyras was thinking of committing suicide by stabbing his heart with a knife if he found that he was capable of enjoying becoming a King solely due to the death of his father.

Note: "To resolve" pain often means "to alleviate or reduce" pain, according to the *Oxford English Dictionary*.

Here are some other paraphrases:

"How hard a heart I should have if I could enjoy my life and the possession of my soul and if my body were not dissolved in extreme pain (l. 187) and sympathetically affected (l. 188) and could still direct the movements of a heart that was touched with joy by such things as earthly dignities."

Source of above: Christopher Marlowe, *Tamburlaine the Great: In Two Parts*. Editor: U.M. Ellis-Fermor. New York: Gordian Press, Inc., 1966. Page 278.

"How hard my heart would be if I could enjoy my life and the possession of my own soul [i.e., with Tamburlaine about to die], or if my body did not dissolve into extreme pain and its affected limbs ('mortified lineaments') were still able to

carry out the prompting of a heart that could be touched to joy by earthly dignities"
(adapted from Ellis-Fermor).

Source of above: Christopher Marlowe, *Tamburlaine: Parts One and Two*. Editor: Anthony B. Dawson. London, New York: A & C Black, 1971. Page 172.

"How hardhearted would be my enjoyment of your gift to me of life and soul if, instead of dissolving into grief and mortification, I should gladden my heart at the prospect of such earthly dignity!"

Source of above: Christopher Marlowe, *Doctor Faustus and Other Plays*. Oxford World Classics. Edited by David Bevington and Eric Rasmussen. Oxford: Oxford University Press, 2008. Page 432.

"i.e. how hardhearted I should be if I were able to enjoy life physically or emotionally, if, instead of dissolving into extreme pain, my heart should be prompted to any joy at the thought of earthly dignity"

Source of above: Christopher Marlowe. *The Complete Works of Christopher Marlowe*. Volume 5. *Tamburlaine: Parts 1 and 2*. Edited by David Fuller. *The Massacre at Paris*. Edited by Edward J. Esche. Oxford: Clarendon Press, 1998. Page 282.

"How hard-hearted I would have to be to enjoy the burden of my life, and if my body, all made up of pain, could still put into action the feelings of a heart that felt joy at a worldly honor!"

Source: Christopher Marlowe. *The Complete Plays*. Edited by Frank Romany and Robert Lindsey. London: Penguin Books, 2003. Page 611.

"Amyras states that he would be hard of heart indeed if his body did not feel the pains experienced by Tamburlaine, and if he could derive pleasure from the prospect of receiving earthly dignities."

Source: Christopher Marlowe. *The Complete Plays*. Edited by Mark Thornton Burnett. London and Vermont: Everyman, 1999. Page 556.

APPENDIX A: FAIR USE

§ 107. Limitations on exclusive rights: Fair use

    Release date: 2004-04-30

Notwithstanding the provisions of sections 106 and 106A, the fair use of a copyrighted work, including such use by reproduction in copies or phonorecords or by any other means specified by that section, for purposes such as criticism, comment, news reporting, teaching (including multiple copies for classroom use), scholarship, or research, is not an infringement of copyright. In determining whether the use made of a work in any particular case is a fair use the factors to be considered shall include —

(1) the purpose and character of the use, including whether such use is of a commercial nature or is for nonprofit educational purposes;

(2) the nature of the copyrighted work;

(3) the amount and substantiality of the portion used in relation to the copyrighted work as a whole; and

(4) the effect of the use upon the potential market for or value of the copyrighted work.

The fact that a work is unpublished shall not itself bar a finding of fair use if such finding is made upon consideration of all the above factors.

Source of Fair Use information:

<http://www.law.cornell.edu/uscode/17/107.html>

APPENDIX C: ABOUT THE AUTHOR

It was a dark and stormy night. Suddenly a cry rang out, and on a hot summer night in 1954, Josephine, wife of Carl Bruce, gave birth to a boy — me. Unfortunately, this young married couple allowed Reuben Saturday, Josephine's brother, to name their first-born. Reuben, aka "The Joker," decided that Bruce was a nice name, so he decided to name me Bruce Bruce. I have gone by my middle name — David — ever since.

Being named Bruce David Bruce hasn't been all bad. Bank tellers remember me very quickly, so I don't often have to show an ID. It can be fun in charades, also. When I was a counselor as a teenager at Camp Echoing Hills in Warsaw, Ohio, a fellow counselor gave the signs for "sounds like" and "two words," then she pointed to a bruise on her leg twice. Bruise Bruise? Oh yeah, Bruce Bruce is the answer!

Uncle Reuben, by the way, gave me a haircut when I was in kindergarten. He cut my hair short and shaved a small bald spot on the back of my head. My mother wouldn't let me go to school until the bald spot grew out again.

Of all my brothers and sisters (six in all), I am the only transplant to Athens, Ohio. I was born in Newark, Ohio, and have lived all around Southeastern Ohio. However, I moved to Athens to go to Ohio University and have never left.

At Ohio U, I never could make up my mind whether to major in English or Philosophy, so I got a bachelor's degree with a double major in both areas, then I added a Master of Arts degree in English and a Master of Arts degree in Philosophy. Yes, I have my MAMA degree.

Currently, and for a long time to come (I eat fruits and veggies), I am spending my retirement writing books such as *Nadia Comaneci: Perfect 10*, *The Funniest People in Dance*, *Homer's* Iliad: *A Retelling in Prose*, and *William Shakespeare's* Othello: *A Retelling in Prose*.

By the way, my sister Brenda Kennedy writes romances such as *A New Beginning* and *Shattered Dreams*.

APPENDIX C: SOME BOOKS BY DAVID BRUCE

Retellings of a Classic Work of Literature

Arden of Faversham: *A Retelling*

Ben Jonson's The Alchemist: *A Retelling*

Ben Jonson's The Arraignment, or Poetaster: *A Retelling*

Ben Jonson's Bartholomew Fair: *A Retelling*

Ben Jonson's The Case is Altered: *A Retelling*

Ben Jonson's Catiline's Conspiracy: *A Retelling*

Ben Jonson's The Devil is an Ass: *A Retelling*

Ben Jonson's Epicene: *A Retelling*

Ben Jonson's Every Man in His Humor: *A Retelling*

Ben Jonson's Every Man Out of His Humor: *A Retelling*

Ben Jonson's The Fountain of Self-Love, or Cynthia's Revels: *A Retelling*

Ben Jonson's The Magnetic Lady, or Humors Reconciled: *A Retelling*

Ben Jonson's The New Inn, or The Light Heart: *A Retelling*

Ben Jonson's Sejanus' Fall: *A Retelling*

Ben Jonson's The Staple of News: *A Retelling*

Ben Jonson's A Tale of a Tub: *A Retelling*

Ben Jonson's Volpone, or the Fox: *A Retelling*

Christopher Marlowe's Complete Plays: Retellings

Christopher Marlowe's Dido, Queen of Carthage: *A Retelling*

Christopher Marlowe's Doctor Faustus: *Retellings of the 1604 A-Text and of the 1616 B-Text*

Christopher Marlowe's Edward II: *A Retelling*

Christopher Marlowe's The Massacre at Paris: *A Retelling*

Christopher Marlowe's The Rich Jew of Malta: *A Retelling*

Christopher Marlowe's Tamburlaine, Parts 1 and 2: *Retellings*

Dante's Divine Comedy: *A Retelling in Prose*

Dante's Inferno: *A Retelling in Prose*

Dante's Purgatory: *A Retelling in Prose*

Dante's Paradise: *A Retelling in Prose*

The Famous Victories of Henry V: *A Retelling*

From the Iliad *to the* Odyssey: *A Retelling in Prose of Quintus of Smyrna's* Posthomerica

George Chapman, Ben Jonson, and John Marston's Eastward Ho! *A Retelling*

George Peele's The Arraignment of Paris: *A Retelling*

George Peele's The Battle of Alcazar: *A Retelling*

George Peele's David and Bathsheba, and the Tragedy of Absalom: *A Retelling*

George Peele's Edward I: *A Retelling*

George Peele's The Old Wives' Tale: *A Retelling*

George-a-Greene: *A Retelling*

The History of King Leir: *A Retelling*

Homer's Iliad: *A Retelling in Prose*

Homer's Odyssey: *A Retelling in Prose*

J.W. Gent.'s The Valiant Scot: *A Retelling*

Jason and the Argonauts: A Retelling in Prose of Apollonius of Rhodes' Argonautica

John Ford: Eight Plays Translated into Modern English

John Ford's The Broken Heart: *A Retelling*

John Ford's The Fancies, Chaste and Noble: *A Retelling*

John Ford's The Lady's Trial: *A Retelling*

John Ford's The Lover's Melancholy: *A Retelling*

John Ford's Love's Sacrifice: *A Retelling*

John Ford's Perkin Warbeck: *A Retelling*

John Ford's The Queen: *A Retelling*

John Ford's 'Tis Pity She's a Whore: *A Retelling*

John Lyly's Campaspe: *A Retelling*

John Lyly's Endymion, The Man in the Moon: *A Retelling*

John Lyly's Galatea: *A Retelling*

John Lyly's Love's Metamorphosis: *A Retelling*

John Lyly's Midas: *A Retelling*

John Lyly's Mother Bombie: *A Retelling*

John Lyly's Sappho and Phao: *A Retelling*

John Lyly's The Woman in the Moon: *A Retelling*

John Webster's The White Devil: *A Retelling*

King Edward III: *A Retelling*

Mankind: *A Medieval Morality Play* (A Retelling)

Margaret Cavendish's The Unnatural Tragedy: *A Retelling*

The Merry Devil of Edmonton: *A Retelling*

The Summoning of Everyman: *A Medieval Morality Play* (A Retelling)

Robert Greene's Friar Bacon and Friar Bungay: *A Retelling*

The Taming of a Shrew: *A Retelling*

Tarlton's Jests: A Retelling

Thomas Middleton's A Chaste Maid in Cheapside: *A Retelling*

Thomas Middleton's Women Beware Women: *A Retelling*

Thomas Middleton and Thomas Dekker's The Roaring Girl: *A Retelling*

Thomas Middleton and William Rowley's The Changeling: *A Retelling*

The Trojan War and Its Aftermath: Four Ancient Epic Poems

Virgil's Aeneid: *A Retelling in Prose*

William Shakespeare's 5 Late Romances: Retellings in Prose

William Shakespeare's 10 Histories: Retellings in Prose

William Shakespeare's 11 Tragedies: Retellings in Prose

William Shakespeare's 12 Comedies: Retellings in Prose

William Shakespeare's 38 Plays: Retellings in Prose
William Shakespeare's 1 Henry IV, aka Henry IV, Part 1: *A Retelling in Prose*
William Shakespeare's 2 Henry IV, aka Henry IV, Part 2: *A Retelling in Prose*
William Shakespeare's 1 Henry VI, aka Henry VI, Part 1: *A Retelling in Prose*
William Shakespeare's 2 Henry VI, aka Henry VI, Part 2: *A Retelling in Prose*
William Shakespeare's 3 Henry VI, aka Henry VI, Part 3: *A Retelling in Prose*
William Shakespeare's All's Well that Ends Well: *A Retelling in Prose*
William Shakespeare's Antony and Cleopatra: *A Retelling in Prose*
William Shakespeare's As You Like It: *A Retelling in Prose*
William Shakespeare's The Comedy of Errors: *A Retelling in Prose*
William Shakespeare's Coriolanus: *A Retelling in Prose*
William Shakespeare's Cymbeline: *A Retelling in Prose*
William Shakespeare's Hamlet: *A Retelling in Prose*
William Shakespeare's Henry V: *A Retelling in Prose*
William Shakespeare's Henry VIII: *A Retelling in Prose*
William Shakespeare's Julius Caesar: *A Retelling in Prose*
William Shakespeare's King John: *A Retelling in Prose*
William Shakespeare's King Lear: *A Retelling in Prose*
William Shakespeare's Love's Labor's Lost: *A Retelling in Prose*
William Shakespeare's Macbeth: *A Retelling in Prose*
William Shakespeare's Measure for Measure: *A Retelling in Prose*
William Shakespeare's The Merchant of Venice: *A Retelling in Prose*
William Shakespeare's The Merry Wives of Windsor: *A Retelling in Prose*
William Shakespeare's A Midsummer Night's Dream: *A Retelling in Prose*
William Shakespeare's Much Ado About Nothing: *A Retelling in Prose*
William Shakespeare's Othello: *A Retelling in Prose*
William Shakespeare's Pericles, Prince of Tyre: *A Retelling in Prose*
William Shakespeare's Richard II: *A Retelling in Prose*
William Shakespeare's Richard III: *A Retelling in Prose*
William Shakespeare's Romeo and Juliet: *A Retelling in Prose*
William Shakespeare's The Taming of the Shrew: *A Retelling in Prose*
William Shakespeare's The Tempest: *A Retelling in Prose*
William Shakespeare's Timon of Athens: *A Retelling in Prose*
William Shakespeare's Titus Andronicus: *A Retelling in Prose*
William Shakespeare's Troilus and Cressida: *A Retelling in Prose*
William Shakespeare's Twelfth Night: *A Retelling in Prose*
William Shakespeare's The Two Gentlemen of Verona: *A Retelling in Prose*
William Shakespeare's The Two Noble Kinsmen: *A Retelling in Prose*
William Shakespeare's The Winter's Tale: *A Retelling in Prose*